GUN MEN

GUN MEN

A Novel

■

Gary Friedman

William Morrow and Company, Inc.
New York

It is the policy of William Morrow and Company, Inc., and its imprints and affili-
ates, recognizing the importance of preserving what has been written, to print the
books we publish on acid-free paper, and we exert our best efforts to that end.

Library of Congress Cataloging-in-Publication Data

Friedman, Gary.
Gun men : a novel / Gary Friedman.
   p.   cm.
ISBN 0-688-11545-4
I. Title.
PS3556.R519G84   1993
813'.54—dc20
                                                                    92-27419
                                                                    CIP

Printed in the United States of America

First Edition

1   2   3   4   5   6   7   8   9   10

To my mother and father

"A well regulated militia, being necessary to the security of a free State, the right of the people to keep and bear arms, shall not be infringed."

—Second Amendment to the Constitution of the United States

THE ACTION

1

The 1978 Chevy Impala turned off Highway 24, east of Oakland, California, and into the town of Laurel Valley. Driving the car was a man dressed in army fatigues and jungle boots. The clothes and boots had come from an army-navy store in Oakland, near where the man lived.

The man was five feet eleven inches tall, thinnish but not skinny. He had straw-blond hair that was neither fine nor coarse, lustrous nor dull. His eyes were an unremarkable blue. And at the end of January he didn't have much of a tan. He was twenty-three years old.

He let the Chevy roll to a stop in front of 406 Blossom Street. He had lived the first eleven years of his life at number 406.

He looked at the door of the house. His father had painted it green. Now, it was white. Above the door his father had painted the family name—Mattox. Now, the name was gone, and nothing had been painted in its place. People were afraid to identify themselves these days. Even the mailboxes, on those roads that *had* mailboxes, only had numbers on them.

Leslie Mattox studied the street. It was empty except for an old man puttering around on a lawn at the very end of the block. Leslie knew the old man—Charles Moulin. He and his friends used to call Moulin "Frenchie" because Moulin spoke with an accent. On Halloween they had splattered his windows with shaving cream and let the air out of his tires.

Leslie, thinking back, decided Moulin had been lucky: They might have spray-painted his house and slashed his tires.

He rolled down the window and took a deep breath. It was warm for January. It was 70°, at least. And with the sun pouring in through the windshield, it was hot; he was sweating under the heavy combat jacket.

He looked at each house on the block. Tommy's house across the street. John's next door. In between, the laurel bush behind which they had undressed John's little sister. They had been too young to know what to do, other than look. The bush was larger now, almost a tree.

So this was what it was like to go back home: everything the same, everything different. All his friends gone, only old Moulin left.

He peered through the windshield. What the hell was the old fart doing down there? He couldn't quite see. Why were old people always fussing?

He remembered his grandmother. She had *lived* with a dust rag in her hand, her head tilted back so she could focus through the bottom of her bifocals. Whenever he had come to visit, she had followed him from room to room to make sure he didn't break anything, or steal anything, like a security guard in a department store.

He rolled up the window and got out of the car. Then he laughed.

He laughed because it was going to be so easy. It was always easy if you were ready to die—he had read that somewhere. He took another look around the neighborhood. Moulin was on his hands and knees facing the other direction.

Leslie walked to the back of the Chevy and unlocked the trunk. The smell of gasoline leapt up at him. He picked up a 9mm Ruger pistol and tucked it in his belt. From under a blanket he pulled out an AKM-47 assault rifle.

They were good guns, guns that would get the job done, not jam or fall apart. He had saved for years to buy these guns, putting away ten or twenty dollars each week from his job stocking shelves in a giant drugstore. He was an assistant manager, which meant he supervised two or three teenagers and got paid an extra dollar-fifty an hour. But, really, he did the same work they did, and he would never make much more; he was a high school dropout.

He looked at his house. His old house. He could live to be a hundred, and he would never have the money to buy a house like that. He would live in Oakland all his life.

He pulled the AKM-47 over his shoulder. He had an extra clip for the rifle; the clip held thirty rounds. He stuck it in his belt next to the Ruger. Then he started to fill his pockets with ammunition.

When his pockets were full, he reached into the trunk and took the cap off the bottle of gasoline. He crammed a rag into the hole, lit the end of the rag, and slammed the trunk closed.

A spot of rust grinned up at him from under the blue paint.

With the trunk closed, there wouldn't be enough air, and the rag would go out. He opened the trunk. The rag flared. It might just suck the gas out of the bottle like a lamp. It might not explode at all.

Leslie cursed, and picked up the bottle and flung it under the car. The bottle broke, and the gas burst into flames. He leapt back.

Charles Moulin looked up.

By then Leslie had turned and was walking away. As he took a right onto Rolinda, the gas tank on the Chevy went.

Charles Moulin ran to call the fire department.

At the end of Rolinda Leslie Mattox turned onto Connair. The shouts from the school yard began to reach him. He would make the Stockton massacre look like a Sunday school outing. Only five dead. Leslie Mattox was planning on an even hundred.

A massacre of the innocents.

He remembered the phrase from church, although he wasn't sure exactly what it meant. He had hated church, stuck inside on a Sunday morning listening to hymns, crammed between older sisters who pinched him.

He was the youngest of four. Seven years younger than

15

Margaret, eight years younger than Joan. His brother was five years older, and had always been off with his friends.

Leslie hated his brother, a stockbroker who wouldn't give him a dime. He smiled. But his brother would never be famous.

He slogged forward, the ammunition in the cargo pockets of his pants banging against his legs. Just across from the school yard he stopped behind a tree.

The Dale R. Boise Elementary School had been built in 1936 for the children of all those people heading west. In 1952 an extension had been added to accommodate the baby boomers; and in 1964 the entire building had been renovated. A modern playground had been added in 1975.

Leslie watched the kids climbing on the chopped-off telephone poles. It was recess, or gym, or something, and the little fuckers were running around screaming and having a good time. He had hated recess because he had always gotten beaten up during recess. There was just no place to hide in a school yard.

A ball banged against the fence, and a girl ran to get it. Other girls were playing hopscotch and jump rope. Some boys were flipping baseball cards.

The jungle gym. The swings. It was all familiar. Even the kids just standing against the fence doing nothing.

That had been Leslie. Leslie the Hammerhead!

Someone had found out that a mattock was a tool. And since Mattox sounded like mattock, and since a hammer was also a tool, Leslie had become "Hammerhead."

Leslie the hammerhead shark. Leslie the girl!

They had pulled down his pants to see if he had a dick. They had pulled down his pants when the girls were watching!

The girls had laughed, and run away.

They wouldn't run away this time.

Leslie jogged forward, suddenly afraid the bell might ring, the bell that had been his salvation as a child.

The children standing against the fence doing nothing were the first to get hit. Leslie fired from thirty feet. One pull of the trigger for each child.

16

GUN MEN

Crack! Crack! Crack!

Each time he fired, the muzzle jumped. He pulled it back down and aimed again. Three for three; he was doing just fine.

The gun cracked, and more children went down. Others came running. It was Chinese New Year, and they wanted to see the firecrackers.

Leslie Mattox stepped through the school-yard gate swinging the gun from side to side. The children fell as before a giant mower.

When David Boatman heard the first cracks, he also thought some child had brought firecrackers to school. It happened every once in a while, often coinciding with holidays such as Chinese New Year.

He sighed and shuffled forward. He was tired of reprimanding the little bastards, and if he dawdled, some other teacher might get there first and have to give the lecture about lost fingers and eyes. He stared over the heads of the running children, looking for the miscreant, and saw Leslie Mattox enter the yard. Boatman grabbed the child nearest to him and fled, screaming for the other children to follow him. About eleven children did. Boatman, in the lead, ran for five blocks before the weight of the child he was carrying proved greater than his fear. He gathered his brood and hid them behind a house, and waited.

Susan Daniels had heard the first cracks, too. She was teaching spelling at the time to her third graders. She walked to the open window, looked down, and saw Mattox in the yard pivoting slowly, the children dropping as he fired. She turned calmly to the class and announced a fire drill.

"Turn your desks over on the floor!" she ordered sharply.

Suddenly afraid, the children obeyed.

"Now angle them toward the door!"

Twenty-two desks were angled toward the door.

"Now get down behind those desks and don't you dare move. Not one of you!"

Twenty-two children crouched behind their desks and held their collective breath.

Susan Daniels shoved her own desk up against the door,

17

then walked to the supply closet, where she removed a large hammer from the top shelf. She returned to her desk and crouched down behind it. She believed in God and God's mercy, but it would be a long day in December before she just stood there and prayed that the bullets missed.

As she knelt, Leslie Mattox was finishing up in the yard. The children, at last realizing there was a man shooting at them, were screaming and running away. Most panicked and were trapped by the fence.

Leslie raised the gun to his shoulder, lined up the sights, and fired. When the second clip ran out, he started to reload.

And that was when he heard the siren.

Dominick Gattuso had been parked on Woodhill Road when the message came in to check out a burning car on Blossom Street. He flipped on the siren and took off. Down Prince, across Rhodes, onto Beaumont. Beaumont was one of four streets that fronted the Dale R. Boise Elementary School. He always drove past the school if he could, both because he liked to watch the kids playing and because he liked to check up on them. His vigilance had once resulted in the arrest of a dope dealer. It made him sick that ten-year-olds were doing dope. And it made him even sicker when the case against the dope dealer got thrown out on a technicality. God bless the courts.

But before the fucker was released, Gattuso managed to have a chat with him, something along the line of broken legs and crushed nuts if he found him by the school again— and never mind police brutality, a man had to do what he had to do.

Dominick Gattuso glanced into the school yard as he drove past and slammed on his brakes. It took him a second to understand what he saw. At first it seemed it must be some game the kids were playing. A moment later the tires of the cruiser were burning as he backed up to the school.

Leslie Mattox looked up and stared at Gattuso. He popped a clip into the rifle, turned, and ran into the school.

"This is car two-oh-eight," Gattuso screamed into the mike. "I'm at the Dale R. Boise Elementary School. I got a male with

18

a rifle who just went into the school. There are kids down everywhere. I need backup and a dozen ambulances right this second. I'm going in after him." He was already out of the car, his .38 service revolver in his hand. At that moment Officer Mario DeLeon pulled up in his cruiser.

"Let's go," Gattuso shouted. "He's inside."

They ran for the door.

As Leslie Mattox stepped into the school, he found the hall empty. He paused, then headed up the stairs. Mark Sanchez, the history teacher, jumped at him, knocking him to the floor.

Sanchez hadn't heard the firing until the very end. He had been in the teachers' lounge grading papers and had stepped out to go to the bathroom just as Leslie Mattox ran out of bullets. Sanchez had been in Vietnam, and he knew the difference between an AK-47 and firecrackers. He had run to the outside door, seen the young man fifty feet away reloading, seen the handgun in his belt, and heard the sirens. He figured the man would come into the school next and planned to ambush him when he did.

As he dropped down on Mattox, fully planning to choke him to death, Leslie jammed a foot up into the older man's crotch. The air went out of Sanchez with a whoosh. Leslie rolled to the side, set the muzzle of the AKM-47 at Sanchez's head, and squeezed off a round. The explosion of blood covered the floor and wall. Leslie turned and raced up the stairs.

Susan Daniels heard the heavy boots coming down the hall and tightened her grip on the hammer. It wasn't over yet. There had been that long silence when she thought the man might have run off. She had nearly gotten up to see what was going on. But Susan Daniels had grown up in Iowa and knew something about the lull in a storm. She had hissed for the class to stay put. Then came the sirens. Then the shot.

Leslie Mattox saw the desk blocking the door. He turned the knob and slammed his shoulder forward. Susan Daniels jumped up, screamed like a banshee, and flung the hammer at him. The window in the door exploded.

Leslie shouted and jumped back, then raised the gun and fired. But by then Daniels had shoved the desk back against the

19

door and ducked down again. Leslie raced down the hall, kicked open another door, and fired into the room.

"Upstairs!" Gattuso whispered, pointing at the stairs.

Mario DeLeon nodded. "I'll go around." He raced down to the other end of the corridor.

Gattuso stepped over Sanchez and padded up the stairs as quickly and as quietly as he could. He peered around the corner. The little turd was facing the other way, reloading again. Gattuso stared at his .38. It would be a long shot, almost forty yards. He didn't want to miss. He raised the gun, steadied it with his left hand, and breathed out, and slowly, so slowly, squeezed off a round.

Leslie Mattox jumped up and turned.

Gattuso fired again.

Mattox was backing up and firing, the AKM-47 cracking like a whip.

Dominick Gattuso fired all six rounds in his revolver as Mattox turned and slowly fell. The AKM-47 skittered to the side.

Gattuso ran forward, but Mario DeLeon reached Leslie first. He had fired three times as Mattox backed past the doors at the top of the stairs. He had his gun leveled at Leslie's head, but Leslie wasn't moving.

Five slugs had hit Mattox. Two had come from DeLeon's gun, but not the one in the back. Dominick Gattuso would wonder for the rest of his life whether his first shot had hit the man.

Ninety-six cartridges were found in the school yard and hallways. Miraculously, only seven children and one teacher died. Forty-two children had been wounded.

Three weeks later Dominick Gattuso and Mario DeLeon were given medals for bravery. It was hard to feel good about it.

No one was smiling at the presentation.

2

In the early hours of Sunday, November 10, 1963, just two weeks before the assassination of John F. Kennedy, Eliot Brod was attacked by two men on the streets of New York City. He was seventeen years old at the time, and the confrontation was something he had been looking for.

Eliot was in New York on an overnight trip with a group of high school seniors. They had come to the big city to visit museums and see a play, and, as one teacher alliteratively phrased it, to scrape some small-town smugness off their souls.

The group arrived by chartered bus Saturday in the middle of the morning. Their first stop was the Metropolitan Museum of Art, where they spent a numbing three hours touring the galleries. After a trek through ancient Egypt, they ate a quick lunch of hot dogs and soda outside on the steps, then they headed downtown to MOMA for two more hours of art. By then even their teacher had museum legs.

A leisurely walk across town brought them to their hotel. They dropped off their overnight bags, washed up, and went to dinner. An hour later, with soy sauce, white rice, and lobster Cantonese swishing in their tummies, they walked down Broadway to the Martinique and saw *Six Characters in Search of an*

Author, a play they were reading in their English class. They were back in their hotel rooms by eleven.

At midnight Eliot slipped out to see the city for himself.

Eliot Brod was ten years old the first time he walked into a martial-arts dojo, and two things struck him about the place: It was dark, and it smelled. He also knew that he was scared—everyone there was bigger than he was.

The dojo was run by an elderly Chinese man named Wa Sung. Whether Wa Sung taught karate, or whether he taught kung fu or jujitsu, was anyone's guess. The sign in the window, with admirable American directness, read simply: LEARN HOW TO FIGHT AND WIN.

Eliot didn't do much winning his first year, or even his second year. But sometime during his third year Wa Sung's words of wisdom began to sink in, and he began to hold his own. Eliot liked winning. It sure beat losing. As he got better, he practiced more. At thirteen, he was starting to show promise. At fourteen, it was *he* who people feared.

Seven years after Eliot joined the dojo, he was still one of the smaller students. He was also top dog.

As he walked around Manhattan, Eliot wasn't sure where he was going. He wasn't even sure exactly what he was doing, or why. He only knew that for all the years he had studied with Wa Sung, he had never been in a fight where his life had truly been in danger. He wanted to know if he would panic. And he wanted to know if what he had learned would really work.

The two men were bigger than he was, not a lot bigger, but bigger. One man stepped in front of him; the other man stepped behind. They smiled. They could afford to smile; they were holding knives, and he wasn't.

"Let's have your wallet, kid," the guy in front said. "And let's have that watch, too."

The man was in his late twenties or early thirties. He was wearing a beat-up black leather jacket and a black longshore-man's cap, and he hadn't shaved for a while.

Eliot told him to get fucked. The man looked offended.

"What'd you have to say that for, kid? Why'd you have to make it personal? Now, I'll have to teach you a lesson."

As the man was finishing up his speech, Eliot threw a whipping roundhouse kick at his head. Ordinarily, a roundhouse kick to the head against a man who is holding a knife is a good way to end up in the girl's choir. But when someone is in the middle of a speech, his next action is *always* predictable: He breathes in. And when you're breathing in, you're dead on your feet for a fraction of a second.

Eliot's kick caught the man just under the ear and knocked him cold. He turned. The second guy was crouched down, his knife low; he licked his lips and started to creep forward like a crab.

Eliot took a step back.

The man thrust the knife at him.

Eliot hopped back again. He considered running. That would have been the smartest thing to do.

But Eliot wasn't really interested in running. He was looking for an initiation. He was seventeen and didn't really think he could die.

The man lunged in.

Eliot shifted to the left.

The knife followed.

As smoothly as he could, Eliot shifted back to the right and punched at the arm holding the knife. Then he twisted quickly and hit the man in the face.

The man grunted, and slashed at him.

Eliot hopped back.

The man shook his head, then smiled and came in quickly: a low feint, a high feint nearly to Eliot's face, a downward slash at his belly.

Just before the downward slash, the man paused; it was all the time Eliot needed. His left hand shot out and smacked the wrist, deflecting the blade; half a moment later a snapping front kick crushed the guy's testicles.

Eliot grabbed the hand holding the knife and pivoted. The man flew forward and landed hard on the concrete. A kick to the ribs broke two of them. Eliot kicked twice more. Each time his foot sank in a little farther.

23

The man went limp.

Eliot kicked one last time. Why take any chances?

He looked around. The street was empty. He walked over and stomped his foot down on the other man's throat.

It hadn't been much of a fight, but then perhaps it never was when you won.

Since then Eliot had killed quite a number of people; it was what he did for a living.

Eliot Brod lived on a dirt road in rural New England, a couple of hours from Boston and New York, and three or four hours from the ski resorts of northern Vermont. He had a wife, a daughter, and a dog, and he owned his own home. His wife, Alison Wilson, was a self-employed graphic artist. *She* went to work during the day; *he* stayed home and took care of the kid. A house husband. A modern man, though now that his daughter spent most of the day at school, being a modern man was no big deal.

Two nights a week Eliot cooked in a restaurant. He did this for two reasons: First, he liked to cook; and second, it kept his friends from asking too many questions about how he paid his bills.

And on those occasions when Eliot was on a job and was gone for a few weeks (this usually happened once or twice a year, though it had been over two years, now, since he had had a job), his absence was explained to their friends—if they even asked—as leftover youthful restlessness. At forty-two Eliot could still get away with that.

Eliot was five feet nine inches tall, weighed 150 pounds, had plain brown hair, brown eyes, and a face right out of *Average American* magazine.

Like countless other members of his generation, Eliot exercised regularly. Every other day he ran six miles, and twice a week he biked to the main post office in Springfield, Massachusetts, sixty miles round trip. He had a P.O. box in Springfield, but not much ever came there except junk mail.

When Eliot first rented the P.O. box, nine years before, he sent out half a dozen postcards requesting a variety of catalogs, all in the name of Michael Smith. The catalogs had come. And then more catalogs had come. Then even more catalogs. Like a chain letter. He had initiated this deluge so that the one legitimate letter he occasionally received wouldn't look out of place. Even the most asleep postal employee couldn't help but be curious about a box that received only one letter every year or two.

This letter looked little different from the rest of Eliot's mail. It was also addressed to Michael Smith, the name and address on a printed label. Perhaps the only thing noteworthy was that the envelope bore a first-class stamp.

Inside the envelope was most often an ad for some vacation paradise, or a free gift, or some other offer too good to be refused. But for Eliot, what set this particular piece of junk mail apart was the line of numbers at the bottom of the ad. These numbers were a code that contained the name and phone number of the person who wished to hire him.

The Springfield P.O. box was one of three systems Eliot had worked out by which he could be contacted.

On January 25, about the time that Dominick Gattuso was taking aim at the middle of Leslie Mattox's back, Eliot Brod was nearing the end of his six-mile run. There were two more houses before his own. He passed them and sprinted the final hundred yards to his driveway. His wife was at work. His daughter was in school. His dog, a huge black monster named White Fang, was hiding under a bush ready to attack. White Fang weighed 120 pounds and loved everyone.

Eliot waited until the beast was launched, then stepped easily to the side. White Fang started to backpedal furiously, and Eliot couldn't help but wonder what the dog was thinking, five feet up in the air and rotating slowly in the wrong direction.

He had bought the dog to protect his wife and daughter, and to guard his earthly goods. But White Fang was only slightly more vigilant than a stone, and hadn't shown the least interest in defending his masters or their property.

Eliot patted him on the head and stepped into the house. It was time to start thinking about dinner. A nice dinner, so his wife would be in a good mood *after* dinner—maybe grilled chicken breasts, finished off in a pan with herbs and mush-rooms, and a splash of wine. They could finish the wine with dessert, *after* his daughter was in bed. A nice dessert. Something rich—maybe a silky custard covered with praline. And then a sip of cognac. And then who could tell?

3

The television flashed: two men talking, a clip from a movie, laughter.

Tran Van Duong raised the teacup to his lips and took a sip of tea. It was bitter, so bitter it seemed to bite the tip of his tongue. He barely noticed. In the week since his daughter Loan had been gunned down by that young madman, he had noticed very little, not the narcissus blooming, not the first daffodil.

He stared at the television, at Berns Hanson, host of *Today in the Bay,* without seeing him, seeing only the flashing light of the screen. The flashing changed, the lights and darks more rapid, more intense. A commercial. *The Extinguisher:* a new weekly drama; or, maybe an ad for a new product, an antismoke device for smokers.

Tran reached for the pack of Lucky Strikes on the table next to him. Americans spent too much time worrying about their health.

Shots rang out, and Charles Bronson scuttled across the screen. Or Arnold Schwarzenegger. He got them confused. U.S. patriots looking for POWs in Vietnam. Still, after fifteen years. Sylvester Pony, or something. Tweety Bird. His daughter had liked that cartoon. Tran had been appalled at the violence.

27

He closed his eyes and saw his wife and daughter, his first wife and his first daughter, saw them as they looked the day they left to visit his in-laws in Saigon. They had flown from Qui Nhon, where he was based and where they were all living, to Tan Son Nhut Air Base.

Tran had been a translator for most of the Vietnam War, attached to the U.S. 1st Cavalry Division. His job had been to assist an American interviewer when Vietnamese civilians came and complained about atrocities committed by the American soldiers.

Tran didn't understand why the Americans wanted to investigate atrocities they themselves had committed. Nor did he understand why they were concerned with atrocities committed during war. What did they think war was?

The television flashed, and Berns Hanson was back.

Tran stared at him for a moment, then stubbed out his cigarette and took another sip of tea. So bitter, like the vegetables that grew in his California garden. He glanced out the window, and noticed for the first time the narcissus, and the single daffodil. The daffodils were Loan's favorite flower, and now she wouldn't see them bloom.

It was in Saigon, in 1960, that he met his first wife. She had come to learn English at the school where he taught. Everyone wanted to learn English. The Americans were beginning to invade Saigon in numbers, and English would be the key to taking their dollars.

After several weeks of sidelong glances and shy smiles, Tran spoke to her. A week later they had their first date, and within a month they were in love. His luck, she was the daughter of wealthy landholders.

A year after they met, they were married. Nine months later a daughter was born.

In 1960 the war against the Viet Cong wasn't going well. President Kennedy, following Eisenhower's lead, sent in more advisers. Then President Johnson sent in even *more* advisers.

Finally, in 1965, the year that Tran was drafted, General West-moreland brought in the marines. Tran, because he spoke English, was assigned to an American unit. Through the influence of his in-laws he was based in Saigon.

But in 1967 Nguyen Van Thieu was "elected" president, and Tran's in-laws found themselves on the wrong side of the ballot box. Tran was transferred north. His wife and daughter went with him.

Around New Year's word came that his mother-in-law had passed away. His wife and daughter returned to Saigon. They planned to stay three weeks, until the Tet truce. But that year there was no truce during Tet.

At first, Tran was not concerned about his wife. Her father's house was like a fortress. And, except for some minor skirmishing, most of the fighting in Saigon was in Cholon, the Chinese ghetto. She was miles from there. Still, as the days passed and he heard nothing, he couldn't help but worry a little.

One week after the fighting had begun, he received the news from his father-in-law. His wife and daughter had been killed by a mortar explosion a short distance from the house. The streets had been quiet for two days, and they had gone to buy ice cream.

Tran was broken. He sat at his desk and wouldn't speak to anyone.

His American friends, eager to find out what they could for him, radioed their III Corps counterparts for details. Several weeks later the report came back: Not one but half a dozen mortars had fallen, and they had not been hostile rounds.

"It's a shitty war," his friends said.

A war in which all he did was file reports of rape and murder, reports that were never acted on. America. A society obsessed with reports and statistics: the number of VC killed each day, the number of U.S. dead. Highway deaths on holiday weekends. The number of people at a demonstration. In America people had violent confrontations disputing the number of protesters who had attended a peace march.

* * *

Tran looked around his living room. There was nothing from Vietnam, just the teacup he was holding. It was all he had brought; that, and the stones.

A year and a half after the death of his wife and daughter, his father-in-law was killed during a political purge. When the will was read, Tran found himself a wealthy man. His wife had had two brothers, but one had been killed in combat, and the other had died in a traffic accident. Tran had always thought his father-in-law would leave his wealth to a cousin, but he had left it to him. He did not know why.

He sold everything. The market was still high, buoyed by the dollars the Americans were pouring into the country. The panic that would ensue as the American pullout became real hadn't yet begun.

For two days Tran walked around Saigon wondering what to do with the mountain of cash he had amassed until, passing a jeweler's, he decided to buy gemstones.

In 1969 the Americans began withdrawing. Two years later the economy of South Vietnam was on the verge of collapse. And by the following year the economy *had* collapsed. Everything had to be imported, even rice; but the dollars to pay for those imports were gone. People were desperate for money, and Tran, with his gemstones, found himself in the unique position of having money. He converted several of the stones to cash, and began to bribe his way out of the country.

It took him eight months to get an exit visa, a piece of paper nearly impossible to obtain. An American soldier he had known agreed to act as his sponsor in the United States. It was November 1972, and Tran was thirty-seven years old.

Swishing around in his stomach as he stepped on board the plane to Hawaii were fifteen gemstones thickly coated with beeswax. Two days later, in a hotel in San Francisco, he shit the stones out into the bathtub. Those stones would help establish him in his new home.

Berns Hanson blathered on.
Outside, the morning was clear and cool.
Tran stared at the bare hills that towered above his house,

30

bright green in the sun. Ribs of dark oaks marked the gullies.

He had been living in the hills of Laurel Valley for five years, and still the view amazed him. To Loan it had just been home; she had been excited that the century plants at the end of the driveway were going to bloom.

In early 1973, after a brief tour of the United States, Tran settled in the Chinatown section of San Francisco. His American friends lived where it would have been difficult for him to find work or fit in. He had few skills. He had the gems, but he was unsure where best to invest them. So he took a job as a cook.

He worked as a cook for two years, then bought his own restaurant, on Piedmont Avenue in Oakland. He sold two diamonds, a ruby, and an emerald to make the down payment.

Tran's House of Flowers was an instant success. The food was hot and spicy, the vegetables crisp, the sauces distinct. Amid the sea of muddy Cantonese restaurants, the House of Flowers stood out. And there was no aching jaw at the end of the meal.

Every morning Tran set out fresh flowers, a different flower on every table. And at the end of the meal, as his guests left, there was a gift for each lady: a delicate silk blossom.

Tran kept the books himself, partly because he didn't trust anyone else, but mostly so he could lift a few dollars from the day's receipts. Once a month he put the cash in a safe-deposit box in the bank.

Five years after the opening of his restaurant a woman came to work for him. She was bright, pretty, and had an infectious laugh. She was also Vietnamese. Six months later they were married, nearly twenty years to the day after his first marriage. Again a daughter was born, Loan.

Four years later they moved to Laurel Valley so Loan could grow up in the country. Tran sold his restaurant and opened a new House of Flowers in Walnut Creek. Again the restaurant was a success. Everything Tran did was a success.

A year before his marriage, with the price of diamonds going through the roof, Tran sold his remaining stones and invested in real estate. His timing was astounding. By 1987 the value of his holdings had increased to such a degree that he was able to sell off two properties and pay off all his mortgages.

But 1987 was also the year his wife suddenly developed a swelling in her abdomen. Eight months later she was dead. He was stunned. This was America, the land of medical miracles: bypass surgery, chemotherapy. But the doctors had been able to do nothing.

Every morning Tran walked his daughter to the school bus.

Why did Mommy die?

He did not know.

Was Mommy happy?

He didn't know that, either.

Was Mommy all alone?

After a month the questions slowed; and, after a year she rarely mentioned her mother. It was frightening how quickly the young healed and forgot.

Every morning he walked his daughter to the school bus, half a mile down the road. It was his pleasure. And then, just a month ago, she decided she was old enough to walk alone. He imagined the other children teased her, always escorted by her father. He struck a compromise. She had a friend a few houses up the road; the two girls would walk together.

Loan. She had only known a few words of Vietnamese, endearments.

The television flashed.

Berns Hanson: resplendent in a three-piece charcoal suit, a picture of health and concern and responsibility, a youngish man. And an older man next to him: George Herbert Brenden.

A word had caught Tran's attention: AK-47. Brenden was there to be interviewed. He was a spokesman for the National Association of Gun Owners, NAGO. Tran turned up the volume.

"...and wasn't it the AK-47 that was used against our boys in Vietnam?"

"That's right, Berns. The AK-47."

Berns Hanson raised his chin. "Well, why do we need the gun that killed so many of our young men—the enemy's gun—available in this country as a 'sporting weapon'? A gun that's being used to kill our children again."

Tran turned the volume up another notch. He wondered

32

whether Berns Hanson even had any children.

George Herbert Brenden crossed his legs. "You might as well ask why we need Toyotas or Mercedes, Berns."

"But why these guns at all, George? Assault rifles aren't used for hunting, or for self-defense."

Brenden leaned forward. "Berns, do you know what the most devastating close-range weapon is?"

Berns Hanson shook his head.

"It's a shotgun, an ordinary shotgun. If that guy Purdy, or that guy Mattox, had been using a shotgun, there would have been five times as many dead kids. It's not the weapon, Berns. It's the guy who picks up the weapon."

Berns Hanson laughed. "Come on, George. You rifle guys have been saying that for twenty years. Look at the statistics: a few handfuls of firearm deaths in most countries, ten thousand in the U.S.A."

Brenden nodded. "It's a trade-off, Berns. No doubt about it. But I'll tell you, there aren't too many countries where an individual's rights are protected as well as in the U.S.A. And that protection is a package: the Constitution. It's lasted for over two hundred years. And the right of citizens to keep and bear arms is part of that package."

"*Any* sort of arms, George?"

"That's what the Constitution says—'the right of the people to keep and bear arms.' "

"A bazooka? A tank?"

Brenden smiled indulgently. "Now, Berns, you know most of us don't even have room for that extra car. Where would we put a tank?"

Tran sighed.

"And consider this, Berns: If guns were outlawed, only the military and the police would have guns. Does that sound a little like our neighbors to the south? Is that what *we* want?"

Tran wondered why total strangers addressed each other by their first names. He found the practice condescending.

An ad for orange juice popped on the screen: smiling children, smiling mother, happy family music. Loan had liked orange juice. Orange juice, and bacon and eggs. An American.

The orange juice was replaced in rapid succession by coffee, lawn fertilizer, and a car. The car happened to be the same-model car Tran owned.

And then Berns Hanson was back, smiling at the audience and announcing his guest again. He turned to George Herbert Brenden.

"Isn't it a fact, George, that it's just too easy to buy a gun in America?"

Brenden nodded. "You're certainly right there, Berns. A criminal can walk down any street in any city in this country and buy any gun he wants."

Berns Hanson crossed his legs. "I had in mind the ease with which someone like Purdy could legally buy an assault rifle."

Tran closed his eyes. The Stockton massacre had been too close, just an hour away. When he had heard about it on the radio, it had made him giddy: a tragedy that had happened to someone else this time, not him.

And then, little more than a week later, the copycat shooting. And this time it *was* his tragedy.

George Brenden pointed his finger at Berns Hanson. "That Purdy fellow should have been in jail, Berns. He had a history of arrests. Not one of you media people ever talk about how the criminal-justice system failed, only about how easy it is to get a gun. It's as if you've given up on locking up criminals. NAGO is in favor of a mandatory jail sentence for the criminal use of a firearm. No exceptions. No excuses. No plea bargaining."

Berns Hanson was ready. "And who's going to pay for all the new jails we'll need, George?"

George Brenden laughed. It was a pleasant laugh, and Tran thought the man would probably be a good neighbor, the sort of man who kept an eye out for your kids when they were on the street.

"*I'd* help pay for those jails, Berns. Would you? Would you give some of your million-dollar salary to lock up a criminal who one day might rape your daughter or sell her drugs?" He pointed at the camera. "I don't think the folks out there would mind paying for those jails."

Tran nodded. He would be happy to write a check.

34

George Brenden looked down at his hands; they were folded in his lap. "You know, Berns, you look at TV today, and all you see is guns and violence, killing and car wrecks. Solve your problems with a gun. That's what our children are learning." He shook his head. "When I was growing up, a gun wasn't something to be proud of; marksmanship was something to be proud of. We need to get hold of our kids. We need to teach them what's right and what's wrong, at home and in school. I'd like to see gun education right there next to sex education. Let's not pretend this stuff doesn't exist. Let's teach our kids. What sort of legacy is ignorance?"

Tran turned off the television. It hissed and popped for a minute and then was silent. He could hear the birds outside, and the distant hum of cars on the freeway.

He had done a great many things in his life, some pleasant, some not so pleasant, many of which, as a child, he would never have imagined he would do. But now, at fifty-four, with maybe another twenty or thirty years before him, his life promised nothing; all he had ever cared about had been taken from him. It was the violence of America that had done this. It had taken his child. Both his children.

And George Herbert Brenden still defended that violence. And he did it well, convincingly; one couldn't help but agree with what he said, even though what he said was madness. A messenger who *was* the message.

Tran lit a cigarette. Well, he would make the messenger think twice about his message. He would offer back a little violence to the country that had become his home.

He sat back and began to plan his revenge, and realized he didn't know where to start. He had never done anything violent, not even in the army. He didn't imagine he could just walk up to Brenden and plunge a knife into his chest. Probably, the man carried a gun.

He drummed his fingers on the arm of the chair. He would have to find someone to help him. Someone who *did* know about violence.

T he dial on the meter of the audio detector jumped.

Peter Weston glanced at the recorder next to the meter: both the time and the intensity of the signal had been noted.

He snapped his fingers again, more softly this time.

Again the dial jumped.

The audio detector was a new item, ultrasensitive for ultrasecurity. That's what the brochure boasted. But Peter Weston, who had been in the security business for nearly twenty years, knew that ultrasensitive was not always ultrasecurity. For one thing, an ultrasensitive audio device was prey to the "cry wolf" syndrome: it gave off so many false alarms it was next to useless. This sort of device required continuous absolute silence, and how many places on earth were *that* quiet? Inevitably, the heating system clanked, or rumbled, or hissed. Or the house groaned, or the floors creaked. Ultrasensitive audio units worked far better as eavesdropping devices than as alarms.

He switched off the machine and walked across the room to retrieve the microphone.

The best security installations were those that were designed for a specific site. Usually, this required a period of location monitoring during which background noise, the changing level of light, and the time and frequency of traffic could be ascertained. Cars, people, dogs, and cats all needed to be taken into consideration; even mice—he would never forget searching for the glitch in *that* job. Only when all the variables of a specific site had been measured could a comprehensive and effective system be devised, one that would signal the presence of a burglar, and not the escape of the family gerbil. A really good installation required balance and imagination. This was the sort of installation Peter did for a living—high-cost custom jobs. Over the years he had achieved a modest reputation.

The phone rang, and Peter reached for it.

It took Peter a moment to recognize the voice on the other end; it had been years since he had spoken with the man. Out of habit he checked the digital analyzer beside his desk. The device automatically and continuously scanned the phone line, letting him know if a tap had been installed. Peter didn't expect anyone to be tapping his phone. Still, it was nice to *know*.

"It must be ten years, Tran."

Tran smiled. "Your memory is very good, Peter. Ten years exactly."

"Is your restaurant still serving the best food in town?"

"Not too many empty tables."

They chatted for a few minutes about nothing. Finally, there was a pause.

"Peter, I need some help."

It was Peter Weston who finally had to tell Tran that U.S. mortar fire had killed his wife and daughter. He hadn't wanted to do it. Tran was his pal. And Tran had once saved his life.

It had happened in a coastal village. They were there interviewing the survivors of a search-and-destroy mission, working their way from hutch to hutch. Usually, these interviews took place on the base in Qui Nhon. But sometimes, when an entire village had been razed, Peter was sent to the site to investigate.

Most of the hutches in this village were still standing, thanks to a downpour that had started in the middle of the torch party.

Peter had been commenting on the villagers' good luck when Tran caught his arm. He pointed at the ground. The dirt in front of the hutch was smooth, pocked only by raindrops. Peter took one giant step back.

Outside the other hutches some villagers stood watching. Peter stared at them.

They stared back.

They had been ready to let him walk in there; they were waiting around to watch him die.

He reached into his pocket and took out a cigarette lighter and touched the flame to the thatching on the hutch. A few minutes later the booby trap exploded.

There were a couple of other close calls. After twelve months, Peter owed Tran.

So when Tran wrote to Peter in 1972, saying that he would like to emigrate to America and that he would like Peter to be his sponsor, Peter was happy to balance the books a little. Six months later the two men stood in the San Francisco Airport shaking hands.

They had seen each other only a few times since, the last time in 1979 when Peter had a job in the Bay area. They had eaten dinner together at Tran's restaurant. It was a terrific meal. But the reunion was awkward, as if the past they shared was more a wedge than a bond. It was the last time Peter had talked to Tran, and, except for a wedding announcement about a year later, the last time Tran had been in touch.

"What sort of help do you need, Tran?" Peter asked.

There was a pause at the other end of the line.

"You do security work, Peter. There must be times when alarms aren't enough."

Peter thought he had a fairly good idea what Tran was going to say next; it was something he was asked from time to time by some of his more desperate clients, something he assumed all security men were occasionally asked.

"I need a certain person taken care of, Peter. Do you know anyone who might do that sort of work?"

* * *

It was a chance encounter that brought Peter Weston and Eliot Brod together. Peter was nineteen at the time. He was in college; it was winter; and he was in the gym, looking for something to do. Eliot was also in the gym, doing some sort of karate kata, and Peter, who had studied karate since he was twelve, and who had never seen anything quite like what Eliot was doing, stopped to watch.

Brod wasn't a large man, and to Peter, who was six feet tall and 180 pounds, it looked like a chance to practice his karate and kick a little ass in a friendly sort of way. But when they started sparring, it was Peter who was getting his ass kicked, and kicked badly. He quite simply *couldn't* hit Brod.

When they stopped, Peter's ribs were sore and already starting to bruise. The only reason he was still on his feet was that Eliot hadn't hit him in the head. And all this punishment from a freshman!

Peter conceded defeat and asked if Eliot would teach him how to fight, and Eliot, who had no one else to work out with, agreed. They practiced nearly every day for two and a half years.

Eliot's suggestions went against everything Peter had ever learned.

"Move more slowly," he urged.

Peter thought it was ridiculous to move slowly. The entire point of fighting was to beat the other guy to the punch, something he just couldn't seem to do.

Eliot made Peter practice walking, just walking for hours breathing in and breathing out. He took Peter's hands and moved him back and forth across the room, as if they were partners in a dance. He made Peter do it with his eyes closed. Peter would never forget the day the wrestling team found them like that.

Just before Peter graduated, Eliot gave him a gift, a small stiletto that had come from Japan. That knife could cut through four layers of cloth. Peter took it with him when he went to Vietnam. But a clerk on an army base doesn't do much fighting.

When Peter had two months remaining to his year in Vietnam, he received a letter from his father informing him that his sister had been gravely injured. He had called home that day.

He would never forget that conversation. His father answered the phone.

"What happened to my sister?" he demanded.

"Is that you, Peter?" His father sounded asleep.

Peter nodded. "Yes, it's me, Peter. What happened to Suzanne? Is she going to be okay?"

"It doesn't look like she's going to die."

"But is she going to be okay?"

There was a long pause at the other end of the line. "We don't know yet."

After that Peter started counting the days. He only wanted to get home. He only wanted to see his baby sister, as if, in his presence, she could not help but mend.

But when he finally saw her, he knew she would never mend.

Suzanne Weston was four years younger than Peter. With straw-blond hair, a pert nose, and an inquisitive manner, she was America's idea of the girl next door. She had idolized Peter all her life (her big brother!), and he, perhaps because four years separated them, or perhaps because she was a girl, had only picked on her occasionally.

He let her play with his old toys. He let her tag along when he went fishing, if his friends weren't around. And when he got his driver's license, he drove her wherever she wanted to go.

But four years is a big gap between children, and when Suzanne was still thirteen, Peter went off to college. It was the fall of 1963, and things were about to change for America. A generation of children who had only known the sunshine and optimism of the fifties was about to grow up and notice that the world wasn't such a nice place. They reacted in an entirely predictable manner: They protested.

Student protests began in California and like a wave moved across the country. There were demonstrations for student rights, and demonstrations against the Vietnam War; and while these protests didn't exactly trickle down to the high schools, they colored the air these children breathed. In 1964 the Beatles

41

arrived, and very definitely trickled down to the high schools. Then the war in Vietnam began to heat up, and for the first time Suzanne Weston, who was sixteen now, realized that her beloved brother might have to go. Each night the number of dead was announced on the evening news. One day soon Peter might be among them.

She began to read the papers, and began to have fights with her parents over politics. These fights grew worse as she grew older and the war escalated. Finally, in 1967, to everyone's relief, Suzanne Weston went off to college, at the University of Chicago.

And to her surprise, mostly because she hadn't really thought about it, she found herself suddenly surrounded by thousands of other young and idealistic youths who felt much the way she did. Energy reinforced energy. The parental anchor was gone. And Suzanne, like all young people, thought that if she shouted loudly enough, things would change.

In October 1967, along with the great and not so great, she went to Washington to march on the Pentagon. She wrote her senators and her congressman protesting the war. And in November she began to write to her brother, who was now in Vietnam. She wrote him three times a week, telling him about the protests and demonstrations. He wrote back and told her not to worry. She worried anyhow.

At the end of January 1968, on the eve of Tet, the Viet Cong and the North Vietnamese Army attempted to overrun South Vietnam. Militarily, this was a disaster for them. But in the United States, the operation was a public-relations triumph. For most Americans it seemed the only thing at the end of the tunnel were more VC.

For the first time the antiwar people tasted blood, the Pentagon's blood. Robert Kennedy had announced he was going to run for president; Lyndon Johnson was stepping down; there was the possibility the war might be brought to an end.

And then the forces of war struck back. In April, Martin Luther King, Jr., was shot dead. In June, Robert Kennedy. And with his death the death of the political hopes of the antiwar movement. There was only one word to describe the mood of these young people now: rage!

GUN MEN

*   *   *

In a way Chicago was Suzanne Weston's home city. Peoria was of course closer, but Peoria was, well, Peoria.

Suzanne didn't like the politics in Chicago; she didn't like Mayor Daley. Had Mayor Daley been standing next to her listening to her thoughts, he would have tapped the ash off the end of his cigar onto her head. He could have cared less about the thoughts of young people; they could take their thoughts to someone else's city. It was the summer of 1968; he had a convention to put on, and he was damned if these kids were going to run riot in his streets. The word went down to the police captains, and from them to the man on the street. By Saturday, August 24, that man on the street had ten thousand buddies, and they weren't going to take any shit.

Suzanne Weston survived the skirmishes with police unscathed until Wednesday, August 28, the day the Democratic Convention voted down the peace plank. That night the TV cameras were live on the streets, and the country watched in horror and glee as the police beat the brains out of young men and women. Suzanne Weston didn't appear on TV that night; she had had her brains beaten out a little while before.

Early that afternoon antiwar protesters had gathered in Grant Park for a rally. There were speeches, and calls for a march, and the usual scuffles with the police. In the late afternoon it was decided a march *would* be held, and, using an unguarded bridge, the protesters made their way out of the park and onto Michigan Avenue. There, they found themselves virtually surrounded by police, and as night fell, the police attacked.

One group of demonstrators, Suzanne among them, attempted to flee down Balbo Avenue. They ran into another line of police. It was impossible to retreat because of the crowd behind them, so they sat down. The police marched right over them, clearing a path with their billy clubs. Unlike the police, the people sitting on the street were not wearing protective helmets.

Suzanne, along with the others who couldn't walk, was picked up and tossed into a paddy wagon and carted away. She was put in a cell and left there, and only later, after she passed out and after the swelling had done its damage, was she taken to a hospital.

By the time her father arrived, the doctors had already operated. The operation had come too late; the swelling inside her skull had crushed her brain. The doctor explained she might have been all right had she been treated immediately; it was the delay in treatment, more than anything, that had caused such extensive injury.

Peter saw her after the second operation. She was in a wheelchair, her chin covered with drool, her eyes rolling wildly. She was babbling away, a horrible slurred monologue that made no sense, yet seemed to send her body into spasms. Every now and then an intelligible phrase popped out.

"She's better," his father said. He tried to smile.

Peter just stared at him. He felt sick.

His mother had refused to come with them. By then she was drowning in the bottle. Four years later she was dead.

The operations on Suzanne Weston continued for a year before the doctors gave up. During those twelve months John Weston grew old and gray, and deeply bitter.

When Peter was discharged from the army, he and his father sat down with a bottle of Jim Beam. They had been to visit Suzanne that day. It had been nearly a year since she had been injured.

Neither man spoke for an hour. Then John Weston began to talk. He talked about his daughter, told Peter about the time she had hit a home run, the smile that had been on her face. He told him about a certain dress she had looked so pretty in. He talked about his daughter for two and a half hours, finally finishing with Suzanne's last summer at home.

"This should never have happened, Peter. Not in America. I'm going to find the man who did this to my daughter. I want the same thing done to him."

Peter looked at him. Did his father expect *him* to carry out this revenge? A family vendetta? He wondered if he could pull it off. Then he thought of the man who could certainly pull it off.

44

GUN MEN

* * *

It would have been nearly impossible for Eliot Brod to do the job John Weston had in mind, except for one thing: Weston had already done most of the job for him.

Six months after Suzanne was injured, John Weston started looking for the man who had clubbed his daughter. The search took him eleven months and five days.

He went to every newspaper, visited every photographer, viewed every piece of film he could find. He told people he was writing a book on the Chicago convention, a street perspective. Those people who had been on the street liked the idea their story would be told and were glad to help. If they wondered why the polite and well-dressed man before them wanted to tell the story—a man who appeared to be in his fifties and who was not at all the sort of person who had actually *been* on the street—they might have figured he was motivated by an old-fashioned American sense of outrage at what had happened. The shrewder among them, or the more cynical, might have wagered he had some personal stake in the project.

At first, John Weston found himself looking for his daughter in each photo. But after three weeks he realized he would never get anywhere if he didn't pick up the pace, and so he began to scan more quickly, looking specifically for the scenes of confrontation.

For appearance's sake, at each newspaper or magazine or photographer's studio, he asked for a copy of several photos. He made careful notes about where and when the picture had been taken, and by whom, so the credit would be correct. And as he was leaving, he always asked the man (or woman) if he (or she) knew the name of any other photographer who had been on the streets. After six months the people he was told to look up were almost always the people he had already visited; and after ten months he was about ready to concede defeat. He had talked to a hundred photographers, had looked through tens of thousands of photos and negatives. It seemed no one had been on Balbo taking pictures that Wednesday night.

And then he found the picture, one of thirty-six images on a contact sheet. The contact sheet, and dozens like it, had been collecting dust in the files of a small Midwest newspaper.

He tracked down the photographer and had him print a few copies: a picture of a young girl with blond hair, her left arm raised to ward off the blow of the nightstick that was already falling. The face of the officer swinging the club could be clearly seen under the light of the flash.

John Weston wondered how the photographer had managed to walk away with his camera after taking that picture.

Then he started to cry. He stared at the picture of his daughter and cried, remembering what she had been like all the years before that terrible night. He cried for what he had lost and would never have again.

John Weston spotted Sergeant Micky O'Connell outside the fifth station house he visited. O'Connell was climbing out of a car, and Weston would have run him over then and there if a bus hadn't pulled in between.

He followed O'Connell to a bar and sat watching as the cop knocked down three whiskeys. When O'Connell left, John Weston stepped to the bar and asked the bartender whether the man who had just walked out the door had once played second base for the White Sox—the name was on the tip of his tongue. The bartender said that as far as he knew, the man had always been a cop—Micky O'Connell.

John Weston shook his head and smiled—another few years and his memory would be as gray as his hair. He ordered another beer.

Michael O'Connell was listed in the phone book.

John Weston didn't want Micky O'Connell killed. He wanted him maimed, badly maimed. He wanted his back broken; and he wanted his hands and arms crushed.

Peter told Eliot.

Eliot didn't want to meet John Weston. He wanted Peter to be the go-between; he would be paid for being the go-between—10 percent.

Peter didn't want the money, but Eliot had insisted. There would be risks: O'Connell's friends might want revenge; and if Eliot was caught, they might *all* wind up in jail.

Eliot wanted the money up front, ten thousand dollars.

John Weston balked at the conditions. He never paid up front; and he always knew who was working for him. It wasn't that he didn't trust his son; it was that he didn't trust his son's judgment of other men. When Peter left with the ten thousand dollars, John Weston had two men follow him.

The tail went smoothly from Chicago to New York and then north, until Peter left the main highway and headed toward the mountains of Vermont. There, at the base of some mountain in the middle of nowhere, Peter parked the car and started up the hill; he had the money in a day pack on his back.

The two detectives looked at each other; between them they had an extra fifty pounds. They got out of the car and surveyed the hill. It was steep and icy, and Peter was already out of sight. So they did the professional thing: They got back in the car and circled the mountain to see if they could find any other cars that were parked. They did—fifteen, plus another sixty-three at various diners and restaurants, plus another forty-two sitting in driveways, plus however many cars are in a small town. The circle took them almost an hour, after which they drove to a store, bought coffee, food, and blankets, filled the gas tank, and went back to wait. Even if they flubbed the job, they still had their retainers.

Half an hour later Peter returned without the pack. He waved at the two detectives and started back to New York, wondering whether he should give the thousand dollars in his pocket to his father.

It was easy for Eliot Brod to find Micky O'Connell. John Weston had given him the man's home address, the station house where he worked, and the bar he drank at. He had also sent along a picture.

What was not so easy was finding a place to do the job. It was going to take him a full minute to maim O'Connell, and if the man struggled, a bit longer. There was also the chance O'Connell might cry out.

At 6:15 on March 12, 1970, Micky O'Connell walked into his favorite bar and parked his ass on his favorite barstool. It had been another bad day, and what he needed was a couple of glasses of booze to make it better. He unbuttoned his coat.

It was raw out, and he was glad to get out of the wind. For the last few years he had feared the wind more than the punks on the street.

He tipped back the shot glass the bartender had set in front of him.

The bar was warm and cozy, with a smell of stale beer and sawdust. A familiar smell. He wondered why the sawdust? The bar was fifty years old and hadn't been remodeled in thirty years.

He signaled Charley to give him a refill.

"How come it smells like sawdust in here, Charley?"

Charley shrugged. "Maybe it's the stuff the cleaning girl uses."

O'Connell nodded. Sure. And maybe hookers had hearts. And maybe crime didn't pay.

Sip by sip the whiskey washed away the day, consigning it to the garbage can that was his life. The whiskey would kill the taste of his wife's dinner. It would be a fog over the evening news and the noise of his kids.

He drained his glass and ordered one for the road.

He was beginning to hate his kids, a bunch of sullen teen-agers who seemed to blame him personally for the fact that the world was fucked up. He had had to bail the oldest one out of jail for dealing drugs. They were all *using* drugs. It pissed him off. A lot of things pissed him off.

It pissed him off that the country was falling apart, and he didn't understand why. There were more cars and meat and whatever-you-wanted-to-buy in America than there was room to put the stuff, yet for the last five years people had been marching and protesting and rioting as if they didn't have enough to eat. He didn't understand it. He didn't understand it at all.

He collected what was left of his ten-dollar bill, waved good-bye to Charley, and headed for the door. The floor was wobbly under his feet. Outside, the wind grabbed for his throat. He buttoned his coat; even with the booze it was freezing out. He hurried up the block and around the corner to his car, the car keys already in his hand.

As he bent down to unlock the door, the wind died, and a sudden warmth took its place. It took him a moment to realize *why* the wind had died.

But before he could turn to see who had snuck up on him, a hand pressed him gently forward. Micky O'Connell lost his balance and tipped against the car, bumping his head on the roof. He giggled. It was an absurd position; he could hardly move. He was about to push himself up when a blow to the lower back sent him to his knees. Two more blows of the short, weighted stick assured that he would never walk again.

O'Connell tore frantically at his coat, trying to get at his gun.

The stick flicked out and cracked his wrist.

His arm went numb.

Another flick, and the other arm was numb.

O'Connell couldn't do a thing as the man dragged him into the space between the cars. Blow after blow rained down.

Micky O'Connell looked up into the face of the man who was doing this to him. All he could see under the ski mask were the eyes. The eyes weren't even looking at him.

Eliot Brod pounded O'Connell's arms and hands until they were pulp; it took a little over a minute. When the job was done, he pocketed the stick and walked away.

By chance, O'Connell had parked on a street that was not much used. It was not chance that Eliot Brod had been there waiting; he had been following O'Connell on and off for a week.

Micky O'Connell would have died of shock if he hadn't been found a little while later. The subsequent investigation was extensive. Everyone O'Connell had ever arrested was dragged in. Every file in the city involving a maiming was pulled. The street, and O'Connell's clothes, were gone over with a microscope.

The detectives came up with nothing.

O'Connell had been a cop for almost thirty years. He had worked Narcotics, Homicide, Theft. He had helped keep order during race riots, peace marches, and various other civil disturbances. There were too many leads and not enough clues. And there was nothing in any of the files that linked him, personally, to the beating of a once-pretty young girl.

When the detectives questioned the bartender, Charley couldn't recall anyone asking after Micky O'Connell; and there hadn't been any strangers in the bar that night. It never crossed his mind that the well-dressed gent from a couple of months back was the man they were looking for. After all, *he* had been wondering about a White Sox second baseman.

Peter Weston tapped his fingers on the desk. He had kept the thousand dollars Eliot had given him. Over the years there had been quite a number of jobs, and the 10 percent had added up. He liked the money, and he liked the little bit of risk that went with knowing a killer. It gave him status. The people he sent to Eliot were the sort of people who liked to show their appreciation. There had been parties, and boat trips, and gifts. Some of the gifts had been quite cute.

He wondered who Tran wanted killed. Maybe the owner of another restaurant.

"I might know someone," he said.

5

The main post office in Springfield, Massachusetts, is a dingy gray, modern brick building that sits like a fort at the north end of the city. The lobby, where the P.O. boxes are located, is open seven days a week, twenty-four hours a day. Outside the lobby, on the sidewalk, a bank of newspaper machines fronts the curb.

On Saturday morning, February 4, William S. Jones was standing inside the Springfield Post Office stuffing mail into the P.O. boxes. He did this every day. First-class mail first, second-class mail, third-class mail. Then more first-class mail. Fourth-class mail. Second-class mail. First-class mail. On and on. An endless stream of mail. A flood of mail that never stopped, as inexorable as the tides, or time, and nearly as oppressive. Men started off at the post office with dark hair; they sorted mail until they grew old and retired, or died; and the mail just kept coming.

William Jones hated the mail. He hated the envelopes with handwriting he couldn't read, and he hated the presorted bulk mail with zip plus four. He hated packages because they were extra work, and he hated postcards because they stuck together. But in particular, he hated third-class mail: those unwanted

51

catalogs offering tools and seeds and clothes and whatnot. The ink on these cheaply printed fliers came off on his fingers and could hardly be scrubbed off. It sat there for hours, seeping through his skin, poisoning him—he could only wonder what sort of cancer he would get.

He'd tried wearing gloves, but the gloves had proved awkward and had made his fingers cramp. And he'd tried washing off the ink, hurrying to the bathroom every time his hands looked gray. But after a week his supervisor had reprimanded him for malingering.

He crammed a piece of junk mail into an already crowded slot, purposefully crushing it. Why didn't people pick up their mail? Where the hell was he supposed to put all this crap?

Had William Jones been a more curious sort of person, or had he worked in a post office that didn't have thousands and thousands of boxes, he might have noticed that the *only* thing that ever arrived at box 8423 was junk mail. No letter addressed by hand ever arrived. Never a postcard. Never a bill. Just a moderate stream of impersonal letters and catalogs and brochures.

He slipped one of these letters into box 8423, a plain white business envelope with a computer-printed paste-on address label. He did not notice the youngish man standing on the other side of the boxes who took the letter out a moment later.

Eliot stared at the envelope. It had a Wisconsin postmark and a first-class stamp, which meant it was from Peter.

The P.O. box was the only way Peter had to get in touch with him. He had never given Peter a phone number, or an address. In fact, he had never even told Peter that he had gotten married; that was his little secret. The two men hadn't seen each other for nine years, not since Eliot had decided to "disappear."

The disappearance had been relatively simple to arrange. When Eliot married Alison, *he* had changed *his* name. A bone for feminism, he had joked at the time. And after some initial kidding by their friends, it had been accepted, and then forgotten.

Eliot tore open the envelope. There, at the bottom of an advertisement for a vacation in Hawaii—Fun in the Sun!—was the line of code—the name and number of the person who wished to hire him. He hadn't gotten a job from Peter in more than three years. He stuffed the letter in his pocket and headed home.

It took Eliot just five minutes to decipher the line of code. A man named Tran Van Duong wished to hire him; his phone number was in the San Francisco area. Chinatown? He might be able to find out at the library.

Eliot finally found Tran Van Duong in the Contra Costa County phone book. The man lived in Laurel Valley. The library didn't have a street map of Laurel Valley, so he walked down the block to the bookstore. The best he could do there was a Rand McNally road atlas of the United States and a street map of the Oakland/Berkeley area. He bought the map of Oakland. He already had the road atlas.

When he got home, he found his daughter parked in front of the TV, watching, of all things, candlepin bowling—and on a sunny Saturday afternoon! He kicked her playfully in the butt.

"Want to go to the zoo tomorrow?"

She turned off the TV. "What zoo?"

"The Bronx Zoo."

"In New York!"

Alison looked up from her book. The only time Eliot went to New York was to make a business call. He always made these calls from New York. When she had asked him why, he had laughed and said nostalgia. Twelve years ago he had stood in a phone booth in Manhattan and called her.

"Can we go see the alligators, Daddy? I want to see the alligators."

Eliot nodded. "Sure. Whatever you want."

They spent the morning looking at the alligators, and the big cats, and the chimps. When Cecelia finally got hungry, Eliot bought her some lunch and sat her down at a table next to a phone booth so he could keep an eye on her while he made his

53

call. A man answered the phone; from the singsong voice Eliot guessed Tran was an immigrant from the Far East.

"My name is Robin," he said clearly. "My friend Peter tells me you have a job you need done."

It took Tran a second to realize who Robin must be and what job he was talking about. "Yes. A job."

"The person's name?"

"George Herbert Brenden."

"His address?"

"I don't know his address. He's the national spokesman for NAGO, the National Association of Gun Owners."

"And your reason for the job?"

Tran sighed. How to answer in less than a thousand words? "He said something that offended me."

"He said this to you personally? Were there witnesses?"

"He was on television. A talk-show interview."

Eliot stared at the phone. Over the years he had been given some pretty thin reasons for wanting someone killed, but this came close to being the thinnest. He was about to hang up when Tran continued.

"Perhaps I should explain *why* I found what Mr. Brenden said offensive." He paused. "You recall the massacre that took place in Laurel Valley eleven days ago?"

Eliot looked at Cecelia, busy picking over her french fries. She waved at him. He waved back. No one who had a child would ever forget the California shootings. He felt like dropping the phone and rushing over to give his daughter a hug.

"My daughter was one of the children killed," Tran said.

Eliot nodded.

"And not a week later this NAGO spokesman was speaking out about the need for *more* guns. And speaking out elegantly, convincingly." Tran felt the anger he had felt at the time return. "You can understand my feelings."

Eliot tried to imagine what *his* feelings would have been, but couldn't. He couldn't bear to think of Cecelia dying. She was too dear to him. It wasn't the natural order of things.

It didn't surprise him that Tran wanted Brenden killed. Several times over the years he had been asked something similar. Mattox was dead, so Tran had focused his anger on Brenden. Brenden's bad luck.

By chance Eliot had seen the same interview with Brenden, or one very much like it. The spokesman *had* been convincing, very convincing.

Eliot didn't know much about NAGO, other than that the organization, along with the NRA, opposed all gun control and wasn't above trying to bribe duly elected officials to get what it wanted. But did a spokesman for NAGO deserve to die? He smiled to himself. There was great historical precedent for killing the messenger.

The coins dropped, and Eliot fed the machine more quarters.

"A hundred thousand dollars."

Tran was silent. He hadn't thought about the cost, which surprised him, for he was a frugal man. He wondered what he had been saving his money for.

"One hundred thousand dollars," he agreed.

"How will you get the money?"

"The money is sitting in a safe-deposit box."

"I'd like it in hundreds."

"That won't be a problem."

"Have you ever contacted Brenden, or made any threats against him or his organization?"

"No, nothing."

"What is your exact address?"

Tran gave him his address.

"And your daily schedule?"

Tran frowned. "Why do you need to know that? It is *I* who am hiring *you*!" He found the questions reminiscent of the immigration and emigration forms he had had to fill out. Endless questions about everything and nothing. And then the interviews, and more questions.

Eliot sighed. This wasn't the first time a client had resented his questions.

"Mr. Duong, it is not *I* who have sought *you* out. Before I take a job, I must evaluate the risk."

Tran recited his schedule. "There is one condition," he added. "I want you to use a handgun."

55

Eliot almost laughed. He could already see the evening news report.

Usually, he didn't allow a client to place him under any constraints, not time, not place, not method. But in this instance he was willing to make an exception. He told Tran a handgun was okay.

"The payment has to be up front. How soon can you have it?"

There was the usual pause; Eliot had come to expect it. People just didn't like paying up front. The only client he had ever had who didn't complain was his wife.

And Tran was about to complain, but then thought better of it. He had already antagonized the man once. The worst that could happen was that he would lose a bit of cash he had no use for anyway.

"You can collect the money anytime; I only need an hour to retrieve it. And, of course, it must be on a weekday."

On Monday morning, after Cecelia had left for school, and after Alison had left for her studio, and after he had done the dishes, Eliot got in his car, a Buick station wagon with imitation-wood side panels, and drove to the library to see what he could find out about NAGO and George Herbert Brenden.

He found out very little. The library had only one book on NAGO: a history of the organization, which was founded in 1924, the result of a schism in the leadership of the NRA. The book, published twenty-two years ago, was mostly an account of shooting competitions, profiles of the leadership, and a history of the relevant legislative issues. There was no reference to Brenden.

In the *Readers' Guide to Periodical Literature,* he found a dozen or so more recent articles. He read them all—mostly recaps of local and state gun-legislation battles. One of the articles mentioned Brenden in passing.

In the *Encyclopedia of Associations,* Eliot got the bare bones of the organization: membership 2,807,486; dues thirty dollars annually; the number of state chapters; the budget (dues times membership); publications—*Guns and Hunters,* monthly; and the phone number and address of NAGO headquarters in Washington, D.C.

Eliot scribbled down the number and address. The library didn't have *Guns and Hunters,* but the library at a nearby state university did.

Things went better at the university. *All* the recent issues of *Guns and Hunters* were on the shelf. Eliot collected about a year's worth and found himself a quiet corner.

Four issues back, tucked between an ad for an assault rifle and a new, compact garden chipper, Eliot found a photo of George Herbert Brenden; he was presenting an award to a high school gun club in Oregon. Eliot read the accompanying article.

He read through an entire year of magazines, and though there were occasional references to speeches Brenden *had* made, there wasn't a single mention of an *upcoming* speech. There was also no note of Brenden's home address, which surprised Eliot, because most of the other NAGO reps *did* have their addresses in the magazine.

Five years back Eliot found Brenden's address: Homewood, Illinois. At that time Brenden had been the Midwest regional rep.

Eliot jotted down the address, and made a copy of the photo and a few other things, then he returned the magazines to the shelf. The library didn't have the Homewood phone book, so he called Illinois information: George Herbert Brenden still lived at the same address. He checked an atlas: Homewood was one of Chicago's south suburbs.

Eliot had done jobs in the suburbs before. He hated them. It was next to impossible to look inconspicuous, which made it next to impossible to do a surveillance, especially for one man working alone. And he had discovered through personal experience that people in the suburbs tended to be suspicious to the point of paranoia, and were not at all shy about calling the police.

He looked over his notes. Considering he had spent most of the day in the library, he didn't have much. Brenden was probably in his fifties (Eliot's guess from the *Guns and Hunters* photo), and he probably traveled a lot (judging from the various places he had given talks).

Eliot dearly wished he could catch the man on the road; it would make the job that much easier, especially if he knew where Brenden was going to be a couple of weeks in advance.

He got up and walked out of the reference room and took the elevator to another part of the library. There were offices here, and Eliot walked into the first one that was empty and closed the door. He seated himself at the desk and tapped out the phone number for NAGO headquarters in Washington.

While the connection was going through, he scanned the office: a room filled with books and papers (naturally); a photo cube of wife and children; various doodads and knickknacks (acquired, no doubt, during a sabbatical trip); a print of a famous painting; a real painting, not very good (the wife's?); a sport coat over the back of a chair. Sooner or later the man who owned that sport coat would be back.

A woman's voice answered the phone.

Eliot asked her if it would be possible to find out the speaking schedule of George Brenden, with the hope of attending one of his talks, as he had heard the man on the radio. And, by the way, could he, Thomas Petarro, get a membership application?

The woman told him whom he would have to speak with and transferred the call.

Another woman answered the phone, and Eliot repeated his request. The woman took his name and address and promised to send out a membership application that day, and wasn't it nice he was signing on. She didn't know George Brenden's schedule herself—she thought he spoke by invitation—but she could pass him on to someone who might be able to help.

The third woman he was passed to listened to his speech and said she knew just who he needed to speak with and could he hold a moment. Precious moments went by. Finally, another woman came on the line. Again, Eliot explained what he wanted. The soft southern voice started chattering away.

From the slight crack in her voice, Eliot knew the woman must be in her fifties or sixties; he also knew that if he laughed at her jokes and was charming, she would tell him everything he needed to know. He prayed he would have the time to get it all.

Brenden was giving a speech tomorrow in Oklahoma.

"And I'm stuck up here in Boston," Eliot said. "I've never been to Oklahoma."

"Me neither," the woman replied.

"I don't suppose he has his schedule made up much in advance?"

She laughed. "Actually, for most of the year. Let's see."

He heard her leafing through what sounded like a sheaf of papers but was probably a desk calendar.

"He's got a vacation coming up, then another tour." She laughed. "A talk in Boston! How about that? Is that your hometown?"

"New York," Eliot said.

She laughed. "I couldn't live in New York myself. All those people and big buildings and crime. Not that we don't have our own big buildings and crime."

Eliot hummed a response.

She gave him the name of the hotel Brenden was going to speak at, as well as the group he was addressing. "It's a shame it's a private affair. But maybe you can oozle your way in. Let's see what else he's got."

Eliot wrote furiously as she ran down the list.

"Are you a veteran?" George was going to address a veterans' group.

Eliot wasn't a veteran.

"How about a member of the American Legion?"

Eliot scribbled down the address. He had taught himself an abbreviated shorthand for just such occasions. It was stupid to miss information because you couldn't write fast enough or remember it all. And it was almost as stupid to pester the person on the other end, asking for a number to be repeated. That was a good way to turn off the tap.

Eliot succeeded in getting Brenden's entire schedule, from Ohio to Massachusetts. He offered his thanks. The woman on the other end laughed.

"And if you miss him at all those places, you can always catch him in Dallas at the annual convention. It's coming up in May."

Eliot had a copy of the convention schedule. He thanked her again and hung up the phone.

As he opened the door to the office, a man stumbled in. Eliot stepped right next to him, his eyes wide.

"My cat!" he exclaimed. He spread his hands wide, palms up, to show that they were empty. "I can't find my cat." He shook his head and walked out of the office.

Bill Wendel watched him disappear down the hall. He *knew* he hadn't closed the door to his office; he never closed the door. And if the man had only been looking for his cat, why had *he* closed the door? It didn't make sense.

He sat down in his chair and looked around the room. It didn't appear that anything was missing. What had the man been doing?

He wondered whether he should notify campus security. The man might be deranged. He might injure someone.

While Eliot Brod was getting his fingers dusty in the library, Tran Van Duong was locked in a cubicle in the bank counting all his money. There would be more than enough, though this "withdrawal" would take most of it.

He counted out ten piles of ten thousand dollars, then carefully recounted each pile twice before placing a rubber band around it. When he had finished checking the number of bills in each bundle, he counted the bundles again to make sure there were ten, then placed a rubber band around the stack. He was surprised; it really wasn't a very big stack, considering how much money was there—enough to buy a house in most parts of the country. He tucked the stack into the box, closed the box, and returned it to the vault. He would leave the money there until Robin called.

Eliot's flight arrived at the Oakland airport in the early afternoon on Sunday, February 12.

He had driven to New York in the dark that morning and left his car in the parking lot. He had a suitcase, garment bag,

60

largish overnight bag, and three very expensive tennis rackets. He was just able to carry it all.

At the counter he paid cash for the ticket he had reserved (in someone else's name), and checked through the suitcase and garment bag. Hidden in the bottom of the overnight bag were ten stacks of paper. The paper weighed a little more than two pounds, and Eliot didn't think it would be noticed even during a careful search, which, of course, there would not be. He had the stacks of paper in his bag because he wanted to make sure the hundred thousand dollars he would be carrying on the way back would pass through the X-ray machine unchallenged.

At the security checkpoint, he dropped the bag and tennis rackets onto the conveyer belt and watched them pass uneventfully through. The security guards barely looked at him. He was white, well dressed, had a conservative haircut, and wasn't wearing any jewelry.

It was warm in California. T-shirt weather.

He took a cab into Oakland, then walked a block and took another cab to a motel in Berkeley. After unpacking, he went for a walk, first along the surrounding streets, then around the university. He had a beer in a neighborhood pub, grabbed an early dinner, went to a movie, and was in bed by ten.

The next morning he placed a set of biking togs in a day pack and walked to a bike store he had seen the previous afternoon. He bought a bike, an air pump, a lock and chain, and a tool kit. It was going to take the bike store an hour to get the bike ready. While they were doing that, Eliot stopped at a supermarket and bought a couple of cans of juice and some granola bars (when in California . . .). He also stopped at a bookstore and bought a street map of Contra Costa County. A bench in a park provided a quiet place to study the map.

He was surprised. There weren't that many roads in and around Laurel Valley. When he thought he knew them all, he went to get his bike.

Half an hour later he was pedaling up Claremont Avenue.

Eliot rode the highways and back roads of Contra Costa County for three hours before he found the spot he was looking for: an isolated section of walking trail that ran between Moraga and Lafayette. He chained his bike to a post, put on his sneakers, and ran for a mile along the trail. He passed one person. He spent ten minutes stretching, then walked slowly back to his bike. This time he didn't pass anyone. He ate a granola bar and drank a bottle of juice, then took the tool kit out of his pack and spent forty minutes tuning the gears, brakes, and wheels of the bike and counting people. When he felt he had a good idea of the traffic on the trail, he packed up his tools and walked the path again, looking for a place to make the drop and looking for an emergency escape route in the unlikely event the drop turned into a trap. Finally, he got back on his bike and began a study of the surrounding streets.

At six o'clock that evening, Tran Van Duong was sitting in a chair in his living room staring into space. On the floor next to him were the day's papers.

All week the papers had been full of articles on NAGO, or the NRA, or assault rifles, or antigun groups. The nation was in an uproar—children had been killed! "Enough is Enough," read one editorial. The California State Legislature was talking about banning assault rifles. There was a movement in Congress to outlaw the guns.

And the gun lobby was fighting back: pressuring legislators and congressmen, rallying the membership; a general advertising campaign had been initiated. In just one week a million dollars had been spent.

Tran looked at the paper at his feet. George Herbert Brenden stared back at him. He was smiling, shaking hands with a U.S. senator. The picture was on the front page of the paper, accompanying an article titled simply "The Counterassault."

The article described the lobbying and advertising efforts of NAGO and the NRA. In California it was thought the legislature would vote to ban assault rifles, but the vote was close, and the gun lobby was fighting hard. Governor Deukmejian hadn't taken a position yet.

Tran knew that the more time that passed, the more unlikely it was that anything would be done. In a few weeks, or months, Laurel Valley and Stockton would be forgotten, and life would go on as it had before.

The phone rang. It was a call he had been expecting.

"Do you know where St. Mary's Road is?" Eliot asked. "It runs from Moraga to Lafayette."

Tran thought for a moment. Five years ago a friend had dragged him to a basketball game at St. Mary's College. He seemed to recall the entrance to the college was off St. Mary's Road.

"I know the road."

"There's an exercise trail that runs along the road."

Eliot told Tran where to park his car and how far to walk along the trail.

"There's a large oak tree on the west side of the path; it's at the top of a small rise. You'll be able to see in both directions."

Eliot described himself and what he would be wearing. Tran was to wait until Eliot was the only one in view, then he was to leave the money by the oak and continue north along the trail, in the direction of Lafayette. He was to have the money in a brown paper bag, the sort of bag used to carry a lunch.

Eliot had Tran repeat everything, then told him what time he wanted him to be at the oak. Eliot estimated it would take seven to eight minutes to walk from the car to the tree.

The next day was clear and cool, a beautiful day, Tran thought. A day that Loan should have been in school.

He stared at the hill above his house, glowing green in the sun. It was Valentine's Day. He had always brought his daughter chocolates on Valentine's Day.

Instead, he went to the bank and collected the bundle of hundred-dollar bills. He got to St. Mary's Road a few minutes early.

Tran left himself eight and a half minutes to make the walk to the oak, and got there a minute early. No one was in sight in front of him, and when he turned, there was "Robin," about a hundred yards back. He appeared exactly as he had described himself: average height, wearing a bright red headband, a green windbreaker, and shorts. At that distance Tran couldn't clearly see his face. He checked the path in the other direction; there was no one, so he set down the bag and walked off.

Tran glanced back once, when Robin was almost to the tree. He had to look twice. The man had taken off the red headband, and in the green windbreaker he was practically invisible against the background foliage. He also didn't seem to move, his head and body floating above his legs. It made Tran shiver; it didn't quite seem the walk of a human being. He turned and hurried on toward Lafayette.

6

About a week after Eliot Brod picked up his hundred thousand dollars, George Herbert Brenden walked into NAGO headquarters in Washington, D.C. He was tan and rested, and he was glad to be getting back to work; a ten-day vacation was just too long, especially when that vacation was in the company of his wife.

They had gone to Florida.

George hated Florida, and Miami in particular (they hadn't gone to Miami this time; they had gone to Boca Raton). He hated the constant glaring sun, and the heat, and the rip-off prices. And he hated having to worry about some unemployed Cuban immigrant trying to mug him. He felt for the .38 special under his arm. A cop's gun. Reliable.

Florida. His wife's favorite place in the world.

They had spent most of the ten days on the beach so she could tan her varicose veins. George's only entertainment had been watching the college kids running around in their bikinis, tits bouncing up and down. He would have liked to have done a little bouncing up and down himself, but his wife wouldn't let him out of her sight. To her a vacation meant spending every minute together.

He paused in the lobby to admire the display of Revolutionary War weapons: "The Guns That Made Us Free." A mural covered the wall behind the guns: Indians and bears in the background; a log cabin in front; British soldiers marching in from the right.

For two weeks in January, and almost that long in February, he had been running around the country nonstop. Most of the time had been spent lobbying the California legislature in the wake of the Laurel Valley and Stockton killings. But he had also been in Washington meeting with senators and congressmen. And he had had to endure any number of radio and TV interviews.

The interviews had been grueling duty: question after question from hostile (and ignorant) talk-show hosts. Most of the questions had focused on assault rifles.

After Stockton, and then again after Laurel Valley, George had met with the president of NAGO to urge that only the briefest public statement be made: an expression of condolence; a condemnation of the illegal use of *any* firearm. He thought the organization should do its lobbying quietly, in private, lest a backlash develop among nongun owners.

But the president of NAGO, Patrick R. Taylor, the man who had picked George to be the national spokesman, had decided this was the moment when gun associations needed to stand tall. The antigun activists were sure to use the California killings to push for restrictive new firearm laws. *Their* lobbying had to be countered by NAGO's own intense lobbying effort— the 60 million gun owners in America had to be warned that their right to keep and bear arms was being threatened.

Rather than lying low, NAGO was going to begin an advertising blitz. Patrick Taylor felt such a campaign, aimed specifically at gun owners, would result in a vast increase in gun-association membership. If NAGO was marching in the forefront of this battle, these gun owners would join NAGO, and not the NRA, or some other group.

So George, good soldier, had gone out and delivered the speeches he was told to deliver.

George had been working for NAGO for nine years. He

started as a state rep, then moved on to regional rep. Now, he was the national spokesman. Mostly, he addressed gun clubs and other groups interested in guns and marksmanship. He went to meetings, dinners, retreats. He talked about gun safety, the history of firearms in America, environmental issues for the hunter, pending antigun legislation. The job involved a lot of travel, and he liked that. When he was on the road, he didn't have to listen to his wife complain.

He took the elevator to the third floor.

There were six floors in the building, plus a basement and subbasement, enough room for about half the NAGO bureaucracy. Patrick Taylor had his office on the top floor. Finance and Membership were on two. Communications and Programs on three. The Legislative Division on four. Senior staff on five. The computer was in the basement. The subbasement housed a shooting range.

George settled into a chair in Dwayne Reginald Hoffmann's office. Hoffmann was an assistant vice president and was about five years younger than George.

They spent fifteen minutes talking about Florida vacations, soft-shell crabs, the state of the economy, the probability of another drought, and the new Glock 9mm handgun.

"We've got a busy two weeks for you, George," Dwayne finally said.

He ran down the list of engagements, mentioning the reasons George had been invited to speak, if any.

George listened with half an ear. He didn't know why Dwayne bothered. The talks he gave were all the same.

When everything had been covered, Dwayne handed George a folder containing his itinerary, the addresses where he was to speak, directions on how to get there, nearby hotels and motels, miscellaneous other information he might need or find useful, and, last, a sheet containing the latest NAGO position on just about everything.

They spent another ten minutes discussing restaurants in the Northeast, then George shook hands good-bye and headed out.

He had a two-week tour in front of him, not too heavy a

schedule; and unless an emergency radio or TV interview came up, not a hostile schedule, either. There would be plenty of time to enjoy himself; and in at least three towns he knew he would have company.

He unlocked the door to the LeBaron (a rent), slid in, tuned the radio to Alan Christian, lit a cigarette, and headed for Ohio.

It was a fine day for a drive. The traffic wasn't bad. And there was a good restaurant about two hours down the road where he could get lunch.

7

The elevator door slid open, and a couple stepped out into the garage.

Eliot Brod leaned forward until he was hidden by the hood of the big Chrysler. He was kneeling in the small triangle of space the front of the car made with the wall, and was nearly invisible.

The footsteps grew louder, then faded as the couple passed. Eliot heard a giggle, the jangle of keys, the click of a lock, a car door opening. The boom of the engine was like thunder.

He didn't straighten up until the car was gone and the garage quiet again.

On the level above him, the level the exit was on, he heard another car pulling in. A minute later the door slammed. The sound echoed wildly along the concrete walls.

The exit on the floor above was the only way in or out of the garage with a car; it was guarded by a man in a cubicle, and by entrance and exit blockades. The only other entrance to the garage was through the hotel, using either the elevator or the stairs.

He tucked his hands under his coat. It was cold in the

garage, very cold. The thin gloves he had on didn't do a thing.

He had been waiting an hour already, and didn't expect Brenden for another half hour. Every fifteen minutes or so, someone entered his section of the garage. He didn't worry that the owner of the Chrysler would appear, because this was George Brenden's car.

Eliot had figured Brenden would drive. The spacing of his talks, both in distance and days, suggested that. It would have taken longer, and been more difficult, to fly.

A week earlier, Eliot had driven to Cortland, New York, to get a look at Brenden and see what sort of car he was driving. He hadn't expected to be able to do the job in Cortland—in the middle of the day with people all around—but he had hoped to get a feel for the man, and maybe learn something that would help him later. He had learned that Brenden was a smoker.

After Cortland, Brenden's next date had been in Albany, a talk before the Tri-City Veterans' Association. The site had looked good, very good, and Eliot had spent an evening familiarizing himself with the alleys and one-way streets.

But Albany had been a bust.

He had found Brenden's car easily enough—on a side street several blocks from the hall where he was speaking. But when Brenden showed up, two other men were with him; it would have been sloppy to kill them all.

Then came two stops in Connecticut: a luncheon with the Northeast Association of Gun Manufacturers (NAGM) and a talk at the Westvale High School.

Neither place had sounded promising, but since they weren't far from his home, Eliot had checked them out anyway. It had been a waste of time. The lunch date with NAGM was in downtown Hartford at noon. And the high school was way out in the country, with no place to leave his car, and kids all around.

Which explained why Eliot was where he was now: in a garage under a hotel in Boston, waiting for George Brenden to finish his talk to a gun collectors' club. Eliot didn't think Brenden was spending the night in the hotel, because there was no room reserved in his name—he had called that morning to check. He just hoped Brenden wasn't staying in a room reserved in someone else's name.

About an hour after Brenden arrived, Eliot had walked into the hotel and crossed the lobby to the elevators. In his camel-hair coat, and with a conservative haircut, he easily passed for a guest and was not challenged. He had taken the elevator to the fourth floor, then back down to the basement, where he had wandered around until he found Brenden's car.

Another couple got off the elevator. He watched as they made their way into a different section of the garage.

He hoped Brenden would be alone. If he missed tonight, he would have to start over, and that would almost certainly mean doing the job in Homewood, or at the NAGO convention in May. Either way, it would involve a great deal more time, and probably considerably more risk.

The couple drove off.

He sat up. He was getting cold. In another half hour he would start to lose his edge. He rubbed his legs, then began a breathing exercise to warm himself, taking slow, deep breaths. The smell of car exhaust suddenly became oppressive. He forced himself to do the breathing exercise anyway.

Another couple passed, then a woman.

He studied the area around him; about a third of the parking spaces were filled, all with new cars. And all the cars were clean; this, despite the fact that it was the middle of winter. Whenever he drove to Boston or New York, he was always struck by how clean the cars were. He had had his own car washed that afternoon so it wouldn't look out of place.

He glanced at his watch: 11:00 P.M. He began the breathing exercise again. He had once had to wait two days to do a job. Waiting was one of the things he did well. It was also something he hated. Waiting for hours and hours stiffened his body; and the waiting gave him time to think, which, for an assassin, was not good. Thinking was a distraction. And being distracted was a good way to botch the job.

A movement caught his eye, a man pausing to light a cigarette. His man.

His man's last cigarette.

He slid the gun from his pocket and lowered himself until he could barely see through the bottom of the windshield. He was lucky; the garage was empty.

Brenden moved forward slowly, trailing a cloud of smoke. He seemed a little unsteady on his feet.

One less drunk on the road.

Eliot stepped out from in front of the car, the gun aimed at Brenden's stomach.

George Brenden looked up in surprise—a moment before there had only been the wall in front of him. He was about to say something when he saw the gun, and the silencer.

He thought about the .38 under his coat and knew he would never have a chance to use it. All that practice on the range wasted.

"Why?" he started to ask.

The first shot hit him in the stomach, knocking him to his knees. As he started to double over, the second shot hit him in the shoulder. The third shot was through the heart.

Eliot took a heavy plastic bag from his pocket and placed the gun in it. Then he picked up the three shells the gun had ejected and added them to the bag. He placed the bag in his right coat pocket.

By then, the spasms shaking Brenden's body were starting to subside.

Eliot grabbed Brenden's arm and tore off his watch and wedding ring. Quickly, but without rushing, he emptied Brenden's pockets, finding his wallet, a bit of cash, and the gun under his arm. He put everything he found in his left coat pocket. Then he dragged Brenden into the space in front of the car and dumped him there. When he checked, there was no pulse.

He looked around to make sure the floor was clear. Except for a small pool of blood, which would probably be mistaken for oil, there was nothing. He brushed himself off, checking his sleeves for blood and his trousers for dust. Then he took an envelope out of his breast pocket and sprinkled the contents over Brenden's body. A little something for the forensic boys.

The week before, Eliot had dressed up in a cheap suit and, sporting a brand-new vacuum cleaner, had walked into a barber shop and begun demonstrating the amazing suction of his machine. He had been promptly thrown out. He did this at three different shops, collecting three different samples of hair.

The hairs he dumped on Brenden were the hairs of a black man. After all, it was Boston, and it was what the police would expect. They would run riot through the ghettos for a week, pressure a lot of people, and, since Brenden wasn't a local, give up quickly.

He checked the floor of the garage again, then headed for the elevator. On the way up he smoothed his hair and straightened his tie. When the elevator door opened, he stepped into the lobby and, with that slightly stiff, belly-forward walk of the rich and self-assured, marched out of the hotel. Three hours later he was home.

He wasn't worried that his pants had left fibers on the concrete floor where he had been kneeling. He had bought those pants off the rack at a nationwide chain.

8

The young woman smiled, a row of snow-white—whiter than white!—teeth, a breeze in her hair. The car—*the* car—in the background.

And then Ted Stanley was back with the news. He gave the TV audience a quick smile before putting on his "serious" face.

Tran hit the Mute button, and Ted Stanley's voice pealed forth.

"A little bit of irony tonight, folks."

The screen behind Ted Stanley filled with the face of George Herbert Brenden.

"NAGO national spokesman George Herbert Brenden was gunned down in a Boston garage late last night, the victim of an apparent robbery. His death, the twenty-seventh murder in Boston this year, comes at a time when many state legislatures are considering stricter gun-control measures."

The picture of Brenden faded, and another picture took its place.

"When contacted in his office today, NAGO president Patrick R. Taylor said George Brenden's murder was exactly the reason Americans needed guns: to protect themselves from the criminals in our society. It is not known whether George Brenden was carrying a gun at the time of his death. Massachusetts has one of the toughest gun-control laws in the nation."

The picture of Patrick Taylor was replaced by a weather map.

Tran flipped off the TV.

The account in the evening paper had been much the same. Brenden was thought to have been killed around midnight, shortly after leaving a dinner party. He had been gunned down while getting into his car. A Lieutenant Manny Bigelow, the detective in charge of the investigation, had refused to speculate how soon it would be before the killer was apprehended.

Tran thought it would probably be a while. A long while.

He smiled. So, it was done. He felt better than he had imagined he would.

He set the remote aside and stood up. It was dinnertime, time to look in on his restaurant. He picked up his hat and opened the door. The last light was just fading from the hills. He watched it disappear. It was a lovely evening. Too nice an evening, really, to spend in his office tallying receipts. He nodded.

Tonight, the restaurant could look after itself. *He* would go out and celebrate. He would have dinner at a French restaurant, food like he used to eat in Saigon.

He recalled his wedding, his first wedding. The tables had been piled with food: tarts and crisps and dumplings, an inspired blend of Vietnamese cooking and French delicacies. And champagne. A river of champagne. He had gotten very drunk.

He would not get drunk tonight, but he would have wine. One had to have wine with French food; it was the only way to dissolve the grease.

He pulled the door closed and locked it.

Have a nice day, America!

The air over Boston was gray with rain. Gray rain over a gray city.

Lieutenant Manny Bigelow of the Boston Homicide Division got up from his chair to look at the rain. Sheets of rain and drizzle and low clouds.

Traffic was backed up past his window.

Whenever it rained, the streets became clogged with cars; people forgot how to drive in the rain. He watched the windshield wipers below flip back and forth, back and forth.

It was Saint Patrick's Day, and Manny Bigelow, looking down on the wet city, suddenly imagined that the gray had turned a little green, an emerald glow. He shook his head. It was appalling the way the mind was open to suggestion.

Today, there would be more than the usual number of fistfights and brawls and traffic accidents; and there would probably be a murder or two, though since it was Friday, it might be unfair to attribute that to Saint Patty.

But Lieutenant Manny Bigelow wouldn't be responsible for any of it. In two hours he would be going home, and the rapists and murderers and muggers would be someone else's problem, at least until Sunday evening when he came on again. But first, he had to meet with Patrick R. Taylor, the president of NAGO.

He lit a cigarette.

Patrick *R*. Taylor. Every CEO had one, a middle initial and a Mercedes.

Manny didn't have a middle initial. He didn't have a middle name. Just plain old Manfred Bigelow. He didn't have a Mercedes, either.

He watched a helicopter zip across the sky. It was going to take forever to get home today. He hoped the airport was socked in. He hoped Patrick R. Taylor had to land in Maine and take a bus to Boston, a bus full of people *without* middle initials.

He flopped down in his chair and poured himself a cup of coffee. Taylor was due in his office in fifteen minutes. He would probably be late. He might even be two hours late, in which case Manny would be gone. That would be tough titty on Taylor.

He leaned back and closed his eyes. He would take the fifteen minutes to relax.

But it had been years since Manny Bigelow had relaxed. Instead, the phone conversation he had had with Taylor played itself back through his head. The man had insisted on a personal interview.

"It's been three weeks since Brenden was killed," Taylor had pointed out.

"Not quite three weeks," Manny had responded, with bureaucratic exactitude.

"And," said Taylor, "the BPD has found out nothing."

"Not quite nothing," Manny had replied.

Taylor had snorted.

And now the man was coming to check up on him in person.

Over the years Manny had come to expect these visits. Usually, they were made by the relatives of the deceased, and had all the solemnity of a pilgrimage. He had long ago decided these people came not to find out how the investigation was going, but because of their own guilt: They could not come to terms with the fact that they were alive and their loved one dead. Manny thought of it as the guilt of the survivor.

But these personal interviews were also demanded by people like Patrick R. Taylor, powerful people who, when things weren't speeding along, felt obligated to come and light a fire under Manny Bigelow's lazy civil-servant ass. Manny usually told these people to go to hell, which was one reason he was still a lieutenant.

He had tried to tell Patrick R. Taylor to go to hell, but the man had obviously not taken the hint, because shortly after his conversation with Taylor, Manny had been called into his captain's office, where he had been informed that those above, those far above, personally wanted Patrick R. Taylor to go home happy. Manny knew exactly why those far above wanted the president of NAGO to go home happy: NAGO controlled thousands and thousands of local votes.

It had been two hours before the body of George Herbert Brenden had been found, or, at least, two hours before anyone had bothered to report the body. You never knew these days.

A search of the corpse had turned up nothing. No wallet, no cash, no I.D., no papers, just a set of car keys in the man's right hand and an empty holster under the left arm.

The empty holster had pissed Manny off. It meant another illegal handgun on the street, a gun that might be used to shoot a cop. He had felt like kicking Brenden's corpse: another gun nut who couldn't hold on to his own weapon. When they searched the car, they found Brenden's half of the garage ticket sitting on the seat.

Brenden had entered the garage at 7:32 P.M. the previous evening. The car was a rent, and a check with the rental agency eventually produced George Brenden's name and who he worked for.

Manny remembered he couldn't help laughing when he found out who the guy was. God sure had a funny sense of humor. He was reminded of a phrase he hadn't heard in twenty years: What goes around comes around. He had always thought the saying a bunch of shit.

When Manny got to the hotel at two o'clock that Sunday morning, the garage was three-quarters empty and dingy gray, though, he supposed, being underground, the garage was always dingy gray. He had his people set up extra lights so nothing would be missed. First, they took photographs; then they went over the body and the scene as carefully as they could. It was a matter of pride with the Homicide squad that they never missed a clue if the clue was there.

After the photographer was finished and the scene examined (there wasn't much to find), Brenden's body was wrapped up and carted away. They scraped up the little pool of dried blood and put it in a plastic bag; and they searched the floor with a magnifying glass—a few fibers were found where Brenden's body had been. The last thing they did was bring in a powerful vacuum cleaner to suck up everything that remained. Then the car, and the wall in front of the car, were dusted for fingerprints, as well as the elevator and the door leading to the stairs. After that Brenden's car was towed away, and everyone went back to the station. There hadn't been very many people to interview, because at midnight the shifts in the hotel had changed.

The next morning Manny sent his detectives out to question those members of the hotel staff who *had* been working at the time Brenden was killed. No one recalled hearing any shots or seeing anyone, or anything, suspicious. At the end of the interview each person was shown a picture of Brenden. A few people remembered seeing him. The management provided a list of hotel guests and dinner guests; the bartender put together a list of those people he could remember serving. A list of those cars that had entered or left the garage between noon and 6:00 A.M. was made. Luckily, it was the policy of the hotel to keep a record of the cars that used the garage.

Two days later Manny had a good idea where George Brenden had been from the time he entered the parking garage at 7:32 P.M. to the time his body was found around 1:30 the next morning.

At about 7:45 Brenden had had a drink at the bar. The bartender distinctly remembered him because they had had a friendly chat, and because, as it turned out, they had both been born in Illinois. After finishing his drink—a whiskey on the rocks—Brenden had gone upstairs to dinner, arriving at ap-

80

proximately 8:05. The dinner, in a private room, had been hosted by an antique-gun collectors' club. Brenden was there to talk about pending antigun legislation in the Massachusetts legislature and the consequences it would have for gun collectors. After the talk he had answered a few questions and had a few more drinks (wine had been served with dinner, and the autopsy revealed that had Brenden managed to drive off that night, he would have been guilty of driving while intoxicated). By 10:45 Brenden had said his good-byes. The coroner placed the time of death before 11:45 P.M.

Manny figured Brenden had been shot about eleven, as he was about to get into his car. He also figured the murderer had been hiding in front of the car, because, as it turned out, the fibers embedded in the concrete did not match those from Brenden's clothes.

He tried to imagine the scene: Brenden fumbling for his keys; the murderer stepping out from his hiding place; Brenden's surprised face; the demand for money; Brenden's hesitation, or refusal, he might have actually tried to go for his gun; the three quick shots.

Manny figured a revolver had been used because they hadn't found any discharged shells. He *knew* the murderer hadn't been standing right next to Brenden, because the lab boys hadn't found any sign of gunpowder on Brenden's clothes. The absence of gunpowder also told him Brenden hadn't managed to fire his own weapon.

It looked like a simple robbery and murder.

Except, two things bothered Manny. The first was that no one had heard any shots, and a gun going off in that garage would have made a ton of noise. The second was how the murderer had managed to get down to the garage and then back out without being seen.

The hotel had a total of five entrances: the main entrance, three service entrances, and the entrance to the garage.

The main entrance was watched twenty-four hours a day by a security guard, porters, and the front-desk clerk. The three service entrances were either locked or full of service personnel; and *they* would have noticed a stranger. That only left the garage entrance.

Manny had inspected the garage entrance the first night. It was up one level from where Brenden's body had been found and on the other side of the building. It was guarded by block-ades, and by a guard in a cubicle. The guard hadn't heard any shots, but given the distance, and the fact that the windows of the cubicle had been closed to keep out the cold, that wasn't surprising. The guard, however, had sworn that no one had walked into or out of the garage that night.

Manny was inclined to believe him. He had stepped inside the cubicle himself and found that the front window offered an unencumbered view of the street. And the cubicle was cold, not the sort of place one drifted off to sleep. It would have been difficult for a rat to slip in without being seen.

Which meant the murderer *must* have been seen, and was either an employee or someone who hadn't looked out of place, like a guest.

About a week after the murder Manny got his first real break: The lab boys had found two hairs on Brenden that didn't belong to Brenden.

Manny had been surprised when he got the call, not that the lab boys had found the hairs (he had expected them to find *something*), but that they were working on Brenden's stuff al-ready. After the autopsy it usually took months to get the rest of the lab results. Obviously, those far above were leaning hard on everyone.

Manny sat back in his chair and thought about the sort of pressure those far above could exert when it suited their pur-pose. It was a lot of pressure, enough pressure to turn big tough cops, heroes on the street, into yes-men. It was also the sort of pressure that disappeared as soon as the guy down below was in a tight spot and needed a little help. Manny knew this from personal experience.

He considered taking the rest of the day off just to annoy his captain.

The two hairs found on Brenden's body belonged to a black male, a black male who had recently had a haircut. The lab boys figured the hairs had fallen off as the killer bent over the body.

Manny was glad to hear that the lab boys had a theory about the murder, because he was still working on one.

In addition to the two hairs found on Brenden, four more hairs had been found in the dust they had vacuumed off the garage floor. Three of the hairs were identical to the two hairs found on Brenden. The fourth hair was long and blond and had apparently been on the floor of the garage for some time.

Unfortunately for Manny Bigelow, the lab had yet to develop a process by which a face could be reconstructed from a few hairs, or even a headful of hair. And the prospect of visiting every barbershop in the city, looking for a black killer, did not thrill Manny; he frankly didn't think it would result in anything more than poor community relations.

That was the good news from the lab.

The bad news was that the cloth the fibers on the floor had come from was a very popular cloth, used by several large clothing manufacturers to make moderately expensive pants and suits sold all over the country.

Which left Manny with a well-dressed black man.

He called the hotel manager and had him draw up a list of guests on the night of the murder who were black (one), and a list of hotel employees who were black (many). Then he sent his detectives back to interview all the people they had interviewed before, asking everyone specifically about a well-dressed black man, and asking the black employees, and the one black guest, specifically about their whereabouts between ten-thirty and midnight, and did they have witnesses. The toughest thing had been convincing these "suspects" to part with a lock of their hair for comparison. There had been curses, and angry reminders about a person's civil rights; but in the end, being innocent and not wanting to be hassled, they had all cooperated.

None of the hairs had matched. And no one remembered seeing a black man at all, well dressed or otherwise. The single black guest had been in his room all evening with his own guest.

And this was something else that bothered Manny. The

lily-white hotels of downtown Boston weren't exactly the sort
of place a black man, however well dressed, could glide through
without being noticed; yet, apparently, the murderer had done
just that. How?

Manny put his feet up on his desk and closed his eyes. He
could think only of two possibilities: either the man had gotten
very lucky, slipping in and out undetected, and shooting Brenden when no one was around to hear (Manny hated it when
the bad guys got lucky), or the killer wasn't black at all.

The possibility of a white man leaving the hairs of a black
man on George Brenden seemed, to Manny Bigelow, bizarre
in the extreme, especially since, during two weeks of investigation, he hadn't found a white man (or anyone else) who was
a likely suspect. Manny had had a check done on Brenden's
family and associates. The man didn't seem to have any obvious
enemies. He wasn't in debt. His wife had an alibi. And there
wasn't much insurance.

So why would someone who wasn't a natural suspect bother
to leave false evidence? Manny couldn't think of a reason. It
seemed more likely that the evidence was genuine, that the killer
had, in fact, been black, that George Herbert Brenden had
simply been unlucky.

Manny believed in luck, especially bad luck. After thirty-
three years as a cop, Manny knew bad luck came like bills, all
at once. Brenden had simply been in the wrong place at the
wrong time. You had to be lucky in life.

You also had to be persistent.

A Sergeant Rodriguez passed Manny's door.

Manny liked Rodriguez. Rodriguez looked like a white guy
with a good tan, and Manny had once suggested (facetiously,
of course) that the younger man had simply borrowed the name
Rodriguez to take advantage of the BPD affirmative-action program.

Perhaps, like Rodriguez, the killer, though black, could
have passed for white.

Manny sent his detectives back to interview everyone all
over again, this time asking about a white man with kinky hair,
maybe a Jew, or an Arab. Jews and Arabs didn't exactly blend

in, in Boston's swankiest hotels, either. His detectives came back with nothing.

It was as if a ghost had killed Brenden.

Manny lit another cigarette and looked at his watch. Taylor was probably stuck in traffic coming from the airport. He could imagine what the Callahan Tunnel was like.

He rubbed his stomach. There was something wrong with him, a slow, nagging pain high up on his left side. His spleen? He didn't want to know, or even think about it. The prospect of being seriously ill made him tired. Thirty-three years as a cop made him tired.

For the last ten years he had been talking about quitting. How many more murders did he need to see? He knew he would never make captain; he was just not a kiss-ass sort of guy.

But for all the complaining, Manny knew he would never quit. He was a third-generation cop. His father had died on the job. His grandfather had died on the job. He was just waiting his turn.

Manny still had his feet up on his desk when Patrick R. Taylor walked in. He didn't bother to move them.

"Have a seat, Mr. Taylor." He waved at the only other chair in the room.

Patrick R. Taylor stared at the two scuffed leather shoes resting on the desk. For a skinny guy Manny had big feet.

"Let's get right to it, Bigelow. I want to see everything you have."

Manny took another drag on his cigarette. He hated when people rushed him. Rushing was a good way to get an upset tummy.

"I'm afraid you can't *see* anything, Mr. Taylor—department regulations." He shrugged apologetically. "I suppose, if you asked nicely, I could *tell* you what we have." He swung his feet to the floor and placed his hands on top of Brenden's file.

Patrick Taylor leaned across the desk. He was big, six foot three, at least, and solid; and Manny could tell he was used to getting what he wanted. He wondered how much Taylor's suit cost. Probably, more than he made in a week, even before taxes.

"Listen, Bigelow, I didn't come up here to get a lesson in etiquette. Didn't your captain tell you to cooperate?"

Stringy Manny Bigelow, five feet ten in shoes with hardly a paunch (nerves kept him thin), rocked forward in his chair until he could smell Taylor's after-shave. "I hope you have a license for that." He pointed at the bulge under Taylor's left arm. "If I could just see your license."

Taylor stood up straight. "The hell you can." He touched the gun to make sure Bigelow hadn't, somehow, filched it. "You fucking well know I have a license for this gun." He stared at the Boston cop.

Manny smiled and opened Brenden's file and began to read the report, leaving out the names of the people interviewed. Patrick Taylor settled into the chair.

It took Manny about ten minutes to cover it all, including the bits and pieces the lab had come up with. When he was finished, Patrick Taylor shook his head.

"That's all you've got, after three weeks?"

"Same as I told you on the phone."

"What about the shots? I stopped at the garage; gunfire would have echoed like a bitch in all that concrete. Are you telling me no one heard anything?"

"So far no one has come forward." He set the report aside. "Frankly, Mr. Taylor, there's not much left to do on this. We've got a few guests still to check out; and we still have to track down the owners of a couple of cars that were in the garage that night. But I ain't holding my breath."

"You find any shell casings?"

"Nope."

Taylor drummed his fingers on the arm of the chair. "So you think some nigger did it?"

Manny Bigelow sat back and lit a cigarette. He didn't even bother to reply.

"Come on, Bigelow. A black guy in a fancy Boston hotel. He would have stuck out like a coffin at a wedding. How come nobody noticed him?"

Manny shrugged. "What I got, you got. Maybe we'll get

lucky, and I'll hear something from one of my snitches."

Taylor stared at him. "And that's it?"

"Your man was in the wrong place at the wrong time. It happens every day."

Patrick R. Taylor stood up. "That seems a little simple, Lieutenant. I'll certainly mention to your captain that your ideas seem a little simple."

Manny smiled. "Y'all have a happy Saint Patrick's Day now."

Patrick Taylor turned and walked out the door.

Manny Bigelow smiled again. It gave him real pleasure to irritate the great and powerful.

He pulled open his desk drawer and took out a pint of whiskey and poured himself a small paper cupful. Then he stood up and put on his coat and got ready to face the traffic on Storrow Drive. It was Friday, and his wife would have fish sticks on the table. He hoped to God they wouldn't be green.

THE
REACTION

10

Down at the end of the long, poorly lit tunnel the target slid into view. Patrick R. Taylor pulled the trigger, and the big Colt boomed. He fired five times, the sound of the gun filling the underground shooting range.

He lifted off his ear protectors and hit a button on the wall. The target slid toward him: Ted Kennedy's grinning face, two holes below the left eye, one through the mouth, two through the nose. Not bad shooting at twenty-five yards.

Taylor chuckled and consigned the youngest Kennedy brother to the incinerator. Then he popped the clip out of the Colt and replaced the five shells. He studied the gun, a perfect example of design efficiency and effectiveness, essentially unchanged after almost eighty years of production. His Colt had never misfired, never fallen apart, never failed him; and all with just ordinary, commonsense care.

He banged the clip home and punched in the code for another target.

NAGO had recently installed a computer-operated target system that allowed the shooter to call up the target of his choice by keying in a number. It worked much the way an old-fashioned jukebox worked. The system could handle up to a hundred different targets and was about half filled.

Patrick Taylor stared down the range at a standard silhouette and carefully squeezed off all eight rounds. This time he was not pleased with his shooting. Two shots had missed the target altogether, and the other six were spaced in a nearly random pattern.

He shook his head. He had never been able to shoot at silhouettes, or at bull's-eyes, either. It was as if a faceless target cause his brain to malfunction.

He considered calling up one of Ted Kennedy's older brothers. Not many people knew about those targets; there would be hell to pay if the public ever found out NAGO was popping holes into pictures of the beloved Kennedy brothers—which was one reason there was no master list of targets. People dropped off their targets and keyed in their own five-number codes. One hundred thousand combinations assured a certain degree of privacy. Besides, it was a man's own business who he wanted to shoot at.

He called up the ayatollah Khomeini and did what every red-blooded American had always wanted to do: He plugged him full of holes.

The code for the ayatollah was posted on the shooting-range bulletin board.

Patrick Taylor shot for half an hour. It was Monday afternoon, and already it was a bad week. And things didn't look as if they were going to get any better.

Legislation was pending in dozens of states and cities to ban assault rifles, each piece of legislation enthusiastically supported by the press (God bless the First Amendment, but to hell with the "liberal" press; did they think the government would tolerate their nagging once the rest of the Constitution had been dismantled?). Even the president, a lifetime member of the NRA, was starting to talk about banning weapons. He had already endorsed a ban on the importation of assault rifles.

It made Taylor shiver. Suddenly, NAGO's war chest looked thin. Where would they get the money for all the fights that were looming? Antigun groups, emboldened by the ranting of the press and the waffling of lily-livered politicians, were on a rampage, proposing all sorts of sweeping new gun-control measures. The polls (if one could believe the polls) showed a shift in public sentiment: suddenly, most Americans were opposed to guns, *all* guns. Rather than seeing themselves as Rambo, most Americans were afraid that *they*, and not the bad guys, would wind up getting shot. Even some people within NAGO had expressed reservations about across-the-counter sales of assault rifles.

Taylor didn't know what to say to these defectors. His arguments sounded lame, especially under the shadow of dead children. Lame, and dusty, and old, a story told too many times. No matter that the argument was still valid and would always be valid—repetition wore on people; it bored them. The whole NAGO countercampaign seemed tired and reactive, not positive at all.

He needed Brenden. Brenden could coax a smile out of a corpse. He could make anyone listen and believe.

That fucking Bigelow.

Patrick Taylor imagined Manny Bigelow's weasel face down at the end of the tunnel, and pumped four bullets into his nose. Quickly, he popped out the empty clip and slammed home his backup clip and fired for the heart. Manny Bigelow slumped to the floor.

If only it were that easy. If only wishing could bring Brenden back.

When Patrick Taylor had been told of George Brenden's murder, a wave of emotion had swept over him. It was a feeling he had almost forgotten. It had been a long time since he had lost a man, almost forty years. Not since Korea.

Patrick Taylor didn't like losing men. He felt a father's responsibility to those under him. And now, somehow, vaguely, he had failed in that responsibility. Maybe he had picked the wrong man for the job? Maybe he should have made sure Brenden had more training; he should have made sure the man better understood the dangers. A leader was only a leader as long as there were men to follow him. Each time one of those men died, a little authority was lost.

He carefully reloaded the two empty clips, slipping one

into his pocket and slapping the other home.

Brenden's death would certainly be used against him at the annual meeting. It would be said that a younger man should have been the national spokesman, just as a younger man had always been the national spokesman. It would be said he had sent Brenden to his death.

Taylor knew that Brenden's death, and the antigun legislation certain to be proposed by May (the time of the annual meeting), might cost him his job. The ultraconservatives were sure to make a move to get him out.

He felt a mixture of bitterness and anger and regret. He felt if *he* had been in that Boston garage, the outcome would have been different. *He* would have been more alert, enough to avoid the killer. George Herbert Brenden had never been in combat; he lacked the sixth sense combat vets had: the ability to sense the enemy, to feel the danger.

When Patrick Taylor was finished killing off the bad guys, he carefully cleaned his gun, reloaded it, and tucked it back in its holster. The gun was warm against his chest; in the cool basement, the warmth felt good.

The basement was always cool, and the range always poorly lit. It was important to simulate bad shooting conditions because, except in the movies, shoot-outs rarely took place at high noon.

He took the elevator to the sixth floor, enjoying the smell of burned gunpowder that rose from his sleeves. It was a pleasant smell. It reminded him of pleasant things: shooting rabbits as a child; hunting with his father.

He settled into his chair and swiveled around to look out the window. It was raining again. It had been raining for a week. He leaned forward and opened the window so he could smell the rain.

Taylor had the only window in the building that opened; he had had it installed the day after he moved into the office. He liked fresh air. He thought windows that didn't open were just plain dumb.

Outside, the very top branches of a tree moved in the breeze. He closed his eyes and breathed in the smell of the rain—rain pattering on the window. Rain on a canvas tent. The Ozarks. He remembered the night he touched the canvas above his dad's sleeping bag, causing the tent to leak; his father had woken in a puddle. It had been a long time since he had slept in a tent. Now, he stayed in lodges when he went hunting.

The central heating kicked on; his open window had triggered the thermostat.

Taylor opened his eyes. The rain was splashing on the sill and getting his papers wet. He closed the window and turned toward the files on his desk: the candidates for national spokesman. He didn't want to be looking for a new national spokesman. He had *had* a national spokesman.

He banged his fist down on the desk. God damn that fucking Manny Bigelow.

It was no mugger who had killed Brenden. He just felt it. And Patrick Taylor had long ago learned to trust his feelings.

He had been expecting something like this for years. Call it paranoia, call it whatever you want; he just knew one of those antigun people would one day slip a screw and try to get even. It was human nature to be violent.

It was also human nature to be predictable. Someone out there had a reason for killing Brenden. He just had to put the reason and the man together.

He hit the intercom button and asked his secretary to send Conners up. Then he opened the top file and began to look for a new national spokesman.

This time the man would be young, an experienced shooter. A combat vet if possible, though that was easier said than done. And he would be single—there was no telling if this killer would try again. The new man would have to be able to handle that sort of stress.

Patrick Taylor narrowed his choice to two men and set the folders aside.

In nine weeks NAGO was going to hold its annual meeting, during which nominations would be taken for president. He shook his head. Just two months ago that process had seemed no more than a formality. Now, he was in trouble.

The killings in California had done him in. The public mood had shifted; now, the momentum was toward gun control. And gun-control legislation meant that Patrick R. Taylor was not doing his job.

He began to understand how Jimmy Carter must have felt, forced to take the rap for events he couldn't control.

Then he decided that he had *nothing* in common with that limp-wrist Democrat. *He* was going to beat this. *He* wasn't going to lose his job. If he couldn't stop the flood of gun-control bills, he would find the man who had killed Brenden.

He began to jot down some possibilities.

Jamison Conners knocked and walked in.

Conners was just forty, just over six feet two inches tall, and just over two hundred pounds, all of it still muscle. He was an ex-marine, a Vietnam combat vet who, in addition to sitting around Khe Sanh clenching his teeth while the NVA dropped in round after round of mortars, had led recon patrols through the countryside. Conners was NAGO's resident detective and security chief. He was also a computer ace. He had been with NAGO for three years and was smart and sharp and mean, which is why Taylor liked him: Mean people got things done.

"We have a problem here, JC," he said, as Conners entered the room.

JC slid into the chair across from Taylor. "George Herbert Brenden."

Taylor nodded. "George Herbert Brenden."

He gave JC a rundown of the police report, including Manny Bigelow's determination.

"I don't happen to agree with him, JC. I don't see it as a robbery. Nobody heard any shots. Nobody saw anything. And how the hell could a black guy just waltz through an all-white hotel?"

JC shrugged. "Maybe he came in with the garbage collectors?"

Taylor waved the idea away. "If Brenden's job had only been handing out shooting medals at Boy Scout jamborees, I might buy a mugging. But his face was everywhere. He *was* NAGO." He leaned forward in his chair. "What I mean to say, JC, is we have a lot of enemies, and Brenden made a good target."

"Shoot the messenger."

"That's right. Shoot the messenger, it's traditional. Don't look for logic in the face of tradition. He was right out there in front."

The point man, JC thought. Except, the point man usually drew a bye.

"We've been beating the pants off these antigun guys for years," Taylor said. He got up and walked to the window. "People get pissed when they never win. It's a humiliation. Those animal-rights nuts aren't above violence."

JC hummed.

Taylor opened the window again. "Listen, suppose the killer used a silencer. That would explain why no one heard any shots. They interviewed everyone in that hotel. No one heard a thing. That wasn't luck. And why Brenden? Why was the guy waiting in front of Brenden's car, and not behind a pillar near the elevator?" He turned around.

JC shrugged.

"Because the guy had targeted Brenden, that's why. A robber doesn't target one person and wait around for him. A robber robs anyone. There must have been twenty people through that garage before Brenden. Why did the guy wait for Brenden? And remember, this happened at one of his scheduled stops; a determined man could have found that out."

A leaf blew in the window, brown and wet and old and crumbling. Taylor stared at it. It was the middle of March, and a fucking leaf had just blown in his window. Was God laughing at him?

"I want you to find this guy, JC. I want him brought to justice."

JC raised his eyebrows. "You want to see him in jail?"

Taylor nodded. "Yeah, I want to see him in jail. Unless, of course, you have to shoot him. I wouldn't want you to take any unnecessary risks." He handed JC a piece of paper. "Here's a partial list of organizations that hate our guts. Add anyone else you can think of. Get hold of their membership lists. And get right on this. We need to find this guy soon."

JC smiled. "*Before* the annual meeting."

"That's right. *Before* the annual meeting."

97

11

The computer screen filled with names. JC hit the Page Down button. More names. He hit the button again. Hundreds of names. Thousands of names.

It had been like this for two days, as he raided the membership lists of all the organizations that hated what NAGO stood for: truth, justice, and a loaded .45, just in case.

He couldn't believe the number of dip-shit groups that were on record as opposing NAGO. Animal-rights groups. Environmentalists. Antigun groups. Pacifists. Conservationists—those organizations that didn't consist primarily of hunters. There were hundreds of groups, with thousands of members. Local, state, national. He had had to set up parallel files just to organize the massive amount of data; it didn't all fit in his program.

He ran the master list down the screen, then totaled the combined membership: just over a million and a half. He cringed. What a lot of people. Patrick Taylor's goose chase might take the rest of his life.

He took a drag on his cigarette and sat back in his chair. Raw data made him tense. Raw data was useless until it got organized, and that didn't always happen.

He stubbed out the butt, then lit another cigarette. The fan in the computer swirled the smoke; in the dim light, it reminded him of mist in the jungle.

Outside, the rain came down.

He sat there smoking and watching the rain. As a kid, he used to sneak outside to play in the rain. The rain was his friend; it hid the sound of his footsteps so he could creep up on things: birds and rabbits, sometimes a cat. The cats were vicious when he caught them.

JC spent most of his childhood getting into trouble. If he wasn't pushing kids off the slide in the playground, he was bullying them for their lunch money.

Finally, his father decided that he wasn't going to just grow out of it. So he signed JC up for boxing lessons. His father hoped the coach, an ex-marine, would whip JC into shape. It was a good plan; it just didn't happen to work.

The first day in boxing, a kid smaller than JC beat the shit out of him when JC wound up to throw a haymaker. After his nose had stopped bleeding, the coach made JC shake hands with the boy. That was fine with JC; shaking hands would put the kid off his guard. As soon as the coach had turned away, JC picked up a chair and whacked the boy in the back of the head. That was good for six months in reform school.

His father refused to give up. When JC got out, he put him in a NAGO youth program. He hoped handling a gun would make JC responsible. This time his plan worked. JC loved guns and didn't want *his* gun taken away. His father spelled out the rules: He didn't care how many birds or rabbits JC shot, but that was *all* he was to shoot; and except for a couple of cats and dogs, JC followed orders. He could afford to be patient. He was almost fifteen; there was a war going on; and in two years he would be old enough to sign up with the marines. He arrived in Vietnam just in time for the Tet Offensive.

Khe Sanh.

Not what he had in mind. Not what he had in mind at all. After a week with nothing to do except sit around and wait for the enemy to attack, he thought he'd go crazy.

100

GUN MEN

He was at Khe Sanh five months before he was transferred to a unit doing sweeps of the countryside. It was like being let out of reform school. But this time there was no one around to lay down the rules—just him and his buddies and the VC, alone in the jungle. The name of the game was no witnesses.

After a month of patrols, JC got promoted to point. He stayed on point. He was good. In a year and a half he only walked into an ambush twice. The first time it was a single sniper, and the man's rifle misfired. The second time it was a reinforced platoon of NVA, and JC and the lieutenant were the only ones to make it back.

At the end of his second tour of duty he was transferred back to the States. He didn't reenlist.

The next three years were a haze of alcohol, and odd jobs, and bar fights. Finally, he wound up back home, in a little town just outside Fort Worth, Texas. He walked in the door one day and parked himself in front of the TV and would have stayed there forever if, after a week, his father hadn't told him to get off his ass and go over and enroll at the university.

"You're not dumb, so stop acting dumb."

JC thought about it, and decided that acting dumb had nothing at all to do with being dumb. He went over and enrolled at the university anyway.

He studied engineering and computer science. He liked the computer; unlike his classmates, the computer didn't have a bunch of questions about what Vietnam had been like.

It took JC five years to get his degree. When he graduated, he got a job in a large detective agency, a firm that specialized in electronic surveillance and the tracing of in-house theft. These thefts were starting to go beyond the pilfering of products and missing petty cash as business records were transferred to computer files. It was JC's job to track down these computer thieves and recover what they had stolen.

JC liked the job. He liked snooping. There was always some clue to find, something that had been left behind; it was only a matter of recognizing it.

JC hunted thieves and snooped for six years before he took the job with NAGO. He took the job because NAGO had a gigantic computer, and he would be in charge. And maybe he also took the job because he had belonged to NAGO as a boy, and he had been happier then.

JC's job at NAGO was simple: learn everything he could about anyone at all who might be in a position to act against NAGO's interests. That included senators, congressmen, governors, as well as thousands of others. He compiled financial records; made lists of social contacts, friends, and associates; dug up whatever background information he could. And if the individual seemed to warrant it, he copied his phone records and tracked down whoever he had been calling. One time he spent a month tailing an antigun activist, eavesdropping on his meetings. It wasn't always interesting; but when it was, it tended to be very interesting. He passed along what he learned to Patrick Taylor.

He looked at the computer screen. It had gone blank while he was daydreaming. He left it blank.

Most people thought computers were fast: Press a few keys, and you got what you wanted. And, of course, that was true, but only after you entered, and entered correctly (the computer didn't differentiate between correct and incorrect data), all the information in the first place, and only after all that information was organized (and organized correctly), and only after you knew what it was you were looking for. And God help you if the information in the computer was incomplete; then all you had was junk.

Which was what he had now. A million and a half pieces of junk.

He looked at the clock. It was three. In two hours he would leave and go to the gym and beat the shit out of the heavy bag. He did that every Wednesday and Saturday. The rest of the week he ran. Five miles every day. He ran in the rain, and he ran in the heat. The running kept the dreams away.

Dreams of the jungle. An endless, pathless jungle. Noisy and quiet and wet and still. Alive.

He was on a path leading to a village. An old papasan grinning at him, half his teeth gone. JC hated the grinning, and the smiles, and the bowing. He hated that they were lies.

Then came the gunfire. And the blood. And the running, his legs like jelly, his gun gone. Darkness. A heavy darkness over him, pressing down.

The Wall.

He couldn't breathe.

Which was when he woke up.

JC had never been to the Wall. He was scared of the Wall. He was afraid the faces that belonged to the names on the Wall would move into his dreams.

He hit a key, and the screen filled with names, the names of people who hated NAGO.

He had organized the names by categories; and he had organized them by their degree of radicalness. All he had gotten was a million and a half names arranged in different ways. That was all he was ever going to get playing with these lists.

He switched off the box and stretched out on the couch. Why Brenden?

He smoked his way through half a pack of cigarettes thinking about the answer. He missed the gym, and he missed his dinner. He had worked straight through the previous night, and now his brain was slowing down. He needed to sleep. Instead, he got up and walked to the closet and pulled out his sweats and went for a run.

He ran farther than usual, making long loops through the empty streets. When he got back, he took a shower (there was a complete bathroom on the fifth floor) and changed into clean clothes. He kept several sets of clothes in his closet because sometimes he was in a hurry and didn't have a chance to make it back to his apartment, a dump on the edge of the ghetto. He had never bothered to fix up the apartment because he had never planned on staying. He'd been there three years now.

He stretched out on the couch again. Why Brenden?

An image of Brenden appeared before his eyes: Brenden smiling. Brenden had never smiled much. That was why he had been so successful; he never seemed like he was trying to con you.

JC had once lost five bucks to the guy when Brenden managed to sell a used condom to a drunk.

"Field-tested!" Brenden had bragged. "It's *better* than new."

Cars, houses, boats, guns. Brenden had sold them all. One night when they were out drinking, he confided his secret to JC: It wasn't the product you were selling, it was yourself.

Why had someone chosen Brenden to kill?

For the life of him, JC couldn't see an antigun fanatic, however humiliated, stripping the body. Only a mugger would do that; or someone who wanted to make it look like a mugging, someone who would naturally come under suspicion. Brenden's wife, for instance.

But JC knew Brenden's wife—an ugly, bitchy woman—and knew she had nothing to gain by her husband's death; there had been almost no insurance, and she had no lover waiting in the wings. Neither had Brenden had one particular mistress to make her jealous. In fact, no one stood to profit by Brenden's death.

Which *only* left a stranger.

He lit a cigarette. He could only think of two reasons why a stranger would kill Brenden: Either the killer *was* a mugger; or the killer hated Brenden because Brenden worked for NAGO.

He rolled off the couch and headed for the library. Maybe something in one of Brenden's speeches would give him a clue.

It took JC twenty-eight hours to read through the transcripts of all the talks and interviews Brenden had given in the last eight months. They were mostly the same. When he was finished, he reread the coversheets: Each gave the date of the speech, the place, and the group addressed.

JC knew that while the speeches had largely been the same, the audiences had varied greatly, from nationwide TV to gun clubs. A speech that seemed timid before the American Machine Gunners' Society might seem radical and offensive to a general audience.

He made a list of subjects Brenden had covered, then ranked those subjects by how controversial they were. Assault rifles headed the list, and almost all *those* references had come in the wake of the two California massacres.

For weeks after the killings Brenden had given his "people

104

kill people" speech, stressing the failure of the criminal-justice system. Maybe his speech had inspired someone, someone who was already pissed off? JC knew it would have pissed *him* off to see someone stand up and defend the weapon that had just killed his child. Better to be quiet and invisible when people were angry.

During his last months in Vietnam JC, on several occasions, had seen large groups of Vietnamese rioting. They had been angry, very angry, and for a lot of reasons. But their anger had been directed at just one target: America, and everything American, particularly American servicemen. There had been murders and maimings.

At the time JC hadn't understood that sort of anger. He did now.

Maybe the person who killed Brenden had just been waiting for a target? Maybe seeing Brenden tipped the scale.

He made a list of everything he could think of that would make him angry enough to kill. Then he made a second list, a list of reasons to target the spokesman of a gun group. He spent an hour organizing the two lists and eliminating those things that, on review, seemed trivial. When he was finished, he surveyed what he had left and suddenly felt calm.

He had found what had been missing: a filter, a key that would organize his data, separating what was useful from what was useless. It was his talent to find these filters, and to sense when he had a filter that would work. Now, he had a profile of his killer.

Suddenly, it didn't seem so crazy that someone had targeted Brenden: someone who had had a friend or relative or spouse killed by a firearm; someone who had no one else to revenge himself on; someone who had not much more to lose.

He called up a directory, and then a file. It was a list of everyone killed by a firearm in the last six months. There were over six thousand names on the list.

NAGO updated the list every month. It was a lot of work and a big expense, but Taylor felt the cost was far outweighed by the value of exact statistics, statistics that could be manipulated to NAGO's advantage.

He was going to have to narrow down that list.

He sat back. It was 7:05 A.M., too early to get any help. Besides, he was hungry. He pulled on his jacket. Organizing the list could wait an hour until he had had some breakfast.

JC had his people eliminate all those victims where the killer had been identified and was still alive. Then they crossed off the victims of accidental shootings. Then the victims of drug crimes, family disputes, and lover's quarrels. Then JC decided to cross off everyone on the list over the age of fifty-five; he thought a spouse would be too tired to take revenge, and a child too preoccupied with the inheritance.

It took all day and most of the evening to pare down the list. When they were done, there were seventy-five names remaining.

JC sat back, satisfied. There were 250 million people in America, and he had narrowed that ocean down to a puddle of seventy-five names. He laughed. His man might even be connected to one of those names. It no longer seemed like such a wild-goose chase.

He read through the information on each of the seventy-five victims, then divided the list one last time. Eighteen of the victims seemed more pathetic, more pitiable, than the others.

He had the computer print out the two lists, along with whatever information he had about each victim. Then he went home and went to sleep.

Saturday morning found him in the library hunting down accounts of the murders. There was not much. The library didn't have many regional papers, and the national papers didn't always list the bereaved. He was going to have to do some traveling.

12

The tail end of lunch was not a difficult time to find people at NAGO headquarters; most were in the subbasement firing off a few rounds.

JC headed past the display of Revolutionary War weapons and down the two flights of stairs. He didn't take off his jacket because the range was cold, and being cold made him tense. As usual, Taylor was next to the far wall.

JC had to admire Taylor. The man had been working seven days a week for two months now and didn't show the strain at all. And he was losing.

The week before had been a disaster: President Bush had banned the import of assault rifles; Colt had announced it was going to discontinue domestic civilian sales of the AR-15; and the California legislature had voted to outlaw the sale of assault rifles.

JC stepped up as Taylor was retrieving a photo of the middle Kennedy brother.

"Not too bad, huh, JC?" Taylor pointed at the target. Half a dozen bullets had shredded Bobby's face.

"Not too bad at all, Patrick."

Patrick tossed the picture of Bobby Kennedy into the incinerator.

JC knew all the pictures in the shooting-range file. He had raided the computer one day for the code numbers, then had gone down to the range and called up each target. Most of the pictures he had recognized: well-known leftist politicians and well-known historical figures (*dead* leftist politicians). Given the political leanings of NAGO members, that wasn't particularly surprising. Still, when the face of Martin Luther King, Jr., appeared, JC had had to admit surprise. Except for a few school kids, who got the day off, who even remembered anymore?

Taylor finished reloading and popped the clip back into his gun. "Care to risk a few bucks?"

JC smiled. "Not much of a risk, Patrick." He slid a .357 magnum Smith & Wesson revolver out of its shoulder holster.

Taylor chuckled. "Still using that relic, huh? What if you need to shoot fast?"

JC smiled. When he needed to shoot fast, he had a two-shot derringer in his pocket, also a .357 magnum.

He pulled on a pair of ear protectors, turned to face the target, and fired five times. Taylor retrieved the silhouette. A group of five holes a good bit smaller than his palm covered what would have been the heart.

He shook his head. "You're a fine shot, JC. No doubt about it."

JC started to clean his gun. "I got something."

"On Brenden?"

JC nodded. "I got a feeling."

"No shit."

Patrick Taylor leaned forward in his chair and set his hands on his desk. "So what have you got?"

JC thought about where to start. "I don't think it was political, Patrick."

"Why not?"

"I don't think an antigun guy would've stripped the body."

Taylor nodded. "So what *do* you think?" He let his eyes settle on the younger man.

The scrutiny made JC uneasy. He figured it was half because Taylor was almost as old as his father, and half because Taylor was a major. JC had never liked officers, even those who had started out in the ranks.

"I think it was a personal thing. I think Brenden said something that pissed someone off."

"Enough to kill him?"

JC shrugged. "I read through Brenden's transcripts going back eight months. Most of it was the same, and not very interesting, until Stockton. Then, that whole assault-rifle business hit the fan. I think that's the key."

Taylor nodded.

"I figure the guy who killed Brenden was pissed off already. I figure he targeted Brenden because there was no one else for him to fix on. And I figure the reason he was pissed off was that someone he loved was killed by a gun."

"Okay."

"I went back six months and checked out everyone who had been killed by a gun. I came up with seventy-five names, and eighteen of those names look a little bit better than the others." He reached for a cigarette.

Taylor shook his finger. Taylor had given up smoking and was feeling righteous. "I don't want to breathe that shit."

JC put the butt away.

"Who's on this shortlist of yours?"

"Mostly the children killed in California."

"Oh, Jesus."

"You could give the list to Bigelow to check out."

Taylor laughed. "I'm sure he'd leap at the chance. I can just see suggesting it."

He swiveled around to stare out the window.

"The police are on the other side, now, JC. They wouldn't care if we *all* got knocked off. Then *they'd* be the only ones with guns."

JC flicked a piece of lint off his sleeve.

Taylor turned back. "You think our man is on this list of yours?"

"He might be related to someone on the list."

"You think you can find him?"

"I don't know. It might take a while."

"I want you to try. Take Szczepanski along. And be discreet. I don't want this getting out. We'll be heroes if we find Brenden's killer."

JC smiled. "You might even get reelected."

"That's right, JC. That's exactly right."

13

About the time JC and Patrick Taylor were finishing up their talk, Tran Van Duong was sitting down to an early lunch in his restaurant.

"Laws are passed, and laws are repealed," said Lee Hong. He scooped up a pile of noodles with his chopsticks and stuffed them in his mouth. Lee Hong was the manager at the House of Flowers. "Take Prohibition, for instance."

Tran crushed a shrimp with his chopsticks.

"Laws are like the seasons," Lee Hong mused.

Tran aimed his chopsticks at his manager. "You should be home composing poems, my friend. Your talents are wasted in this restaurant."

Lee Hong laughed and aimed his chopsticks right back at Tran. "You will see, all these new gun-control laws they're proposing—the proposals will disappear like a puddle under the sun." He circled his chopsticks to describe the disappearing puddle.

"Laws!" Tran shot back. "No longer just proposals! Cleveland. Los Angeles. The entire state of California!"

Lee Hong smirked. "The governor has yet to sign the bill."

"A matter of formality!" Tran dismissed the concern with a wave.

Lee Hong scooped up more noodles. "That, we will see. The NRA hasn't given up yet. Nor has NAGO."

Tran stared at the morning paper sitting open on the table. Darrel Honeywell, the new NAGO national spokesman, stared back at him. Honeywell had been in California all week. It seemed there was still some chance the bill to ban assault rifles could die in committee.

Immediately after the two California massacres legislation to ban assault rifles had been introduced in half the states in the country; and with the police actively supporting the legislation, for once it looked like the antigun forces would be victorious. People were outraged.

But now, two months later, things were slowing down. Much of the legislation that had been proposed had since been withdrawn, or was locked up in committee. People were losing interest—assault rifles were old news.

Tran glanced at NAGO's new national spokesman again: The man had the face of a pig. A hungry pig. And his voice—like a meat grinder clogged with gristle.

Tran set his head in his hands. Where would it end? Was there no sanity in the world?

"Are you all right, my friend?" Lee Hong asked.

He filled Tran's cup with tea. Perhaps his remarks had been injudicious. After all, the man had lost his only child to gunfire just a few months before.

Darrel Honeywell was Patrick Taylor's peace offering to the ultraconservative wing of NAGO. It was from this quarter that he expected a challenge, and he hoped the appointment of Honeywell, a rabid-dog, progun nut, would get him re-elected.

Honeywell was twenty-nine years old. He was a fourth-generation Californian who thought the rest of the country sucked, and who wasn't too crazy about most of the people in his own state. And he wasn't afraid to let them know it.

He had spent his childhood riding his tricycle, and then

112

his bicycle, around Orange County, cursing out the niggers and spics and kikes and wops and chinks. On the night favorite son Richard Nixon got elected president, Darrel, along with the entire neighborhood, ran screaming into the street. They celebrated all night. He even got to miss school the next day.

Things didn't get that good again for a while. First, Nixon got forced out of office. Then Jimmy Carter got elected president. On that black day Darrel decided that if he personally didn't do something, the country would certainly go down the tubes. He gave up being a juvenile delinquent and started studying, and managed to get into UC Irvine, majoring in political science.

In 1980 he had the pleasure of watching Ronald Reagan whip that pussy Carter's ass. It was a pleasure that was particularly sweet because Darrel had spent three months working with the Reagan campaign.

In '82 he went to work for Pete Wilson. Wilson was running for the senate against faggot-lover, and governor, Jerry Brown. Victory again.

And in '84 victory yet again, with the Gipper's reelection. Not much of a race against Mondale and a woman.

Two years later Darrel started working for NAGO as a local spokesman, mostly warning gun clubs about the need to be vigilant, and Boy Scouts about the need to shoot straight.

Darrel took great pleasure in demonstrating to these young men exactly how to shoot straight. He would draw his Desert Eagle out of its holster and hold it up for them to admire. Then he would explain in detail how the gun worked, finishing up by flipping off the safety and dropping five straight into the bull's-eye. Darrel knew how to shoot straight. He had been a junior state champion.

Nineteen eighty-eight was another fine year for conservatives: Pete Wilson got reelected senator, something no Republican had done for quite a while; and George Bush put the screws to that socialist from Massachusetts.

It was good to be a winner.

14

United flight 933 from Washington, D.C., to Oakland, California, with a stop in Denver, was going to arrive late. JC didn't like when planes that left on time arrived late; it suggested something was wrong.

He leaned over Szczepanski, who was snoring lightly, and peered out the window. It was clear below; he could easily see the ground: the cars on the road; the snakelike wandering of rivers and streams; the giant circles formed by center-pivot irrigators. To the south a city glittered in the sun. It didn't seem that far away, even though they were flying at thirty-four thousand feet.

They were going to be twenty-five minutes late into Denver, the result of an erratic jet stream. Forecasters were predicting another year of drought.

JC thought these gloom-and-doom predictions were several months premature. The jet stream, notoriously capricious, could easily move again. A month of rain, and people would forget about the dust and start complaining about the mosquitoes.

He took a last look at the dry heartland of America, then settled back into his seat.

Another year of drought and there would be worldwide panic, and everyone and his brother would head out to buy a gun. Uncertain times always resulted in increased gun sales; that was what "civilization" was about.

The flight attendants rolled by with their cart of soda and booze. He asked for an orange juice. The woman dutifully served him.

He could remember when it had been service with a smile. Then, they had been called stewardesses. These flight attendants were probably the same women now sagging toward middle age, tired after twenty years of smiling. Chalk one up for women's lib and the union.

He shoved Szczepanski's arm off the elbow rest. Szczepanski snored on. A pair of sunglasses hid his eyes.

JC couldn't stand people who wore sunglasses all the time. And he hated people who could sleep anywhere. He had trouble sleeping in his own bed.

He took off his sweater and closed his eyes. He could hear the sound track of the movie humming out from the earphones around him, like a subliminal message. It blended with the whir of the air blower and the vibration of the engines, and Szczepanski's light snoring.

When JC and Szczepanski arrived in Oakland, they rented a car and drove to Stockton. JC wanted to start with Stockton because he suspected the Stockton massacre was the beginning of this whole mess.

But Stockton turned out to be a bust.

He had tracked down the parents of the victims and followed them around for three days, occasionally asking neighbors a discreet question or two (and getting stared at), occasionally chatting it up with a local store owner (and getting stared at). He had discovered nothing out of the ordinary, and he was beginning to wonder if he had spinach on his teeth. And his gut was as cold as ice.

Suddenly, spying on the parents of dead kids didn't seem so clever. What it seemed like was macabre. He was reminded of walking through Vietnamese villages after a bombing raid. Insult to injury. Better to have just finished burning the village.

116

He closed his eyes as Szczepanski walked into their room at the Holiday Inn in Walnut Creek.

"Come on, JC. Time to party."

They had just finished a late dinner at a Chinese restaurant, and Szczepanski was ready to burn up the town.

"I'm feeling kind of tired, Taddy."

Taddy was checking his hair in the mirror. "Come on, JC. I got the word from the bellhop; the local hot spot's only a couple of minutes down the road."

JC laughed to himself. What sort of action did the kid expect to find in Walnut Creek? A housewife out moonlighting? A teenager painted up to look twenty-one?

"You go on ahead, Taddy. I'm going to turn in."

"What you need, JC, is a wiggly little thing to make your little thing wiggle."

"Don't stay out too late."

"Right, Mom." And he was gone.

JC opened his eyes and stared at the ceiling: a crusted, textured "paint" that looked like it would take the skin off your arm faster than a belt sander. A faded landscape sat on the wall to his left. A dresser sat across from him. He lit a cigarette.

Stockton had been a waste of time. And now he was going to do the same thing again. It was possible he might have to move on to his second list, or even his third list. The prospect of checking out aggrieved relatives for the next two years made him want to go out and buy a bottle.

But JC knew if he bought a bottle, he would buy a second bottle, and then a third, just like before. And then the dreams would come. Dreams in which his gun misfired, dreams of the dead. He didn't want those dreams.

He dragged himself off the bed, changed, and went for a run. He ran for two hours, until the pain in his side was so bad he had to stop. Then he threw up his dinner—greasy fried pork and vegetables and rice—and walked back to the hotel. Szczepanski was already asleep.

Two days later JC thought he had something. The father of one of the Laurel Valley victims was a widower; and the victim had been an only child.

He copied down all the information in the newspaper article; among other things, it gave him Tran Van Duong's home address and his business address.

That night JC padded up the dead-end road that Tran lived on, past the Jaguars and Mercedes, past the gardens kept green with scarce water, past the horses and beef cattle, and shimmied up the utility pole that carried Tran's phone line. JC wasn't afraid of being spotted or sniffed out by curious dogs, because it was pouring rain; he was afraid of getting electrocuted.

The eavesdropping device he installed on Tran's phone line was a battery-powered transmitter that turned itself on and off automatically. It had a range of several miles, but because Tran's house was located on a hill, JC knew the signal would carry farther than that. He had a receiver in his car and a receiver in his motel room. The receiver in the motel room had an alarm in case a call came in at night.

JC had learned how to use a number of these devices during his years as a private eye and had worked on customizing several of them. The device he installed on Tran's phone line looked like a clamp. It was wrapped with black tape, and to the casual observer was indistinguishable from the equipment the phone company used. It took him ten minutes to attach it, mostly because the rain had made everything wet.

An hour later he had a similar device clamped around the line coming out of Tran's office at the restaurant. And the next morning, while Tran was going over the books inside the House of Flowers, JC placed a beeper under his car. The beeper was held in place by a magnet and took four seconds to install.

JC waited all afternoon for something to happen. But nobody called Tran, and Tran didn't place any calls. He didn't even go home for a siesta, as he had the day before.

At five JC decided Tran was going to work straight through, so he sent Szczepanski for some sandwiches. The previous evening Tran had worked until nine-thirty.

But at six-fifteen, just as JC was peeling the lid off his cup of coffee, Tran walked out the door. JC pressed the lid back on and stowed the cup.

"What do you think, Taddy? He's calling it quits kind of early tonight."

"Maybe he's got a date?"

"Mah-jongg?"

They followed loosely, letting the beeper guide them as Tran headed west on Highway 24, and then down into Berkeley. He stopped at the College Bowl.

Szczepanski laughed. "Mah-jongg! He's going bowling."

JC picked up his coffee.

It sure looked like Tran was going bowling. Except he wasn't carrying a bowling ball. Was his ball inside? in a locker? That would make him a regular.

He climbed out of the car. "Come on, Taddy. Let's go bowling, too."

Szczepanski hopped out of the car. Bowling was his middle name.

"And you can just leave those fucking sunglasses in the car."

The bowling alley smelled of unwashed socks and wax. They rented shoes from a guy named Marty and bowled a game, then walked back to the desk to pay.

"Only one game?" Marty asked. He handed them their shoes.

"I whupped his ass so bad," JC said, "he didn't want to bowl anymore."

Marty laughed.

JC handed him a ten-dollar bill and turned to face the lanes. "You know, it's amazing those little guys can even throw the ball." He nodded at the group Tran was with. They were all Orientals.

Marty nodded. "Some of my best customers."

"No kidding?"

"Been bowling here six, seven years. Every Saturday night."

"Every Saturday, huh?"

"Haven't missed a night in a year and a half."

"Is that right?"

The news didn't make JC's day. Brenden had been shot on a Saturday night.

119

They said good night to Marty and went back to the car.

In the two days JC had been following Tran around, a feeling had been growing that he didn't want to admit: Tran wasn't a killer. The man moved wrong, his aura was wrong, everything was wrong. And now he knew Tran had been in California the night Brenden was shot.

Which meant it was time to move on to the next person on his list.

But JC didn't want to move on, because Tran fit his profile so perfectly.

He wondered if Tran might have hired someone to do the job, some Chinese ninja, or whatever, from Chinatown. That would explain why nobody had seen anything in Boston; the guy had probably crawled into the garage through an electric outlet.

"Let's get some pizza," Szczepanski said.

"You eat like a fucking teenager, Taddy boy."

"Come on, JC. Those guys are going to be another hour, at least."

JC pointed down the road at an orange light. It was barely visible.

Forty minutes later Szczepanski was back with three chili dogs and an extra large milk shake.

The smell made JC gag. He lit a cigarette.

He would have to prove that Tran had hired a pro, and that meant finding some evidence of a payment—maybe a cash withdrawal from his bank account, or a new mortgage on his house, or the sale of something valuable. He hoped the killer had cost a pile, because it was sure easier to detect the transfer of fifty thousand dollars than five thousand dollars. And he hoped to God the killer hadn't been some kid off the street, someone from *Boston's* Chinatown who had been called up by his California cousin to do the job for fifty bucks (like sending flowers).

On Sunday, when it looked like JC was going to be a regular in the shopping-center parking lot at the bottom of Tran's road, he gave a call to the detective agency where he used to work and asked if they would let the local cops know he was on a surveillance. His old employers were happy to help out.

And on Monday, when the county offices opened, JC left Szczepanski to follow Tran, while he headed over to Martinez to see what the public record held.

Tran Van Duong was a wealthy man. A very wealthy man. JC was envious. Tran owned four properties in Contra Costa County. And when he checked the neighboring counties, JC found two more places.

Tran had made his first purchase in Oakland, in 1975. Eight months later he had bought a second property, also in Oakland.

JC wondered how he had managed that, right off the boat. When *he* had come back from Vietnam, he had had nothing, just bad dreams.

Over the course of his investigation JC confirmed that Tran's wife had died two years before, and that there had only been the one child, the one killed by Mattox: Loan.

He thought about that. First the wife, then the daughter. That must have been some kind of pain, probably enough to unhinge anyone.

He wondered what Tran's life had been like in Vietnam. Probably more pain.

JC followed Tran around for a week.

The man led a boring life: In the morning, around ten, he went to his restaurant; around two he returned home; at five he returned to the restaurant; around nine he returned home. Once, he stopped at the local market for some groceries. Once, he brought a package of food back from the restaurant.

In seven days he had received a total of eight phone calls. One had been a wrong number. Three had been sales pitches. The other four had been in Vietnamese, and, after JC got them translated, turned out to be nothing more than friends saying hello. Tran had called the restaurant twice.

But there was no evidence, not even a hint, that the man had hired a killer. There had not been any sale, or mortgage, of property; nor had he withdrawn any money from the bank.

JC knew this because he had gotten a NAGO member who worked at a credit agency to call up Tran's bank and (saying that Tran had applied for a million-dollar loan) get a run down on his account. Tran had not withdrawn a dime for six months, which didn't really surprise JC, because Tran owned a restaurant, and restaurant owners skimmed. They skimmed a lot. JC knew that because when he was working as a detective, he had once checked out a restaurant. After fourteen years Tran must have had enough to pay the killer cash.

Which left him with nothing, just a feeling in his gut.

"How long are we going to follow this guy around, JC?"

They were sitting in the parking lot, waiting for Tran to leave for the restaurant. It was still early, and not many other cars were around.

"You got something better to do, Taddy boy?"

"I got a wife, JC."

JC smiled. "Are you saying you have a hard-on, Taddy? Is that your problem? Why don't you just hop in the back and take care of it. I don't mind."

"How much longer, JC?"

"Till I get bored."

On Thursday morning, April 6, nearly two months exactly from the day he had watched George Brenden on *Today in the Bay*, Tran Van Duong had an eerie experience. He turned on the TV and found Darrel Honeywell staring back at him.

The same time. The same program. The same questions and answers as before. He stared in disbelief as Berns Hanson repeated the interview.

"What about a 'well regulated militia,' Darrel?"

"Where do we draw the line, Darrel? Bazookas? Tanks?"

"And who's going to pay for all those jails, Darrel?"

And Darrel Honeywell rasping back the answers, the same answers Brenden had given, but in a taunting, condescending voice, a miserable gravelly whine.

The Founding Fathers. The Constitution. The criminal-justice system.

Tran flung his teacup across the room.

How much could one listen to? How long could a man sit silent? He turned off the TV.

How could one man fight a group like NAGO? How could a single person stop such a Gargantuan organization, an organization that thought nothing of threatening senators and congressmen, that had millions of members, all of them running around with guns. He could only think of one answer: terror. He knew it wasn't a very good answer, but then he didn't really care.

He would hire this assassin again. He would pay him to kill Darrel Honeywell. And when NAGO appointed a new national spokesman, he would pay to have him killed, too, until his money ran out. He would make NAGO afraid, just as the ayatollah Khomeini had made the writers and publishers of the world afraid. It was one thing when terrorism threatened strangers in Beirut, quite another when *your* name was on the list. Maybe he would have Berns Hanson killed, too.

He pulled on his coat and left the house.

"There he goes," Szczepanski said, as the beeper started to grow louder.

JC glanced at his watch. "He's early, today."

As they watched, Tran pulled his BMW into the lot where they were sitting, not two hundred feet away. He got out of his car and stepped into a phone booth.

"You think his phone is broken?" Szczepanski asked.

JC was leaning over the backseat, frantically pulling at something. Finally, he got the case open and the listening horn out and aimed at the phone booth. He flipped on the tape recorder and pulled the earphones over his head, trying to look as inconspicuous as possible. He was in luck. Tran was facing the other way.

"Holy shit!"

It was the moment every detective knows, when persistence and patience and intuition combine with luck for the payoff. He had beaten that grumbling little voice of boredom, that voice that had been suggesting, respectfully, that perhaps this time his instincts were off, that perhaps the feeling in his gut was only the Mexican food he had eaten the night before, that perhaps it was time to get the fuck out of there and go home. He had proved that voice wrong. He had been lucky.

Oh, yes, it was good to be lucky. He laughed, and cuffed Szczepanski on the chin.

"It's good to be lucky, Taddy boy. So good to be lucky."

When Tran drove off, JC disconnected the tape recorder from the mike and hurried over to the phone booth.

15

"I found him, Patrick! I found the guy who killed Brenden."

JC cradled the phone between his shoulder and his ear as he fiddled with the tape recorder.

"At least, I found the guy who had Brenden killed. His name is Tran Van Duong."

"A chink?"

"Vietnamese."

Patrick Taylor swung his chair around to stare out the window. It was raining.

"Looks like we're still fighting that war, huh, JC?" He drummed his fingers on the arm of his chair. "So the guy was on your list."

"Listen to this, Patrick."

JC played him the tape; it took about twenty-five seconds.

Taylor leaned forward in his chair. "How come there's only one side of the conversation?"

"He called from a pay phone. I had to use a mike."

"That tape doesn't say very much, JC."

"Patrick, this is our guy. I know."

"JC, that tape wouldn't convict Nixon."

125

"Listen, his daughter was one of the kids killed in the Laurel Valley massacre. He's all alone now. He's got no wife, no family, nothing. And he's got money. A lot of money. He's worth millions."

"Where'd he get it?"

"He started off with it. He bought a restaurant and house right off the boat. He's got a pile of property. And his restaurant is always packed. Chinese food."

"He mortgage any property in the last couple of months?" Taylor asked the question as innocently as he could.

JC started rocking back and forth, the way a snake rocks back and forth when it's testing the air. Taylor wasn't buying it. He turned and looked at Szczepanski. The deadbeat was asleep; his mouth was hanging open catching flies.

The phone started clicking. JC dropped in another pile of quarters.

"Patrick, this is our man. I know it. He's setting up another hit. He didn't need to mortgage anything; he paid the killer cash. He runs a restaurant, Patrick. He's been in business fourteen years."

Patrick Taylor closed his eyes and tried to picture JC standing in a phone booth in California. The image that rose before him was, strangely, not of JC in jeans and long-sleeve T-shirt, his usual office dress, but of JC in jungle fatigues, camo paint all over his face. Taylor had never seen JC in camo fatigues and was surprised that this picture and not the other, more familiar, one had come to mind. He decided it was because NAGO was at war and JC was on point.

Taylor knew the hardest thing for a leader was to trust that he had picked good men, and then to trust the men he had picked.

"Does Tran know you're following him around?"

JC stopped rocking and relaxed. "I don't think so."

Taylor shook his head. "I can't believe he's setting up another job. How soon you think the killer will get in touch?"

"A couple of days. Maybe a week."

"And the target?"

"I can guess."

"Yeah, me, too. Play me the tape again." He flipped on his own tape recorder.

JC rewound the tape and played it again:
"Mr. Weston, please."

. . .

"Tran Van Duong."
(a pause of ten seconds)
"I have some more work for your friend."

. . .

"Yes, the same sort of job."

. . .

Taylor started drumming his fingers again. "God damn, that's not much. I didn't hear him dialing."

"Push-button."

"You think this Weston is the killer?"

"I think he's just the contact. Otherwise, they would have talked about the target and the money, or set up a meeting."

"You think you could get the name of the killer out of Weston?"

"I could sure try."

Taylor leaned back in his chair. "Where's Tran?"

"He's home."

"And he was in California the night Brenden was killed?"

"He was out bowling with friends."

"A regular American. Call me back in an hour." He swung his chair around and set the phone in its cradle.

Weston.

He pulled out the D.C. phone book and flipped through the pages until he got to *W*. Almost forty Westons in Washington alone.

He rapped his fingers on the desk. He could call in the cops now. He could play them the tape and explain how they had found Tran. If they threatened Tran with a murder charge, he would give them Weston; and Weston would give them the killer.

He picked up the phone and started to dial Boston. Then he thought of Manny Bigelow sitting at the other end, his feet up on his desk, and set the phone down.

127

Tran had just lost his kid to a maniac. The Boston cop would laugh at the idea of having a talk with him.

He would have to call the brass and have Bigelow ordered out to California. Even then, the man would probably do nothing more than ask a few routine questions and maybe check Tran's alibi. He would discover that Tran had been bowling. Probably, Bigelow bowled, too. They would compare averages.

Then Tran would call up Weston, and Weston would alert the killer.

Taylor got up and began to pace the room. A smiling Ronald Reagan, his hand wrapped around Patrick Taylor's paw, stared down at him. On the opposite wall an almost identical picture featured George Bush. Taylor had placed the pictures in his office because he wanted visitors to think the president of the United States supported NAGO and that that support was enduring.

But Taylor had no illusions about George Bush's loyalty. The man, like all politicians, was only loyal to whatever position got him the most votes; and right now that position had nothing to do with defending assault rifles. If he hoped to win this battle, he was going to have to mobilize every one of the 60 million gun owners in America.

And Patrick Taylor intended to win. Winning was just a matter of tenacity and courage, and dirty fighting. It was fine to feel righteous, but in the long run it was much better to feel rotten and have won.

He walked to the window and stared down at the street. People were on their way to lunch.

The easiest thing would be to kill Tran and declare the score settled; but he didn't like that idea. It felt incomplete.

And killing Tran wouldn't get him reelected. He wouldn't be able to tell anyone. And even if he could, it would look like he had knocked off the dink because the dink was the easy target; he would look bad. He needed the killer, too.

He began to pace the office again, finally stopping in front of a Civil War rifle that was mounted on the wall. The gun worked perfectly; every year he fired it at a Civil War weapons competition.

If they grabbed Tran, eventually he would give them Weston. And if they grabbed Weston, eventually they would get the killer. But would they get him before he discovered that Tran was missing? Taylor wasn't sure. They didn't have much to threaten Tran with, just pain; and at this point in his life, Tran might just eat the pain.

Taylor had once watched a man die under torture. It took six hours, and the man never talked; he didn't even cry out. His eyes just grew bright, then brighter, then feverish. Then his eyes grew dull. Then the eyes didn't have any light in them at all.

If Tran didn't give them Weston, they would have nothing *and* the killer would be alerted. Better to try for Weston themselves, without any help from Tran. They could always grab Tran later. And maybe the killer when he came for the money.

He sat down in his chair. One way or another they would get this guy.

The phone rang.

"I want Weston, JC. You think you can find him without Tran?"

JC felt his shoulders bunching up. Taylor was heading in the wrong direction.

"Listen, Patrick, we don't really need Weston. The killer has to contact Tran. And then he has to pick up his money. I can just wait for him."

"Szczepanski can wait. It could be weeks before the killer shows up. By then we could have Weston."

"What about the police?"

"Fuck the police. They can't find their own dicks. Just make sure Szczepanski knows what to do."

As JC and Patrick Taylor were making their plans, Peter Weston was adding a line of code to the bottom of a travel brochure. When he was done, he stuck the brochure in an envelope, pressed on an address label, and dropped the letter off at the post office. It went out with the afternoon mail.

Two days later the letter arrived at the main post office in Springfield, Massachusetts. It was sunny, and cold, and William

Jones wasn't thinking about much of anything as he pushed another piece of junk mail into box 8423.

No one picked up the letter that day, or the next. Eliot Brod was away on a skiing trip with his wife and daughter in northern Vermont. The letter would sit there for almost a week.

16

JC stared at the screen of the computer. How to find a Weston in a haystack?

Either Tran knew Weston, or Weston was a friend of a friend.

JC hoped Tran knew Weston, because he knew he would never find the man if he was a friend of a friend.

But if Tran knew Weston, then some time, somewhere, their paths must have crossed. If he could recreate Tran's past accurately enough (and if he got lucky), he might find that crossing. And then from Weston to the killer, like a hinge.

He typed in a few commands, and Tran's file appeared on the screen.

In 1975 Tran bought a restaurant. The place was still a restaurant, and still a Chinese restaurant. JC had visited the joint and, after dinner, had spent a couple of minutes chatting it up with the woman behind the cash register, praising the food and asking a few innocent questions. Tran had run the restaurant for almost ten years before moving to Walnut Creek.

Tran purchased a second property in 1976, also in Oak-

131

---

land, a home. He still owned it; a Chinese family lived there now. JC figured the place had once been Tran's home, and when he finally tracked down an old phone book at a historical society, he discovered he was right.

The phone listing for the House of Flowers and the Oakland home continued until 1984. That was the year Tran moved to Laurel Valley, and the year he moved his restaurant to Walnut Creek. In 1985 the two listings appeared in the Contra Costa County phone book.

There was no listing for Tran, or the House of Flowers, before 1976 in either Alameda or Contra Costa countries. And there had never been a listing for Tran in the San Francisco phone book. JC had checked as far back as 1965. He couldn't know that Tran, living in a boardinghouse, hadn't bothered to get a phone.

In 1979 Tran bought three more properties, all homes. In 1980 he got married. In 1981 he bought another two properties: a piece of land and a commercial building. Nineteen eighty-one was also the year Tran registered to vote.

JC figured that was just about right. If the man had come over with the first wave of Vietnamese immigrants in 1975, he would have been naturalized about five years later and eligible to vote.

In 1982 Tran's daughter was born. In 1984 the family moved, probably so the kid could grow up in the suburbs and not in scuzzy Oakland. In 1987 Tran sold a house and the commercial building and paid off all his mortgages. That same year his wife died.

So where did Weston fit in?

JC thought he knew.

He had followed Tran around for a week and hadn't seen the man so much as speak to an Anglo. Probably, that had been Tran's pattern since coming to America. Probably, Tran knew Weston from another time. Vietnam.

JC had gotten to know a couple of Vietnamese while in-country; a lot of soldiers had. Vietnam would have been the natural place for Tran and Weston to have met, and the natural place to find a killer.

He saved the file on Tran, and called up the membership file.

NAGO was a huge organization, with close to 3 million members, and as with any organization that size, its main strength lay not so much in its financial resources, though they were considerable, as in the membership itself. NAGO's members were spread across every layer of society, from military leaders to garbage collectors to the cop on the beat. But the group of members that particularly interested JC were those people who sat in front of computer terminals. You could find out a lot very quickly at a computer terminal, information that might otherwise be difficult to obtain.

To encourage their cooperation, these "drones," as JC thought of them, received benefits from NAGO beyond what the average member received. There were shooting trips and outings and dinners; and once a year, a private party with wine, women, and firearms.

JC tapped "Pacific Bell" into the computer, and a name popped up: Stephen Ballard.

JC knew the phone company kept old phone records, but he wasn't sure for how long; it varied from state to state. He was ecstatic when he learned California kept the records for seven years.

"They're stored in a warehouse," Ballard told him.

"Can you get at them?"

"Sure, no sweat. I got a friend who works there."

Loyalty (to the phone company), and legality, were no problem, because Ballard, like most phone-company employees, hated the phone company and broke the rules whenever he could.

"I want to know if this guy Tran ever called a guy named Weston."

Ballard whistled. "I'll have to check each number. That'll take a while."

"He has a business phone, too." JC gave him both numbers. "And thanks a lot."

He sat back and lit a cigarette and watched the smoke float around the room.

The room was small, which was good, because he didn't have much stuff. There was the computer, which sat on a low desk; and the couch, which he used as a bed when he didn't feel like going home; and a bookcase with empty shelves. He used the bookcase to hold his ashtrays.

The only other item in the room was a photograph of three men, all in camouflage fatigues, and all heavily armed. The photo had been taken during the Vietnam War, and only one of the three was still alive.

JC punched in another command.

Tran must have been in the war. Maybe he had served with U.S. forces? Maybe there was some record of that? God knew, the military kept enough records. Maybe Tran had even served with a Weston? One could always hope.

The machine hummed out a name: Janis Williamson.

Two hours later he had talked to Williamson and explained what he needed to know: any record of a Tran Van Duong associated with any U.S. military unit in Vietnam any time from 1960 to 1975. And all Westons in the same time frame.

"First name?" Williamson had asked.

JC didn't have a first name.

Williamson had groaned.

Which was exactly how JC felt. It would be a miracle if they found the right Weston.

He was sick to hear that most Vietnam War records were not in the computer. That time frame was B.C.—before computerization.

"It's going to take a while."

"Work backward from '75. And let me know as soon as you find stuff."

"Ground forces were out by '73," Williamson noted. "Most by '72."

JC had forgotten that. The image of U.S. helicopters fleeing the embassy was so potent in his memory, he had forgotten that for the United States the war was all over by '73.

"I'll start in on it first thing Monday," Williamson said.

It was Saturday, and JC had been lucky to get hold of him at all.

Williamson was in the army, but he had friends who were

his counterparts in the other services; they spent their time faxing each other information, and dirty jokes.

The first report came back Tuesday afternoon, and much to JC's surprise, it looked as though his hunch was going to pay off.

Six Westons had been found, and one Tran Van Duong.

To celebrate, JC went for a long run, then out to dinner. After dinner he visited the house of a friend of his, a woman who rented rooms to other women. JC always came for one particular woman. She was small and lithe, with tiny breasts and dark hair and dark eyes. She was Vietnamese.

JC never spoke to her; he just stretched himself out on the bed and let her work on him. And at the end, right at the end, when he couldn't contain himself any longer, he reached out and grabbed her thighs and squeezed. He squeezed as hard as he could. She never cried out, never showed the pain at all, just kept up her slow rocking, her vulva swollen and hard, her thighs all wet.

He loved that she didn't show the pain. It was why he kept coming back.

At 3:00 A.M. he called Szczepanski to see how things were going. Nothing had changed, and nothing out of the ordinary had happened.

"The killer hasn't called?"

"I already told you, JC. How long you going to keep me out here?"

"Hang tight, Taddy boy. You'll get a raise out of this."

By the end of the week JC was feeling less triumphant. The killer still hadn't called, and the phone check on Tran had been completed: There was no record of Tran ever having called someone named Weston, not within the last seven years.

He learned that on Wednesday.

On Friday Williamson called with the last of the military info he and his buddies had found: There were scores of Westons, and five Tran Van Duongs. Tran was apparently the Vietnamese equivalent to Smith.

JC thanked Williamson for his efficiency and told him he'd see him at the convention.

"You can buy me a drink."

JC laughed. "I'll buy you a bottle."

He wondered how much of his own work Williamson had gotten done that week—probably not much. JC figured there must be hundreds of private groups that pestered government employees for favors. That was probably the reason the government ran such a big deficit.

He began to match up the Westons and Trans. Two Trans dropped out, and about three quarters of the Westons.

The three remaining Trans had all been translators. Two had worked with platoons, while the third had been assigned to group headquarters. The two that had worked with platoons had been privates, eventually reaching corporal. The third had started out as a sergeant and had remained a sergeant.

He swung his chair around to face the window.

Beneath the lowered shade he could see the tree limbs swaying in the wind. The buds looked about ready to burst out.

The sergeant must have had some pull. He must have known someone, or had some money.

JC had a theory about life: There were the people who did well, the people who fumbled, and everyone else in between. And never mind the exceptions. The theory applied to jobs, relationships, everything.

Tran was a wealthy man. He had done all right in America. Probably, he had been doing all right in Vietnam, too.

The Tran who had been a sergeant served from 1965 to 1972. Then the records stopped. Probably, at that point, the U.S. unit had been pulled out, and Tran had been reassigned to an ARVN unit. There was no mention of his death.

JC cross-checked this Tran against the remaining Westons. Most of the rest dropped out. Only four left.

He needed another connection. Even if one of the four *was* his man, he didn't think he could necessarily pick him out. They were all Vietnam vets—just walking around, they probably looked guilty. And more than one might have known Tran personally.

He punched a few buttons, and Tran's file appeared on the screen:

The phone records—his best shot—had been a bust.

Tran's circle of friends, another zero.

Served with U.S. forces from '65 to '72.

In the United States from '75 on.

A three-year gap.

It was natural that those years should be missing; those were the years the Republic of Vietnam was falling apart. Still, a gap was a gap. Maybe Immigration had something on the guy; he must have filled out a few forms.

JC typed in the information he wanted—and was presented with a blank screen. He couldn't believe it. With nearly 3 million members, NAGO didn't have a single man in Immigration and Naturalization. He cursed for three minutes, then punched in a different command. The best he could do was a border guard: Phillip Morris.

What a name to be stuck with. Instinctively, he glanced down at the pack of Camels on his desk.

Phillip Morris was in a bad mood. It was Friday, April 14, and he hadn't finished his taxes yet. In fact, he hadn't even put together the information he needed to *begin* his taxes. Somehow, he had misplaced his W-2.

The fact that this year April 15 came on a Saturday, and that he therefore had until April 17 to mail in his return, did nothing to lighten his mood. He already *had* something planned for the weekend. Her name was Juanita.

So when JC called with some cock-and-bull story about how he needed to get a look at the records of a guy who had been a citizen for almost ten years, Phillip Morris (two *l*'s, the cigarette only had one) wasn't too interested.

"It'll take a while," he said.

"I need to know *now*," JC countered.

"Sure," Phillip Morris shot back, "everyone needs to know now. It'll still take a while. I gotta call my friend, then he gotta find out what you need to know, then everybody gotta call everybody again. You gotta have patience in life." And he hung up.

JC was livid. He scanned the files again, looking for some-one else to call, but couldn't find anyone better situated than Phillip Morris.

While JC was on the phone with Phillip Morris, Eliot Brod was driving south on Route 91 in Massachusetts. He had been on the road for four hours, driving through rain and sleet; he was stiff from a week of skiing in northern Vermont; and all he wanted was to be home.

When they finally got there, wife, child, and father had a light supper and climbed into bed.

The next morning Eliot had planned to bike down to Springfield; but when he woke at eight, his wife slipped a leg across his hip, and after a few minutes of playful wrestling, he knew he wasn't going anywhere.

At nine Cecelia bounced in with a pile of books that had to be read. After that, it was time for breakfast. Then the dog had to be picked up at the kennel, a good bit thinner but grate-ful, nonetheless, to be retrieved—dogs, unlike cats, don't harbor a grudge for half a week.

There was laundry to do; they were having guests the next day; it had started to rain; and Eliot had to cook in the restau-rant that evening. He didn't get the letter from Peter until Monday morning.

He wasn't happy with what he found. He had never been contacted by a client more than once, and the possibility that something was wrong set off all kinds of alarms. He wondered if his luck was changing.

Just before he had left for Vermont, he had been contacted about a job, a shitty job—some business tycoon wanted his mother-in-law knocked off for the insurance and the inheri-tance. She was worth a pile. She also happened to know that he was cheating on her daughter.

"I'll pay you a quarter of a million dollars to do the job, but it has to look like an accident."

Eliot didn't want the job.

"Half a million, then. In cash." A note of triumph had begun to creep into the guy's voice. *Everyone* had a price.

Eliot had hung up the phone.

It had been a little more than six weeks since he had done the job on Brenden, plenty of time for someone to have tracked down Tran. However carefully one did a job, there was always a chance the other side might refuse to believe the death had been either an accident or a random attack. The opposition could, with logic and persistence, trace the murder back to the person, or persons, most likely to have wanted the victim dead; and, if they were good, they came up with a suspect.

But if no one admitted anything, and if there weren't any loose ends, like a large cash withdrawal from the bank, then they could never be completely sure they had the right man.

And now Tran was ready to provide that evidence. Why?

Eliot thought he knew why. He had seen Darrel Honeywell on TV. Tran must have seen him, too. Tran was on a crusade and was obviously planning to drag Eliot along.

But a crusade wasn't something Eliot wanted any part of; judging from past crusades, that seemed like a good way to die.

He picked up the letter and envelope and dropped them in the wood stove. He would go to California and check up on Tran; and if things looked okay, he would take the job. But after the payment, it wouldn't be Darrel Honeywell who would die. Tran Van Duong had become a risk.

He put the dog outside, then drove to town to make a plane reservation. The earliest ticket he could get was for Wednesday morning.

As Eliot Brod was petting his dog good-bye, JC was putting in a call to Phillip Morris.

"What have you got, Phillip?"

"I got a hangover, and my dick is sore. How about you?"

There was silence on the other end of the line.

"I haven't talked to my friend yet."

JC exploded. "What the fuck do you mean you haven't talked to your friend yet?"

"I called him on Friday; he wasn't in."

"Well, call him right now. Listen up, Phillip, someone's life is on the line here."

"Whose?"

"None of your goddamn business. Just get me the info on this guy."

"Gimme his name again."

JC spelled out Tran's full name and slammed down the phone. The son of a bitch. When this was over, he was going to go down to New Mexico and fling this fucker's ass right over the border. Let him explain in person to the Mexicans how come they weren't welcome in this country.

The next morning around eleven JC got a call. Tran Van Duong had entered the country in November 1972. Naturalized eight years later.

"You sure you got the date right?"

"Yup. Nineteen Seventy-two."

Jesus, JC thought, he had missed three years of the guy's life in America. Where the hell had he been? He kicked himself for having assumed that Tran had come over in '75.

"I thought it was five years to be naturalized?"

"So the guy didn't run right down and sign up."

"You find out anything else?"

"Yeah, a guy named Weston sponsored him."

"Weston?"

"Peter Alfred Weston. Guy lives in Spring Bay, Illinois."

JC nearly fainted. He hung up and called Illinois information. But there was no Peter Weston listed in Spring Bay.

"Any other Westons?"

"I'm sorry, sir. You'll have to give me a first name."

He hung up.

Did Weston have an unlisted number?

It took him three minutes to find the name of the man he wanted, and fifteen to get him on the phone (thank God the guy was in). He checked the records while JC waited.

There was no Peter Weston in Spring Bay.

JC smashed down his fist. Why wasn't anything easy in life? Peter Alfred Weston.

He called back the army guy and gave him the name. Two hours later JC had Weston's Social Security number. He had the fucker now; he had only to locate him.

"You got an address on this guy?"

140

"Spring Bay, Illinois. But that could be out-of-date."

"Send me a copy of his file, with a photo. Send it express mail."

He broke open another pack of Camels and started looking through the membership file for another name.

Internal Revenue Service.

He had once broken into an IRS computer, looking for bank and stock information during an investigation. Somehow the IRS had discovered the intrusion and had come looking for him. It had been a close call.

Now, he had a drone.

He called the man at work, but it was lunchtime, and he was out. JC cursed for five minutes.

He finally got the guy in at two-thirty and told him what he wanted. ASAP. The man said he would call right back.

But Joey Waltham had other things to do, and he was still pissed about the case of clap he had gotten at the last NAGO convention. There had been hell to pay for that, especially since he had passed it on to his wife.

ASAP his ass.

It took him five minutes to get the address. He tucked it away in his pocket and forgot about it.

When JC called at four-thirty, Joey Waltham had left for the day.

When he called the man at home, his wife said he was out.

And when he called at nine-thirty the next morning, Mr. Waltham hadn't come in yet. Joey Waltham was obviously a salaried employee.

JC finally got through to the man a little after ten.

"It took longer to find than I thought," Waltham explained. "He lives in Wisconsin." He gave JC the address, and all the other information on Weston's tax return. Last year, Peter Weston netted eighty-eight thousand dollars. "Want to know what he does?"

"What?"

"He sells burglar alarms. You want his business address, too?" Joey didn't want JC to think he wasn't trying. After all, this year's convention was coming up soon.

"Of course I want that address."

141

* * *

It took JC just a minute to scan through a road atlas and locate the town Peter Weston lived in: It looked to be about an hour from the Dane County Regional Airport. Five minutes later he had two plane tickets. The flight left at 1:15 and arrived in Madison at 4:35. There was a change in Chicago.

He would probably miss the guy at the office.

He called Avis and reserved a car. Then he called Taylor and let him know what was happening. Then JC dug up the name of a phone-company employee in Wisconsin and had him start working on Weston's phone records. Then he called Big Mike Mooney.

He would bring Big Mike and his three hundred pounds of fat and muscle along to help convince Weston it was in his own interest to tell them the name of the killer. Big Mike was the only man JC knew who could lift a fully loaded fifty-five-gallon drum of oil off the back of a pickup truck and walk with it. He also carried a .44 magnum Smith & Wesson revolver with a six-inch barrel. Hi-ho, Silver!

He jabbed out his cigarette, took a deep breath, and started to cough. When the coughing fit was over, he went down to the basement to fire a few rounds. Big Mike was already there.

17

The clock chimed ten times.

Tran Van Duong, standing in front of the picture window in his living room, turned to stare at it.

Ten o'clock, already. Time to leave for the restaurant. He glanced at the phone, tempted to check again for a dial tone; but there was nothing wrong with his phone.

He turned back to the view out the window.

Why didn't the man call? It had been almost two weeks.

For two weeks he had been staring out the window in his living room, not at the flowers below the house dying in the heat, not at the vegetables that needed thinning, not even at Mount Diablo, standing huge in the distance. Tran Van Duong was staring out the window at the landscapes and faces of his past, landscapes and faces he would never see again.

Except to go to the restaurant, he had not left the house for over a week, even missing his Saturday night bowling. The killer knew his schedule. The killer knew practically everything about him. Why didn't he call? Would he refuse the second job?

He picked up the tea he had poured for himself. It was cold again.

All week he had sensed someone following him. But whenever he had turned to look—stopping abruptly on the street, or casually glancing over his shoulder—no one was ever there. A ghost. The ghost of George Herbert Brenden, come back to torment him.

He set aside the cup of tea and pulled on his jacket.

Well, Brenden's ghost could just keep following him around. Pretty soon it would have company.

Down in the parking lot of the shopping center Szczepanski heard the beeper change. He set his Egg McMuffin back in its box and put the lid on his Coke. Half a minute later Tran's BMW rolled into view. The man was like a clock.

Szczepanski started up the big Ford.

18

As JC was tightening his seat belt in preparation for landing in Chicago, USAir flight 129 was approaching the runway in San Francisco. All Eliot Brod could see was water—water, and more water, until it seemed the plane *must* land in the bay. And then, finally, thankfully, the ground. Eliot congratulated himself on having survived another flight.

The captain seemed pleased, too. He welcomed everyone to San Francisco, gave a quick weather report, and wished them all a nice stay.

It took Eliot an hour to get into Berkeley. He found a motel and dropped off his bag, then walked to a bike store and bought a bike. While they were dusting off the seat and tightening the brakes, he grabbed a light lunch. At 1:10 he picked up the bike and headed for Laurel Valley. It was an unbelievably hot day, and he was sweating even before he reached the hills.

At 2:00 P.M. exactly Eliot pedaled past the road that led to Tran's house, eyes nearly forward, peripheral vision taking in the gas station, shopping area, and parking lot. It looked the same as it had two months before. He didn't slow down; but five minutes later he was back, stopping in front of the deli.

He locked his bike to a post, went inside, and bought a can

145

of juice and took it outside to drink. If someone wanted to keep an eye on Tran, this was the place to do it; here, or the hills overlooking his house, or the restaurant.

He scanned the parking lot, letting his eyes drift over the big Ford a second time. The man inside was definitely eating a hamburger. That in itself was no big deal; except there wasn't any place to buy a hamburger anywhere nearby.

So what was Wimpy doing there? He didn't exactly look like the Laurel Valley type.

Eliot finished his juice, dropped the can in the garbage, and pedaled off.

Szczepanski didn't even notice him; the man looked like every other health nut in California. Jogging, biking, granola. After three weeks, they were all a blur. Except the girls. Tadeusz definitely noticed the girls, with their long, tanned legs and sun-bleached hair.

It took Eliot half an hour to find the place he wanted. He needed to know if the guy in the Ford was keeping an eye on Tran. And he needed to talk to Tran, but not on one of Tran's phones.

He dropped a quarter into the slot of the pay phone.

Tran answered on the first ring.

"This is Robin," Eliot said. "I'd like to get together."

Tran's heart started to beat faster. At last!

"When?"

"Twenty minutes?"

Tran nodded. "Twenty minutes is good."

Eliot gave him exact directions to the spot where he wanted to meet. "Just off the intersection. The corner by the phone booth."

Twenty minutes later Tran was standing next to the phone booth looking around for a man he had seen only at a distance and only half remembered. The phone started to ring. He stared at it. A coincidence? He couldn't decide. On the sixth ring he picked it up.

"Don't say a word," Eliot said.

Tran swallowed his hello.

"Put a coin in the phone."

Tran reached into his pocket and fished out a coin and dropped it in the slot.

"Dial a number."

Tran punched in seven numbers.

"I want you to go shopping. There's a market right across from you. Take about twenty-five minutes. After you're done, put your packages in the car, then walk down to the steak place; it's five stores to the right of the market. Go inside and walk to the back. There's a phone there. Wait for my call. And when you hang up now, make sure you take your coin."

Tran hung up the phone and slipped his finger into the coin slot. The man was ridiculously cautious.

Eliot Brod set down the receiver. He was tempted to hop on his bike, pedal right back to his motel, collect his stuff, and fly home.

All the while he had been talking with Tran, the buffoon in the big Ford had been fumbling with a snooper scope that was unmistakably aimed at the phone booth Tran was in. What if he had been there for the call to Peter? What if they already had Peter? The thought made Eliot sick, because if they found Peter, they would eventually find him.

He dropped in another quarter, dialed a number, then started dropping more quarters into the phone.

Peter Weston closed the file on his desk and glanced at the clock on the wall. It was four-thirty, and four-thirty was late enough for any self-respecting self-employed man to call it a day, especially if that man hoped to be at a certain bar by five for the arrival of a particularly attractive young lady.

Peter didn't know the name of this young lady, not yet; he only knew that Wednesday afternoons had suddenly become her happy hour. He had always been partial to Wednesdays.

He got up and dropped the file he had been working on back into its slot in the drawer; then he closed and locked the cabinet. He pulled on his jacket, set the security alarm for the inner office, and was almost to the door, when the phone rang.

A second later his secretary buzzed him. He considered being out, then decided Miss Beautiful could wait; next Wednesday was only a week away.

Forty minutes later he had sealed a deal for a security installation at a jewelry shop. A complete custom job. New everything. The owner was fed up. His place had been hit twice in the last six months. Both times the alarm system had been disabled. The police hadn't found a thing, and the owner, in his darker moments, suspected that *they* were in on the thefts. And now his insurance agent was starting to make noises about canceling his policy.

Peter assured the man that not one of *his* alarm systems had ever been disabled. He made an appointment to look the place over that Friday.

He had just hung up the phone and was on his way to the door again, when his other phone rang. Not too many people had that number. He stepped across the room and caught it on the second ring.

"Long time no see," the voice on the other end said.

Peter Weston smiled. It was a common phrase, but also, in this instance, a code.

"That's so," he responded.

"Is the line secure?" the man asked.

Peter checked the scanner next to the phone. The readings were all normal. "Like talking down a well. What's up?"

"Tran is being watched; and they may be looking for you. You'd better disappear for a while."

Peter sat down in his chair. "Disappear where? And for how long?"

"Probably just a couple of weeks."

"What about my business?"

"No business if you're dead."

Peter Weston breathed out slowly. He found it nearly incomprehensible that someone might try to kill him. He had left that in Vietnam. "You're kidding?"

"I want you to go to Calgary, in Canada. Drive there. You can go skiing and get a tan."

"I don't know how to ski."

"Find some cutie pie to teach you."

148

"I hate the snow."

"Do you have some cash?"

"Yes."

"Make sure you use it. And leave as soon as you can. I'll let you know when it's safe."

"How will you find me?"

"You can send me a postcard. And check your car for a bug or a beeper."

"That second call."

"Yes."

"God damn."

"What's your connection with Tran?"

"I was his sponsor when he immigrated. We knew each other over in Nam."

"Okay. Have fun skiing."

Peter Weston dropped the phone in its cradle. He would probably break his leg skiing.

He picked up an attaché case and dropped his date book and a pair of electronic-scanning devices inside. Then he crossed the room to the closet where his safe was hidden. He had $11,500 in the safe. He put fifteen hundred in his pocket, and the rest in the case. He had more cash in a safe-deposit box in the bank, but he doubted he would need that. Besides, the bank was closed for the day.

He locked the case and picked it up. It made him a little heady to have all that cash under his arm. It was one thing to have money sitting in a safe for a rainy day, quite another thing to actually put that money in your pocket to spend.

He wrote a note to his secretary (who had left at five), locked the office and set the main office alarm, and headed home to pack a suitcase. The sky was just starting to cloud up.

At a little after seven that evening JC and Big Mike pulled into Peter Weston's driveway. They hopped out of the car, walked to the front door, and rang the bell.

They had been delayed twice along the way. The first time at O'Hare, when their plane had been half an hour late getting off the ground—so what else was new? The second time, outside

Madison, when a misleading road sign sent them north when they wanted to go west.

Now, it was starting to get dark.

JC rang the bell again, then turned to look over Weston's yard. There was a small lawn, mostly shaded by large trees, a few flower beds, mostly clogged with shrubs, and an old apple tree. He noticed the road was clearly visible from where he stood, which was strange, because he had had trouble spotting the house at first, maybe because it was painted brown. It was a small house, a ranch, similar to most of the other houses on the road. A dense stand of evergreens, and some woods, offered a little privacy from the neighbors.

JC leaned on the bell again, but nobody answered. After another minute he walked over to the garage and peeked in. It was empty. He wandered around to the back. There was another lawn, a little larger, another apple tree, and more flower beds filled with shrubs. A built-in brick grill sat on the corner of a small slate patio. JC didn't see any lights on anywhere.

He walked back to the front. A shovel was resting against the wall near the door. He strolled down to the road and took a quick peek in the mailbox. It was empty. So Weston was around. Probably, he was having dinner somewhere; or, maybe he went back to the office; or, maybe he was balling his chick. He collected Big Mike, and they piled back into the car.

Half an hour later they had checked out Weston's office. It was located on the second floor of a four-story building that also held the offices of a few lawyers, a couple of psychologists, one doctor, a travel agency, and a number of consultants. It appeared Weston had two or three rooms on the second floor, but JC couldn't be sure because the door into the building was locked, and all he could see was the directory. He *was* sure Weston wasn't in his office, because there weren't any lights on on the second floor. Which didn't leave him many options.

So, he and Big Mike picked up a pile of sandwiches and drove back to Weston's house and settled in. By then Peter was on Interstate 94 closing in on Eau Claire.

At two in the morning, when Peter Weston still hadn't shown up, JC decided it was time to check out the house more carefully. He crept out of the car and around to the back and tried the door. It was locked. He tried the side door; it was locked, too. So was the front door, and all the windows. He couldn't believe it. In the middle of Wisconsin. America was growing up.

He turned on a flashlight and peered in a window. The usual assortment of couches and chairs and tables stared back at him. The house was neat, with most things put away.

He couldn't see any sign of an alarm system, though that didn't mean there wasn't one. It would be risky breaking in, and at this point a tour of Weston's house would just be to satisfy his curiosity.

He padded around the house again, looking for anything he might have overlooked the first time. It seemed a typical suburban house. It was neat and clean, which surprised him, because he knew Weston wasn't married. Maybe the guy had a girlfriend who helped clean the place? Maybe that was where he was now?

He peeked in the living-room window again, studying the large fish mounted over the fireplace. Was Weston a fisherman? Or had he picked up the trophy at an antique dealer? JC had no idea what sort of fish it was.

He turned off the flashlight and walked over to the garage and opened the garbage can. He found a TV dinner tray sitting on top, some empty Coke cans, miscellaneous junk mail, a lot of plastic wrapping mostly from food products, some scraps of food that had once called the plastic wrapping home, a juice bottle, a few newspapers. Your average garbage in your average garbage can. He noticed Weston didn't bother to recycle. Peter was a bad boy.

He closed the can and climbed back into the car. "Home, James."

Big Mike drove them to a motel they had seen near the highway.

The next morning Peter Weston still wasn't in evidence at his house, so they cruised over to the office. At eight-thirty on the dot a woman showed up and unlocked the door. JC practically followed her in.

"Peter Weston, please," he asked. He tried to look like a normal human being.

151

The woman looked up. "It appears he'll be gone for a few days."

JC noticed the note beside her right hand. "I have a rather pressing job. Do you know how *long* he'll be gone?" He leaned forward for emphasis.

The woman began to eye him more carefully.

"Until he gets back." She picked up a pencil that looked as if it had been sharpened on a strop. "Would you care to leave your name?"

"I'll stop in again."

What JC *did* leave was a small bug under the edge of the desk that would pick up any sound in the room—like a telephone conversation with the boss—and transmit it to a recorder. He hid the recorder under a dumpster outside the building. Then he went looking for a phone to see how Szczepanski was doing.

Szczepanski was not doing well.

He had spent the last twelve days in the Ford following Tran around: twice a day to the restaurant, twice a day back home; no variations, no changes; the man had even stopped bowling. Twelve days sitting in a parking lot watching the parade of suburbia.

Szczepanski was bored, restless, horny, and depressed. It seemed to him the surveillance would go on forever, and, strangely, in the last few days he had come to accept that. Which is to say, Szczepanski was asleep on his feet.

So when the tape recorder kicked on and he heard Tran speaking in English instead of Vietnamese, he thought at first he had inadvertently jarred the tuner and was receiving the wrong signal. And when he realized the receiver didn't have a tuner, and that the voice he was listening to had to be Tran's, he panicked.

Who the hell was Robin? And why did he want to meet Tran in twenty minutes?

There was no time to call JC. He wasn't even sure where JC was.

Ten minutes later Tran was at the bottom of the road turning onto the main drag. Szczepanski pulled right out after him.

But Tran didn't race off. If anything, he was driving more slowly than usual. Szczepanski got a grip on himself and dropped back so he wouldn't be spotted. A minute later Tran pulled into a shopping plaza; it was almost identical to the plaza Szczepanski had been haunting for the last couple of weeks.

Szczepanski watched as Tran got out of the car and walked back to the street. He checked his watch. The Viet was a couple of minutes early.

What if Robin was the guy JC was looking for? What if he was the killer?

He checked the Beretta under his left arm. He could just shoot the guy. Wouldn't that just burn JC, after all the work he'd done—to miss out on the kill. Szczepanski couldn't help but grin, until he realized that if Robin *was* the killer, he might also be carrying a gun. Tadeusz wasn't so sure he was ready to shoot it out with an assassin across fifty yards of parking lot.

He pulled the shotgun mike off the floor of the car and set it on his lap. Then he dug out a camera with a telephoto lens from under the seat. First, he would take the guy's picture. Then he would listen to what they were saying. *Then* he would decide what to do.

But after five minutes nothing had happened, and Tran, looking impatient, stepped into a nearby phone booth.

Szczepanski aimed the mike at the phone booth as Tran dropped in his coin. Who was he calling? Weston again? Where the hell was Robin?

There was nothing on the mike.

He tapped the receiver and turned up the volume. Still nothing. He turned up the volume some more, just in time to hear Tran hang up the phone. The concussion practically ruptured his eardrums.

He stared as the Viet walked across the parking lot and into the supermarket.

Why the hell was the man going shopping? What if he escaped out the back door?

He got out of the car, then got back in. He would be spotted in a second in the supermarket.

Tadeusz sat in the car for three minutes before the waiting became unbearable. Then he got out of the car again and strolled over to the supermarket and peered in the window. It was hard to see anything through his sunglasses. He lifted them up: There was Tran at the end of an aisle putting a can of soup, or something, into his cart. The guy was just shopping. He let out a sigh and went back to the car.

Twenty minutes later Tran came out with his groceries.

Szczepanski watched as he loaded the bags into the trunk of the BMW. Then he watched as Tran walked back to the line of shops and into a steak-and-ale place. He looked at his watch again. It was a little late for lunch and a little early for dinner. Cocktail hour.

He thought how nice it would be to have a cocktail, to get out of the fucking Ford for an hour and sit in a booth and stretch out his legs and have a drink. Several drinks. Something tall and cool—like a rum and Coke with lots of ice.

But by then, Tran was on his way out. Probably, he had just needed to pee.

Szczepanski realized *he* needed to pee, too.

When Tran first stepped up to the phone booth at the back of the restaurant, he had a moment's panic: The booth was occupied. Worse yet, the booth was occupied by a young man, and Tran knew from experience that young men could be both rude and long-winded; it might be twenty minutes before he was off.

He tapped his foot and looked at his watch to let the fellow know he was in a hurry. The man smiled and raised a forefinger; a moment later he was off. Tran didn't even say thank you.

Just as he was closing the door to the booth, the phone rang.

"You have another job," Eliot said.

"Yes."

"The new spokesman, Darrel Honeywell."

"Yes."

"Half a million dollars."

Tran's throat went dry. "That will take a while."

"Three weeks exactly."

"That's not much time."

"Three weeks. How will you get the cash?"

"I'll have to sell some property."

"Have the police talked to you?"

"No, why?"

"You were followed here. Don't call Peter Weston again."

And the line went dead.

By the time Tran left the pub, Eliot was pedaling back toward Berkeley. He chained his bike to a bike rack outside a dorm at the university. If he was lucky, it might still be there in three weeks.

In three weeks he would be half a million dollars richer, Darrel Honeywell would still be pestering lawmakers, and Tran Van Duong would be among his forefathers.

He walked to a convenience store and bought an apple and a paper, then strolled back to his motel. Four hours later he was on a flight home.

19

When JC called Szczepanski and learned that something "a little strange" had happened the day before, he felt his stomach tighten.

And when he learned what exactly that something strange was, he thought he was going to be sick.

His first impulse was to jump out the other end of the phone and strangle Szczepanski, because the boob had certainly missed the killer, who must have been standing right in front of him. The second thing he wanted to do was call Taylor and tell him what an idiot he was for having hired Szczepanski at all. And the third thing he wanted to do was kick himself, both because he had let Taylor stick him with Szczepanski, and because he had let Taylor talk him into tracking Weston when he should have been watching Tran.

Tran had the money, and the money was the bait. A hunter had to have patience; he had to endure.

Six months before his second tour in Vietnam was up, JC's unit started getting hit by ambushes. The pattern was always the same: A small patrol would start off on a one- or two-day reconnaissance and would get hit within a mile of the base. In thirty days half the patrols had been ambushed.

So JC volunteered to check it out.

He had to wait three days for his man. Three days sitting in the jungle without moving. When he had to shit, he shit in a can and buried it. The same with the piss. He ate crackers and water; and after three days, there wasn't much left of that.

He spotted his man just at dusk on the third day: a Vietnamese corporal, one of the translators. JC knew the man, but not well. He had never liked him; the guy smiled too much.

As the corporal came abreast of him, JC stood up. The man stopped, a smile already beginning to form.

JC didn't say anything; he just fired. Four times. There was only one reason the man would be in the jungle alone at night, and it wasn't to collect worms for fishing.

Patience. He had followed Taylor's hunch instead of his own.

He fished a cigarette out of his pocket and lit it. Had the killer spotted Szczepanski? Was that why Weston was gone?

"Taddy, tell me again what happened."

Szczepanski repeated his story two more times, then JC listened to the tape of the conversation again.

So the killer was using the name Robin. And for some reason, he hadn't wanted to talk about the job on Tran's phone. Why? Was he already suspicious? Or was he just a cautious sort of guy?

There must have been a second conversation at the phone booth that Szczepanski missed, and then a contact in either the supermarket or the restaurant.

And all the while Szczepanski staring at Tran like a setter at a pheasant. Where had the killer been?

Why, watching Szczepanski, of course.

Now, the man knew he was being hunted. Wasn't that a happy thought?

"You still there, JC?"

"Still here, Taddy boy. You hang in there. Pretty soon you get to go home."

He hung up. The killer was alerted, and Weston was gone. One more strike and he was out.

He gave his contact in the Wisconsin phone company a

ring, but the guy was still working on Weston's calls. Somehow JC didn't think that one was going to work out anyway. That would be too easy. He punched in Patrick Taylor's number.

"Weston is gone."

"What do you mean, he's gone?"

"He's gone. His secretary says for a few days, but she doesn't know; he left her a note. I think he's just gone."

"Why would he suddenly disappear?"

"I think the killer spotted Szczepanski."

He told Taylor about the phone call, and Szczepanski's pursuit.

"You better start thinking about some help, Patrick. Pretty soon this guy Robin is going to start shooting again."

"God damn, JC. We're so close."

"Not anymore."

"Can't you find this fucker Weston? He must be somewhere. You're a detective."

"It would be a lot easier to find him if the police were helping."

"I don't want to call in the police. Not yet."

There was a long silence as JC wondered why he had so much trouble telling Patrick Taylor to fuck off. "I'll tell you, Patrick, if I could go through Weston's office, and his home, and if I could get his secretary to help me out, and if I could talk with all his friends, then *maybe* I could find him eventually. But I can't get into his office, or his home, and I don't know who his friends are, and his secretary is already giving me the hairy eyeball. I don't know if I can find him or not."

"How long before you *do* know?"

"Maybe a few days."

"How long before the killer makes the pickup?"

"That depends on how much money Tran has to get together. If he has the cash, it could be tomorrow."

"Let's hope it's not. You try to find Weston."

"I need you to do something for me."

"What?"

"Weston used to live in Spring Bay, Illinois. See if you can find some relatives. Maybe he went to visit one of them."

"I'll have it for you by tonight."

* * *

JC lit another cigarette and stared out at Main Street. It was a small town, and in small towns there was always someone watching you.

He scanned the streets, and then the windows overlooking the streets, to see who was watching him: a shopkeeper, who turned away when JC stared back; and a cleaning lady in a third-floor window, who was not the least bit embarrassed about staring. He was a stranger and counted for nothing.

What he needed was the person who had been watching Peter Weston when he left the office yesterday, which JC figured must have been after, say, four or five, and before seven-thirty, when he and Big Mike had come by. They had been so close to grabbing the guy it made JC shiver just to think about it. If the timing of any of a dozen things had been a little different, he would have had the killer's name already. Instead, he had nothing; and Weston was gone.

He started walking the streets to get a feel for the place that Peter Weston called home.

The downtown section consisted of half a dozen streets of shops and offices and banks. There was a modern police station, an old courthouse, an imposing city hall, and a school built in the fifties. There were also a number of bars and luncheonettes, a pizza place, and a few restaurants.

Probably, Weston had a favorite place to eat lunch. Probably, the waitress knew him and his friends. He might have even mentioned where he was going. Wouldn't that be nice?

JC stopped. He had wandered into a residential area, a well-to-do part of town with large houses and manicured lawns. Chestnut Street. Maybe chestnuts had once grown there? He turned onto Elm and walked in a different direction.

Residential areas surrounded the town on all sides. The most run-down houses were by the river, the most expensive up on the hills. There were several major roads that reinforced these divisions; these roads were lined with the usual variety of commercial businesses: car dealerships; fast-food emporiums; minimalls; gas stations; and supermarkets.

160

He glanced at his watch. It was time to start his rounds. He walked back to the car.

At the town clerk's office JC learned that Weston had been born in Spring Bay, Illinois. At the Register of Deeds he learned the name of the bank that held Weston's mortgage—he had bought the house twelve years ago. At the Department of Motor Vehicles he learned that Weston drove a brand-new Ford Thunderbird (he made a note of the license number). He also discovered that Weston had put on fifteen pounds since his army days.

Then it was lunchtime, so he went to find out where Peter Weston chowed down.

It turned out quite a few people knew Peter Weston, and they were all sorry they couldn't help JC out. Everyone agreed it was terrible when a relative took sick suddenly, and even worse when you couldn't locate the family to tell them.

By two o'clock JC had checked out every restaurant in town. No one knew where Weston was, and no one had heard him talking about taking a trip. JC did manage to find out the names of a few of Weston's friends and the names of two women he had occasionally been seen with.

He walked over to the coffee shop where he had parked Big Mike that morning.

Big Mike was still sitting there, still working his way through the morning paper. He had a hearing aid in his left ear and a cup of coffee in his right hand. The hearing aid was a receiver that picked up whatever was going on in Peter Weston's office. If the boss called to check in, and maybe say where he was, JC wanted to know right away.

But Weston had not called; and except for an hourlong conversation with her mother, the secretary hadn't done much talking at all.

JC listened to Big Mike's report, then left him to continue the surveillance while he drove over to the local airport. Peter Weston's car wasn't there. It was too far to drive to the airport at Madison before five; there was no train station to check out; and JC didn't think that a guy who tooled around

161

in a Thunderbird would take the bus anywhere. So he drove back to town and began to check out the bars. He learned zippo.

At four, he was down the street from Weston's office, waiting to see what time the secretary left and looking for someone who might have seen Peter Weston leaving the day before.

The secretary walked out the door of the building at 5:03 along with a handful of other people. Probably, she had left at exactly the same time yesterday.

He scanned the street. A minute later he spotted his informant, sitting on a bench half a block away. JC strolled over and plopped down next to the man, an old geezer who needed a bath and who, after sullenly studying JC for about ten seconds, made a point of turning in the opposite direction.

"I'm a detective," JC said. He casually flipped his I.D. open and shut. "And I'm having a shit of a time finding this guy."

The old geezer worked his gums and screwed up his face a little tighter.

"Guy named Weston. You know him?"

The old geezer started to work his gums again. "'Course I know him. Been living in this town sixty-seven years. Born here. All these newcomers." He spit, a long, arching gob that easily made it past the curb.

JC nodded. "His brother's sick, maybe dying. Happened just like that." He snapped his fingers. "When the family called last night to tell him, he didn't answer his phone. So they hired me. Except, I can't find him, either."

"I guess you won't get paid."

"I already *been* paid."

The old fart snorted. "Used to be you had to do a job to get paid. Thing's different now." He spit again.

"You see Weston leaving last night? He left about this time."

The old geezer turned to stare at JC, his eyes squinted nearly closed. "Now how do you know when he left last night? You weren't here to see him."

JC smiled, just a little smile, partly because he had guessed right, and partly for the old man's benefit. "That's why I get paid to find people, because even though I wasn't here, I still know when he left."

162

The old man nodded. "Well, you're right. He left just about this time yesterday."

"You notice anything different about him? He look different?"

"Looked the same as always."

"Was he carrying anything?"

"He had one of those attaché cases."

"He always carry one?"

"Sometimes yes, sometimes not."

"Was he in a hurry?"

"Young folks is always in a hurry."

"Was he carrying anything else? Anything at all? A jacket? A coat?"

"He was wearing a jacket. Same as always. Sporty leather thing. Fancy. Musta cost a bunch."

"What about his car?"

"He has a car."

"Was it parked somewhere different? Did he drive off in a different direction?"

"Didn't see. His car was parked round back. Same as always."

When JC finally got bored of sparring with the old buzzard, he found Big Mike and began another tour of the bars and restaurants. They came up with nothing, except that Weston taught karate at a local health club. When they swung by the club, Weston wasn't there and hadn't called to say he wasn't coming. Calls to Weston's friends, and the two women he had been seen with, were also a washout. So JC and Big Mike drove back to Madison and began walking through the parking lot of the airport looking for Weston's car. Three hours later they had sore feet and nothing for their work. Wherever Peter Weston was, he didn't fly there out of Madison, not unless he took a cab to the airport.

JC found a phone and rang up Patrick Taylor, and got more good news.

Weston's relatives were all dead.

The last to go, a sister, had died two years earlier after almost twenty years in an institution.

JC didn't want to know why she had been there.

* * *

An hour later, JC and Big Mike were outside Weston's office changing the tape in the recorder under the dumpster. JC would have dearly loved to read the note Weston had left for his secretary, but he had no intention of picking his way through a dumpster full of garbage in the middle of the night, especially since a restaurant also used the dumpster, and especially since the note might not even be there.

They found a motel on the outskirts of town, grabbed a coffee and a piece of pie at an all-night diner, checked out Weston's place again, and gave Szczepanski a call.

Szczepanski was all worked up. Tran had been on the phone all day, and all the calls were in Vietnamese.

JC smiled. He was going to have the time he needed after all—Tran didn't have the cash.

"Just calm down, Taddy. It's no big deal. Just go and get the tapes translated."

The next morning JC was on the phone to the local travel agencies.

He told each agent he reached that he had been talking with Peter Weston, and Peter had told him about this great fishing trip he had taken. But now he couldn't remember the name of the hotel Peter had stayed at, and Peter was out of town.

On the third call he got lucky. The woman knew Peter and remembered setting up the trip. She gave JC the name and phone number of the hotel. It was in Florida.

And no, she didn't happen to know where Peter was off to this time.

JC pressed down the receiver button, waited ten seconds, then called the hotel in Florida and asked for Peter Weston. After a minute the clerk informed him that there was no guest by the name of Peter Weston staying at the hotel. None of the other travel agents could remember booking a flight for Weston.

And that was all JC had in his bag of tricks, so he gave Big Mike Weston's photograph and left him to carry on the surveillance—checking Weston's home and office, and switching the tapes in the recorder.

The first thing JC did when he got back to Washington was switch on his computer. The second thing he did was call up the membership file and find someone who worked for a credit agency.

It took Lewis Stimpson ten minutes to get a list of Peter Weston's credit cards, and half an hour to find people at the issuing banks who would let him know if any of the accounts were used. He promised JC he would call the minute *he* was called.

Then JC called his drone in Wisconsin Bell and had the guy fax him Weston's calls. Thank God there weren't all that many.

At two-thirty Szczepanski called. Tran was trying to sell his property. *All* his property.

20

"I don't like that Tran is selling everything," JC said. "The job couldn't possibly cost that much." He was slumped in a chair in Patrick Taylor's office.

Taylor wasn't facing him but was staring out the window. It was a perfect day: warm and breezy and sunny. The trees were just starting to blossom.

"I think Tran's getting ready to take off."

Taylor drummed his fingers on the arm of his chair. "You think so?"

"Let the police talk to him, Patrick. A first-degree murder charge will get things moving." He started to reach for a cigarette, then stopped himself.

Taylor swung around to face him. "God damn, JC. I don't want to call in the police. They're not going to threaten Tran; the guy just lost his kid. They'll spend the whole time apologizing for bothering him." Up on the wall the photo of Ronald Reagan agreed.

"Once the killer has his money, Darrel's a dead duck."

"Then we'll have to make sure he doesn't *get* the money."

"The cops could find Weston."

"Yeah? How?"

"They could put out a bulletin on his car."

"Across the whole country? Why would they do that?"

"He's a suspect in a murder investigation."

Taylor shook his head. "No, he's not. He's only a suspect in *your* investigation."

"Talk to Bigelow. Pull a few strings."

"I'm running out of strings. My credit's not so good anymore." He swung around to face the window again. "I want the killer, JC. The rest of these guys are nothing. Are you going to be able to do it?"

"We'll know pretty soon."

"My money's riding on you, JC. Don't disappoint me."

While JC was getting ready to fly back to California, Tran Van Duong was busy calling his friends and acquaintances. Each call was the same.

He wanted to sell his property. Right away. For cash. And at a good discount for the haste. He was contemplating a move.

"Where?" his friends asked, half out of concern, half with a gossip's curiosity.

He hadn't yet decided.

"Paris?"

He chuckled. Paris was a lovely city.

They chuckled.

Tran knew he would never see Paris.

In three days he sold three properties. The paperwork would take a little time, but not long. Seven to ten days. His friends trusted him, but titles had to be checked. After all, business was business.

On Tuesday, around eleven, Tran took the train into San Francisco and walked over to Chinatown.

Szczepanski followed, loopy with the effort. First, the BART station in Lafayette had been nearly empty. Then the streets of Chinatown had been so crowded he had had trouble keeping Tran in view.

He breathed a sigh of relief when the Viet finally walked into a restaurant: C. H. Han's.

GUN MEN

* * *

C. H. Han was waiting for Tran; he was expected.

Tran bowed.

C. H. Han bowed.

They both smiled.

In their three-piece suits they looked like the successful businessmen they were. Both wore gold wedding rings. Both wore gold tie clips. Both wore gold watches. They had known each other for over sixteen years.

It was in C. H. Han's restaurant that Tran went to work when he arrived in America; and right from the start Han liked him. The man was self-possessed, and patient. And there was something else, something hidden—a mystery. It made Han curious. An uncle-nephew relationship developed.

And as Tran struck out on his own and prospered, C. H. Han stood back and smiled, the way a mentor smiles at the cleverness of a favored pupil. Good fortune among one's associates was something that rubbed off, like warts.

Typically, the two men saw each other once a year, always to share a meal. At each reunion C. H. Han offered to buy Tran's restaurant. It was a standing joke.

"Twice in six months," Han said.

Tran smiled. "Our blessings increase with our years."

"Yes," Han agreed, "but only because we continue to earn them."

He led Tran to a private room at the rear of the restaurant, a room that could comfortably seat two or ten, depending on the setting of the lamps.

Tran loved that room. For all the years he had known Han, that room had not been changed: the chairs and tables just where he had first seen them; the scrolls of misty landscapes still covering the walls; the large, cushioned couch, for those most private meetings; and the rug, such a dark red, in the shadows it seemed black.

"Please," Han said, "sit here."

He indicated the chair in which he customarily sat, the chair that faced east.

169

Almost immediately a platter of roast smoked porksticks was brought. The meat had been stripped from between the ribs.

Han poured tea.

C. H. Han had planned a banquet for his friend, an expression of condolence for the loss of his child. He had never spoken to Tran about Loan's death; any words he might have offered would have been insufficient, because *he* had never lost a child.

A plate of crab dumplings was set out.

Tran tasted one.

"I hope the fish is fresh enough," Han said.

Tran prodded one of the dumplings with his chopsticks. "That piece just moved."

Han sighed. "I'll have to beat the cook again."

They both laughed.

Salt-fried shrimps were brought. And rice. And vegetables. Then Peking duck. Han served the pancakes himself.

"I think I still remember how to fold these."

Tran smiled, as Han deftly filled and folded the pancakes using just a single set of chopsticks. The duck wasn't fatty in the least.

When all the food was gone, Tran set down his chopsticks. "Your chef has outdone himself this time." He patted his stomach and breathed out contentedly.

Han surveyed the half-dozen empty platters. "I fear he didn't make enough."

Tran laughed. "I was stuffed half an hour ago, but I didn't want to insult you by leaving any." He belched, then leaned forward. "My friend, while it's always a pleasure to eat your food and not pay for it, I must confess, today I am also here on business."

Han looked surprised. "Who spoke about a gift? Your tab is waiting out front."

Tran laughed.

Han poured more tea. "How can I help you?"

"You haven't offered to buy my restaurant yet."

"I hear your restaurant isn't doing well."

170

"Who told you that?"

Han laughed. "I was coming to an offer. Are you so eager to sell?"

"I am considering a move."

"I knew you had no stamina."

Tran smiled.

C. H. Han did not. "I am sorry to buy it like this."

"When you see the receipts, you will forget your sorrow."

Han chuckled. "Send me the paperwork."

"And the price?"

"You decide the price."

Tran looked surprised.

Han smiled slyly. "If you try to cheat me, I'll just send the papers back to you."

Tran laughed. "You are old, but still clever. Even now you find new ways to make an extra dollar."

"Let us toast the contract."

Han picked up a crystal decanter of amber liquid and filled two small glasses to the brim. When Tran tasted the wine, tears came to his eyes. It was a rare pear wine, thick and sweet and redolent. It brought to mind all the happy moments of his life.

"You are too kind," he said.

21

J C scanned the trail in front of him, then checked the trail behind. No one was around.

"Down here," he said. He started down the hill.

The young man next to him followed. They were in Briones Regional Park, on the ridge above Tran's house.

Forty yards down the slope JC stopped. He had found the spot he was looking for. He pulled out his binoculars and ran them over Tran's house, a sprawling Spanish-style house with a terra-cotta barrel-tile roof. Past the house he could see Highway 24, Interstate 680, the town of Walnut Creek, and Mount Diablo. Not too bad a view. He could think of lots worse. He figured the house, with its gardens and flower beds and fruit trees, must be worth over a million bucks.

A hawk drifted past hardly moving at all, just hanging on the wind. He aimed his finger at the bird and turned to the young man crouched beside him.

"There you go, Kenny baby. You're going to do just what that bird is doing."

Kenneth Hawks looked up at the bird, trying to decide if JC was poking fun at him.

173

Kenneth Hawks was twenty years old, an Eagle Scout, a marksman, a member of NAGO since his sixth birthday, and about as gung-ho as anyone JC had ever met. Kenneth Hawks thirsted for hard work and hardship the way range cattle thirst for water, and for the life of him JC couldn't figure why the kid wasn't in the marines.

"That's the house, Kenny baby. Right there." He pointed at Tran's house. "I want you to keep your eyes on it all the time. You understand?"

"Sure, JC. Surveillance. I got it."

"Never take your eyes off the house, except to survey the road, and the grounds around the house; then check the house again."

"Roger, wilco, ten-four. I gotcha."

"We want to always know where the gook is. And if he drives off, we want to make sure no one pays him a visit while he's gone. Any visitors, you give me a call."

They ran through the radio procedure again.

JC had two men on the restaurant. He had a car, and Szczepanski had a car, and the following day two more men were coming to ride along. Three cars, seven men. He thought that would be enough, if not to catch the killer then at least to stop him from making the pickup. God damn, but he wanted to beat this guy.

He gave Tran's house another sweep with the high-powered binoculars. The garage and front door, the sides of the house, and the grounds to the rear were all clearly visible. It would be difficult for Tran, or anyone else, to come or go without being seen.

"Let's get the packs."

They scampered back up to the ridge and along the trail until they reached the gully where they had hidden their packs. JC pulled the two big bags from behind a bush; then they hunkered down to wait for it to get dark.

An hour later they were back above Tran's house digging out a hole for Kenneth to hide in; they covered the hole with camo cloth. He would be out of sight from above, and screened from below by a few low shrubs.

JC pulled a night scope out of one of the packs and set it up. "You got four days of food here, Kenny. I'll be back in three days with more."

Kenneth grinned. "Just like being on patrol."

JC smiled. "Yeah, just like on patrol."

He reached forward with both hands and pulled Kenneth Hawks out of the hole.

"You don't know fuck about being on patrol, Kenny baby. On patrol *you're* the target, and it's the other guys sitting around. You think you'd like that?" He twisted his hands so his knuckles dug into Hawks's chest.

Kenneth Hawks shook his head.

"This guy killed Brenden, Kenny. He hunted him down and shot him like a dog. And now he's going after Honeywell. You think he'd mind adding *you* to his list?" JC dug his knuckles in a little more.

Hawks shook his head.

"Your only chance is to stay hidden. Which is exactly what you're going to do. Don't budge from this hole. You understand?"

He nodded.

JC shoved him back into the hole. "Don't fuck this up, Kenneth. You stay in the hole, and you watch the house. That's all you gotta do. Now, gimme the gun."

Kenneth Hawks handed over the Colt revolver his father had given him on his eighteenth birthday.

"You shoot someone, Kenneth, and it turns out to be some hiker lost in the dark, you'll wish the killer *had* popped you. You'll spend the rest of your life in a cell, convinced your asshole is a cunt. You understand what I'm saying?"

Kenneth Hawks nodded.

"Now, run through the radio procedure again."

Kenneth ran through the routine. He was not to radio JC unless he thought something was wrong, or unless he was in trouble.

"There's a beeper in Tran's car. I'll hear him coming. Don't tell me what I already know."

"Right, JC."

"I'll give you a call each night to see how you're doing."

"What if I have to take a shit during the day?"

JC smiled. "Hold it in. Or shit in a can."

"What about sleeping?"

"I'll send Szczepanski up each morning, just before it gets light. He'll spell you until Tran leaves for the restaurant."

"How the hell is he going to find me in the dark?"

"He'll smell your food."

And JC was gone, disappearing into the darkness of the park like a bear after berries.

Kenneth Hawks peered through the scope at Tran's house: It was almost as bright as during the day. He'd have to get one of these scopes for deer hunting.

He opened one of the packs and pulled out a sweater. Then he dug out a ground cloth, spread it in front of the scope, and set his sleeping bag on top. He opened a chocolate bar.

It was going to be a long night.

Three days later the sale of one of Tran's properties was entered at the Recorder's Office. It gave JC the chills to see it. Two days after that, two more sales had been recorded. Tran was cashing in the chips, and it was going to be a big pile.

JC wondered how much Tran was paying to have Honeywell killed. Whatever it was, it was more than Darrel was worth.

Darrel might have had other ideas, but nobody asked him, and he was too busy to worry about it: He was trying to save the Second Amendment for our kids, so *they* could walk around with guns.

Most of his time was spent in California, where he still had connections from his days in politics, and where it looked almost hopeful that the bill banning assault rifles might be killed after all.

He met with legislators and right-wing activists and conservatives. He met with anyone who would listen and who might be sympathetic. His message was simple: First they were going to take away your semiautomatic rifle, then they were going to

176

take away your handgun, then they were going to take away your shotgun.

Pretty soon it would even be against the law to own a kitchen knife. It was already against the law to carry a knife; try taking one on an airplane.

22

It took Peter Weston four days to drive to Calgary. He was in no particular hurry, and each day he killed was a day he wouldn't have to go skiing.

He stayed on 94 until he reached Jamestown, North Dakota, then he swung north on 52. In Canada he picked up Highway 1, which took him into Calgary.

He slept in motels off the highway. He paid cash. Near St. Cloud he bought a sweater. In Fargo he bought some toilet supplies. In Moose Jaw, a day pack and a pair of boots. And in Medicine Hat, a ski parka.

But after four days he was wondering if he would even need the parka; he hadn't seen a speck of snow. In fact, in a great many places it had looked like spring.

Nevertheless, when Calgary finally rose above the plains, the Rockies rose with it, huge and high and pointy-peaked, and covered with snow. He decided no one was going to get him to the top of one of those things, he didn't care how cute she was. Maybe he would just spend the time fishing.

He pulled off the highway and walked into a tourist-information office. After chatting with the woman inside for half an hour (Canadian girls, with their rosy cheeks, were really

179

quite cute), he went back to his car to study the pamphlets. Then he continued on into town.

It was off-season, and he had no problem getting a room. He paid for two nights. He told the desk clerk his plans were up in the air; it was his first trip to Canada, and he was going where the mood took him. The clerk assured him that, should he wish to stay on longer, there would be no problem keeping the room.

Peter spent the rest of the day wandering around the city. There was a lot to see; and he decided, in all fairness to the city, that he should spend several days (even a week) touring the sights before heading into the mountains, which were actually not all that close. He wondered—staring at the peaks—whether the broad patches of white scarring the sides of the hills were ski trails, or the swathes cut by avalanches.

Just then a young woman with an armful of packages stopped to ask him directions. When he confessed to being lost himself, she laughed. It was a nice laugh. He asked her which part of town *she* had been lost in. They compared notes. Then he asked if she was visiting friends in Calgary. She wasn't. She was with friends—two. So he asked if she would have dinner with him. After a brief pause, during which she studied his eyes (he had nice eyes), she said yes.

Sometimes it was that simple.

While Peter Weston was making time in Calgary, Big Mike was in a motel room in Wisconsin sinning with some floozy.

Her name was Sally Ann, and Big Mike had picked her up the day after JC had flown back to Washington.

Not that Big Mike was a shirker; it was just that sitting in a coffee shop nursing a cup of coffee, waiting for a man to show who was obviously never going to show, was not his idea of a productive life. Twice a day he checked Weston's house: in the early morning and around seven in the evening. At five he watched the secretary go home. And at 3:00 A.M. he changed the tape in the recorder under the dumpster. The rest of the time he spent with Sally Ann: playing cards, drinking, going out for cheap dinners, watching movies on TV, and balling. The weather had turned cold and wet, and frankly he couldn't think of a better way to spend his time even if he had other options, which he didn't.

Which is why Eliot Brod did not see him when he went pedaling past Peter Weston's office; and why he didn't see him when he went pedaling past Weston's house, though he did notice numerous sets of tire prints in the soft driveway.

That evening, after the sun was gone, Eliot ditched his bike in the woods next to Peter's house and crawled through the trees until he had a clear view of the front door and driveway. He laid out the piece of plastic he had brought, settled onto it, and covered himself with a rust-colored rain tarp. It had been raining all day, and it was still raining. It was going to be an uncomfortable evening, but he needed to know who was visiting Peter so often. He hoped it was a girlfriend.

He had been to Peter's house once before, shortly after Peter bought the place. Everything looked about the same: The trees were bigger, and the shrubs more grown in; but that was it. The house was still brown.

No one came by that night; and Eliot was just beginning to think he would have to wait all day to catch a glimpse of the mystery guest, when a car pulled into the driveway. The man who got out was the size of a small mountain.

The Hulk walked straight up to the front door, rang the bell, and knocked. He waited three minutes exactly, patiently, without so much as swaying; Eliot, watching him, thought he had taken root. At the end of three minutes he rang the bell again and knocked again. At the end of eight minutes the Hulk turned around, walked back to the car, and drove off. Not very subtle.

Of course, the Hulk probably didn't need to be very subtle. If Peter had been home, the Hulk would have grabbed him the way a large spider grabs a fly.

After the Hulk was gone, Eliot edged back into the woods. He carefully folded the tarp and piece of plastic he had lain on and tucked them into his pack. Then he peed and collected his bike. A minute later he was pedaling toward the airport.

He felt tired, and not because he had sat up all night in

181

the rain and cold. He felt tired because the job had turned sour.

If they found Peter, they would eventually find him; they only needed his name. Once someone had your name, the name on your Social Security card, he just about had you. Social Security would spit out a list of numbers to go with that name (and with a name like Eliot Brod, the list was sure to be short), the Internal Revenue Service would attach an address to each number, and that would be that. It wouldn't even matter that his name was now Eliot Wilson, because Social Security would have *both* names in its file.

He stopped at a diner to have some breakfast and get warm.

He was surprised the police hadn't been to see Tran. Were the boys at NAGO planning to do the job themselves? Real law-and-order types.

He wondered if they would kill Tran. There was no longer any reason for *him* to kill Tran; the man had already done all the damage he could.

And Darrel Honeywell?

He sprinkled a little salt on his eggs. He hadn't planned on killing Honeywell in the first place; he had only planned on taking the money from Tran. Besides, going after Honeywell now would be dangerous, because NAGO would be expecting him.

He nodded when the waitress offered more coffee.

He had never failed to complete a job before; this would be the first time. The thought left him feeling a little guilty, like a thief. He didn't like that feeling. He didn't like it at all. He wondered if what he was feeling was really fear?

One had to guard against fear. Fear was like the water outside a dike: ready to rush over you at the first sign of weakness.

He had been afraid when he first started studying karate. He had been afraid of getting hurt.

Wa Sung had smiled. It was natural to be afraid. He would learn how to control his fear. He would learn how *not* to fear.

Training. Years and years of training. And at the end, a curious indifference. The warrior's state of mind.

It was who he was now. It was who he wanted to be.

If he didn't kill Darrel Honeywell, he would always wonder

if he had been afraid; and then he would wonder what he would be afraid of next, for the rest of his life.

The next day he was back at the university library seeing what he could learn about Darrel Honeywell. As with George Herbert Brenden, there was a nice picture of Darrel Honeywell in *Guns and Hunters;* also Honeywell's home address: Orange County, California.

Eliot knew Honeywell had recently been in California, because he had read about it in the paper. The man had been crisscrossing the state lobbying legislators and meeting with gun groups. Eliot figured it was a good bet Honeywell would be staying at home if he was in the L.A. area. It wasn't that far from Laurel Valley to L.A.

Eliot spent all day reading through back issues of *Guns and Hunters.*

The NAGO Annual Convention was coming up in Dallas the third weekend in May. Friday night was the opening session. Saturday, the annual meeting; and in the evening, the banquet. Monday and Tuesday, executive committee meetings, and a meeting of the board. The Exhibit Hall—booth after booth of guns, ammunition, knives, and other sporting equipment—was going to be open Friday evening, all day Saturday, and all day Sunday. There was a shooting competition Saturday afternoon at a nearby rifle range; the rest of the weekend the range was open to NAGO members. A test-firing of assault rifles, courtesy of the world's gun manufacturers, would take place on Sunday.

Crowds, chaos, guns.

He looked over the schedule again. Honeywell was going to be opening the opening session Friday night; it was a task the national spokesman had performed for the last nine years.

Dallas, home of assassins.

He liked the idea. Dallas could be his backup site if Honeywell wasn't in L.A.

He made a copy of the schedule of events, then went to find a phone to make the necessary plane reservations.

23

If Kenneth Hawks had ever thought about joining the marines, the last two weeks had killed that idea.

He was cold and wet, and completely exhausted, which he found absolutely strange, since he had been doing nothing more than sitting on his ass the whole time. And he was hungry. Unbelievably hungry. No matter how much he ate, his stomach wanted more. JC had had to resupply him five times.

He looked at the pile of food and chocolate bars JC had dropped off a little while before. He had just finished four Big Macs and two large fries, and his stomach was still growling. He opened a can of peaches and drank the whole mess down. Then he crept out to take a shit.

The worst was when he had to shit during the day. Then he had to hold it in. One time he had had to shit so bad, he tried shitting in a can, like JC had suggested. Some had gotten on his hand. He almost cried. He didn't have anything to clean it off with, none of those wet-wipe things his mother always carried around in the car. All he had was toilet paper. He had wound up rubbing his hand with dirt for hours.

And his hole stank of piss. He couldn't pee far enough to the side; some always dribbled back in. The one time he had peed in a can, he had accidentally knocked it over.

JC had laughed at the stink. "Just like a real patrol, huh, Kenny baby?"

Then he had hunkered down a little ways away and told a story about a real patrol. In Vietnam. In the jungle. The gooks hiding here, hiding there. Whole gook camps hidden in the bush, the hutches blending right in.

"We got hit, Kenny baby. My third patrol. Small-arms fire—no big deal. So the hotshots up front decided to push forward a little, test the resistance. That's when the machine gun opened up.

"We had our noses right down in the dirt. Except it wasn't dirt; it was shit. We were lying in the latrine." He laughed. "You should have seen the bugs in there. Big bugs, little bugs. Ever see a wound go gangrenous, Kenny? It happens fast in the heat. First the colors, then the smell."

All Hawks could smell was his own B.O.

He waited for JC to tell him about the air strike they must have called in. But JC was quiet, because there hadn't been any air strike.

"Vietnam, Kenny baby. A real vacationland."

And he was gone.

Kenneth didn't even hear him leave; he just sensed JC wasn't there anymore.

Mr. Tough Guy. Mr. War Stories.

He wondered whether JC had even been in Vietnam. Probably, he had sat on a base in Texas the whole time playing with himself.

Kenneth Hawks reached down and started to rub his own dick. Shit, there was nothing else to do.

The next morning, while Kenneth Hawks was catching his forty winks, Eliot Brod was getting organized in a motel room in Berkeley. He had flown in three days earlier and had spent the time pedaling around and looking around. He had seen exactly what he had expected to see: a lot of NAGO heavies.

Wimpy and a friend seemed to be permanently moored in the parking lot at the bottom of Tran's road. Two more guys were camped out directly across from Tran's restaurant. Probably, there were more. Certainly, there was someone watching Tran's house.

He picked up a medium-sized backpack and started filling it with the things he had laid out on the bed. When everything was tucked away, he closed the pack and dropped it in the closet. It was time to pay Tran a visit.

He pulled on a pair of khaki trousers and an off-white, button-down cotton shirt. A beige tie, a beige sport jacket, a pair of tasseled off-white loafers, and tinted glasses completed the outfit. He had bought the clothes a couple of days before. An hour in a Laundromat, followed by a trip to the dry cleaner's, had made everything look lived in.

He practiced walking back and forth across the room a few times: a slightly bouncy, slightly stiff-legged athletic walk. When he was comfortable with the walk, he headed over to the Berkeley BART station and caught the 10:09 to MacArthur, switched trains at MacArthur, and caught the 10:26 to Walnut Creek. The train arrived at 10:48, three minutes after it should have; the train out of Daly City had been late.

For an hour he wandered around Walnut Creek, buying a trinket here, a doodad there, finally arriving at Tran's House of Flowers a little before twelve.

He didn't notice JC sitting in a nearby pastry shop sipping coffee, though JC noticed him. JC figured him for a crooked lawyer who played a lot of tennis.

Eliot found Tran's restaurant pleasant enough. It was clean, and relatively quiet. The chairs were comfortable, and spaced so nobody was bumping elbows. Paintings of flowers hung on the walls. And on each table a small vase held a single fresh flower. Looking around, Eliot realized the flowers were all different.

He had fried dumplings, Szechuan shrimp and vegetables, and the house fried rice. The food was good, which explained why the place was packed, because the prices weren't all that cheap.

By twelve-thirty he was done. He got up and paid for his

187

lunch, and after the woman at the cash register had given him his change, he handed her a card and said he had an appointment with Tran.

She looked at the card—Royal Security Systems, R. Hartwick, with a picture of a robin in the upper right corner—and then at Eliot, and said she'd be right back.

As she left, Eliot picked up a take-out menu and stepped around to the side so he couldn't be seen from the dining room.

A moment later she was showing him into the office: a hole in the wall filled entirely by a desk and a couple of file cabinets.

The man Tran saw step into his office was not the same man he had seen three months before. This man was older, and his walk was wrong: too bouncy.

He was about to say something, when Eliot raised a finger. He pulled out a piece of paper and held it up for Tran to read.

It was a list of instructions, and a timetable.

Tran read through everything twice, and the timetable a third time. When he was finished, he nodded.

Eliot turned and walked out of the office.

A minute later JC glanced at his watch. Forty-three minutes for the tennis-playing lawyer, six minutes longer than the average. Probably, the bum had had a drink or two to start with.

He made a note of the time of departure, checked to make sure the man had been carrying a small bag when he entered, and crossed him off the list.

Tran was still staring at the door.

The meeting, if you could call it that, had been so brief, so strange and unexpected, it seemed half a dream.

He sat down at his desk and picked up a photograph of his daughter. His beautiful daughter. She was wearing a white dress with a red bow. He remembered the day he had bought it. He remembered a lot of things. It was all he had left. He placed the picture in his pocket.

Then he put away the ledger he had been working on, collected a few papers, and left for the bank.

By then, Eliot was on the train to Daly City. Forty-five minutes later he was in his motel room getting ready.

24

JC scanned the parking lot of the shopping center looking for something that was a little off—a car he hadn't seen before; an unfamiliar delivery van. His eyes came to rest on Szczepanski, as, he was sure, the killer's had.

The man knew they were waiting for him, and he was going to try for the money, anyway. Tonight. That was some kind of confidence.

JC sorely hoped he would be able to disappoint the guy. He wished he could just drive up to Tran's house, park himself in the Viet's lap, and wait for the killer there.

But that might not be the guy's plan. He might not like dead-end roads with nowhere to run.

A couple walked out of the supermarket carrying a bag of takeout from the deli. They had eaten deli last Thursday, too. It was dinnertime, but the thought of eating made him nauseous.

He got out of the car to catch some air.

It had been over a month since he had intercepted Tran's call to Weston, a month of hard work, and chasing around, and bad luck; and nothing to show for any of it. And now it was

189

going to happen tonight. As simple as that, with lots of warning.

JC didn't like things that were simple; things that were simple usually went wrong.

He scanned the parking lot again, trying to sense the presence of the killer.

But he had never been any good at sensing the enemy, only at finding the telltale signs the enemy left, and this man left very little.

JC knew what his plan would be: a shell game. Maybe, several identical suitcases. Maybe, some sort of diversion. That was always the plan. The trick was to figure out the variation. He was hoping Tran wouldn't let the money out of his sight until he handed it over to the killer. He always hoped for the best. Why not?

He got back in the car, checked his gun again, and thought through his coverage. He thought it was pretty good. He had a few wild cards the killer couldn't know about, and he had the guy outnumbered.

He wondered how the man had contacted Tran. There hadn't been any suspicious phone calls to Tran's house, or to his office. Had he used the mail? That would be brave.

JC supposed the guy might have made his plans three weeks before, when Szczepanski was supposed to be guarding the fort. The only other possibility was that the man had met with Tran in person, and that could have happened only at the restaurant. That day? Cause and effect? That was some kind of balls, walking right in. Who the hell did this guy think he was, the Sundance Kid?

He pulled out his restaurant list. Thirteen people had eaten lunch alone that day: eight women and five men. Two had stayed longer than the average. Five had left early. None had set off any bells. He couldn't decide whether or not to be a sexist pig and ignore the possibility that a woman might be the assassin, not that it mattered. If one of the thirteen *was* the killer, the disguise had worked; it was too late to start tracking them all down.

That afternoon JC had followed Tran to the bank. The Viet had walked in with a large leather briefcase that was ob-

190

viously empty, stayed about ten minutes, then walked out with the same briefcase banging against his leg. He had driven straight home.

JC had called Hawks on the radio, and Hawks had watched the car coming up the road. There were two spots where Tran's car was out of sight, but Kenneth didn't think the car had stopped or even slowed down. And he had definitely seen Tran carry a case into the house.

"Does it look heavy in his hand, Kenny baby?"

"He's leaning a little to one side."

"Well, look alive. There could be two cases. The money might still be in the car."

"I can see the whole car."

"Good."

Then JC had walked up the road and searched the gullies to make sure Tran hadn't tossed the cash out the window. There was nothing, so he had walked back down to the parking lot.

Now, he was waiting again.

He had Hawks watching the house. He had the phone tapped. The beeper in Tran's car was working perfectly. He and his partner, and Szczepanski and *his* partner, would cover any road races. And the two guys who had been watching the restaurant, and who were now also in the parking lot, would be back up if anyone needed help.

He couldn't think of anything else to do.

He hit the button on his radio and checked in with Szczepanski, and then with the two guys in the third car. It was getting on toward dusk, and in a few minutes he was going to send one of those guys up the road toward Tran's house to help cover the road and keep an eye out.

He buzzed Kenneth to see what the word was from above.

"His house is lit up like a Christmas tree."

"How's that?"

"He's got all the lights on. And he's been walking from room to room for the last two hours."

"What's he doing?"

"I can't tell because of the angle. I only see him when he's passing a window."

"What's he doing then?"

"Just walking."

"He's been walking around for two hours?"

"Maybe he's nervous?"

"Anything else? Did he move his car at all, or go outside?"

"He's been inside the whole time."

"Can you see the briefcase?"

"No."

JC thought about it. The guy could be nervous. He was sitting on a pile of money, waiting. For what? A phone call?

"You look sharp, now, Kenny baby. Anything else strange happens, or someone shows up there, you give a call right away."

"Right."

"And don't fall asleep on me. And don't you be playing with yourself, either."

"Fuck you, JC."

Fifteen minutes later the whine of the bumper beeper coming over the receiver in JC's car started to get louder. At the same moment the radio sang.

"He's got the briefcase in the car, JC."

"The same case as before?"

"The same case; and he's still lugging it around."

"Okay, you stay sharp, now. This could be a fake. You need help, there's two guys down here at the bottom of the hill."

He called Szczepanski with the news, just as Tran hit the main road and took off. He was already doing forty by the time JC got out of the parking lot. JC slammed down on the gas. Szczepanski was right after him. The bumper beeper hummed reassuringly.

JC pulled just close enough to see Tran's car. It was going to be tough in the dark, but the bumper beeper would warn him of any turns. He fixed the BMW's rear light pattern in his mind, then dropped back a little.

Tran was driving fast, but not evasively, which worried him. Maybe he didn't *need* to drive evasively? Maybe the money was still in the house? Or maybe he was planning to drop the case over the Bay bridge? There were lots of ways to lose a tail. He called Hawks to see if anything was up.

"Nothing you'd care to know about, JC."

GUN MEN

JC didn't even bother to reply. He dropped back and let Szczepanski follow Tran for a while, just in case Tran *was* watching for a tail. After a few minutes he pulled forward again.

For over an hour Tran drove around Contra Costa County: east on 24, north on 680, south on Taylor Boulevard, back onto 24 heading west, south on Moraga. Then onto Canyon Road and up into the Oakland hills until he hit Pinehurst. North on Pinehurst, south on Skyline Boulevard, and finally down into Oakland.

By then, JC was ready to run him off the road and shoot him. He was sure he would be able to think of something to do with the money.

Just then Tran started to slow down. JC closed the gap a little.

"Look alive, Taddy," he called over the radio.

At that moment Tran swerved into the left lane and flung the briefcase out the window of the car. It sailed over the rail of an overpass and disappeared.

"Stay with him," JC shouted.

Szczepanski took off after Tran.

JC was already running toward the overpass, the Smith & Wesson in his hand. He hopped the low guardrail and scuttled down the incline a few feet, stopping behind a bush. He could hear something moving down below, but in the dark he couldn't see what it was; he was still night-blind from staring at Tran's taillights. He cocked the .357 and inched forward. If the killer was down there, *his* eyes would already be accustomed to the dark.

A stone rolled from under his foot; it tumbled down the slope and hit another stone. He stayed where he was for five minutes.

Fifteen minutes later JC was at the bottom of the gully. The briefcase lay open just in front of him, the bundles of money all around. He wondered where the hell the killer was. All he could see was a goddamn cat.

He reached forward and picked up one of the bundles— it was exactly as heavy as a brick. He threw it at the cat and ran for the car.

193

25

Eliot Brod had spent that afternoon trotting around Briones Regional Park, scouting out the trails, and making his final plans.

By six he had seen what he needed to. He hiked back to the parking area, collected his bike, ate a few candy bars, and started toward the park entrance. Halfway to the entrance he passed a brushy gully. He looked around for cars, then pedaled down the incline.

It took less than a minute to hide the bike. When he was finished, he crept back to the road, smoothing out the bike track with his foot.

The gully in which his bike was hidden was opposite a good-sized oak, and 283 steps from a road sign; it would be dark when he returned, and he didn't want to spend half the night searching for his means of escape.

Half an hour later he was standing on the ridge above Tran's house. The sun was just setting.

If someone was watching Tran's place from the park, Eliot figured this was where he would be, probably just below the lip of the hill so he could see the entire house.

He scanned the hillside but couldn't see anything. He had

scanned the hillside earlier that afternoon, with the same results. If the guy was there, he was well hidden.

He took a last look at Mount Diablo—just the tip of the peak was still in the sun—then continued along the trail. When Tran's house was out of sight, he slid down the hill and into a gully. He opened his pack and pulled out a black shirt and black pants and put them on. Then he blackened his face and ears. The last thing he did was pull on a pair of very thin black leather gloves. Not exactly a ninja, but close enough.

It took him ten minutes to get to the bottom of the gully, mostly because he was memorizing the path for the way back. By the time he reached the bottom, he was muddy and wet.

He slid under a barbed-wire fence and into the drainage ditch that ran alongside the road. Three minutes later he was across from Tran's house. He checked his watch. Tran would be leaving in five minutes. He had timed it just right.

Fifteen minutes after Tran drove off, Eliot crept out of the ditch and, using the shrubs along the driveway as cover, scampered up to the house and in the side door. Just inside the door was a plastic bag filled with hundred-dollar bills. It only weighed eleven pounds but was somewhat bulky. Eliot stuffed the bag into his pack, walked to the front door, and took off.

Kenneth Hawks had a fit.

After Tran had left, he had swung the scope around, checking the grounds and the road. They were as empty as ever, so he gave a quick peek at the neighbors: The couple next door was at it again, busy performing lewd and, Kenneth Hawks suspected, illegal acts on one another. He zoomed in with the scope and carefully adjusted the focus. Certainly, no one had ever done that to him. He zoomed in a little more. Except for the smells, it was like being in the room with them.

And that would have been Kenneth Hawks's evening entertainment, if not for the fact that after about ten minutes the two lovebirds grew shy and pulled the curtains. Kenneth wondered what they were planning that demanded *more* privacy. He couldn't imagine.

But since he couldn't see anything anymore, he turned the scope back to Tran's—just in time to see someone walking out the front door. The guy was dressed all in black, like Bruce Lee or something; he had nearly swung the scope right past him.

Where the hell had he come from?

He swiveled the scope to make sure he had the right house, then hit the radio button to call JC—and got nothing.

"You pig!" he cried, banging the box as hard as he could. "You *will* work." He hit the button again.

Kenneth Hawks was feeling what every soldier feels the first time he's in the field and in trouble and the radio doesn't work: He felt panic.

He jumped out of the hole and ran back and forth. The fucker was going to get away. He jumped back into the hole and stared through the scope: The guy was gone.

Kenneth Hawks cursed and swept the scope along the road in both directions. The road was empty. He cursed again and swept the scope along the ditch that ran next to the road. It was hidden by trees. He cursed some more. Instinctively, he began to search the uphill section of the ditch, very slowly and very carefully. Deer ran uphill. Hares ran uphill. Everything ran uphill. Each time he reached an opening in the trees over the ditch, he paused, and finally picked up a shadowy figure scurrying along.

He didn't know whether to go after him or stay in the hole. JC hadn't covered this possibility.

Kenneth didn't know it at the time, but he was in the middle of his first real leadership test: The man in command was down, and it was up to *him* to decide what to do. Much to his credit as a soldier, he took off after Brod.

Eliot had retraced his steps exactly, and was nearly to the top of the ridge, when Kenneth Hawks jumped out at him from behind a tree. Even in the dark Eliot could see the knife, a long, mean-looking thing. He stopped where he was.

It was what Kenneth Hawks had been expecting; the sudden move had startled the man. If that jerk JC hadn't taken his gun, it would have all been over except for the applause.

He lunged forward, the knife like a divining stick, and landed flat on his face.

197

Eliot had stood his ground until the last moment. By then Kenneth Hawks *knew* he had the man and lunged extra hard. He never saw Eliot step to the side. He never even saw him move.

Kenneth was just pushing himself up when the punch to the back of the head landed. An experienced fighter would have rolled.

But Kenneth didn't have time to think about his mistake; he was out cold.

Eliot slid a knife out of the sheath along his back and sliced up a few strips of the kid's clothes. Then he hog-tied the boy, checking the pulses in the thumbs and ankles to make sure the blood was still flowing.

There was no point in killing the kid. He hadn't seen anything. And why risk a murder investigation for nothing?

He checked the knots again, then trotted up the rest of the hill and back to his bike. A little cold cream removed the blackening on his face. A minute later he was out of his ninja costume.

The lights of Orinda greeted him as he coasted down the hill from the park. By God, a little fresh air and half a million dollars made a man feel good. He laughed.

He was back at the motel by ten-thirty.

26

JC was doing eighty-five when he reached the Caldecott Tunnel. And he was in a rage, partly because he had gone for the fake, but mostly because that idiot Szczepanski hadn't followed Tran all the way home but only as far as the parking lot. The conversation kept running through his head.

"Where's Tran?" he had called over the radio.

"He's home," Szczepanski had replied. "Up the hill."

"You're in the parking lot?" he had screamed. "I told you to stay with him."

"I went where I always go."

"Can Hawks see him?"

"I can't get through to Hawks."

It was then that he decided he really *was* going to strangle Szczepanski.

"What the fuck do you mean, you can't get through to Hawks?"

He hadn't waited for an answer, but had called Hawks himself, and gotten nothing.

"Tadeusz, get your ass up that road right away and see what's going on."

* * *

Which is where JC finally found him: sitting in the car on the side of the road just below Tran's house. He pulled his car in behind Szczepanski's and walked forward. Szczepanski rolled down the window.

"Is he in there?"

Szczepanski shrugged. "I haven't seen him yet. You get the killer?"

"I told you to stay with him."

"Hawks is supposed to be watching the house. I went where I always go."

"That's good, Taddy. Real good. At least I'll always know where to find you. Gimme the fucking radio."

But Kenneth Hawks was not at home on Szczepanski's radio, either. JC went back to his car and tried *his* radio again. Where the fuck was the kid? He walked back to Szczepanski's car. Tran's BMW was sitting in the middle of the driveway.

"You see anything suspicious while you were in the parking lot?"

"Nope, nothing."

"Nobody walking down the road? No taxicabs?"

Szczepanski shook his head.

"Tran come straight back?"

"Right back. Drove like a bat out of hell the whole way. You get the killer?"

"The bag was full of bricks."

"Oh."

JC stared at the house. The whole time he had been following Tran around, the cash had been inside. He didn't imagine it was still there. But Hawks must have seen the pickup. Where the hell was he?

He knew one thing: If the killer had the money, Tran was shit now.

A car came whipping around the curve below them, swerved, and went zipping past. The driver stared at them.

JC pointed at Szczepanski's partner. "Take my car and wait in the parking lot." He waved Szczepanski over to the passenger seat, pulled the car farther up the road, and let it roll back into Tran's driveway. Just then, a light went on in the house.

JC relaxed a little. "Looks like you didn't fuck it up too

bad, Taddy boy. Let's go have a talk with our friend." He caught Szczepanski by the arm as he reached for the door. "And we're going to do it quietly. You understand? No guns. And put your fucking gloves on and don't take them off, not even to scratch. You go around back."

The moon was gone, but the stars were bright enough to see the ground. JC crept forward slowly, peering in the windows as he went. Where the hell was Tran? Was he taking a crap?

The perfume of a flower drifted past him. Overhead, an airplane buzzed. He was glad the guy didn't have any dogs.

He tried the door; maybe, in the excitement, Tran had forgotten to lock it.

The door didn't budge.

He pulled out his pick tools and selected a pick and tension wrench. Two and a half minutes later he had the door unlocked. He pushed it open an inch and listened. He couldn't hear a thing.

He withdrew the tools from the lock and put them away. Then he eased the door open, ready to stop it if it started to squeak. The door swung wide without a sound. He left it ajar and crept into the foyer. All he could hear was the low rumble of the refrigerator and the hum of an electric clock. He turned around and eased the door mostly closed, then crept toward the room with the light on.

The room was empty.

He crept back into the foyer and headed down a hall. The hall was dark, very dark, like a tunnel.

He had crawled into a tunnel once, a blackness like a hole in the universe. Black, and quiet, and still. And not a breath of air. He didn't go in very far. He couldn't; he was too big. Just thirty feet. After that the tunnel turned and tightened. He was pissed, because he knew there were VC in that tunnel. And then he was scared, because when he tried to back out, he realized he was stuck.

It was an hour before Gomez finally dragged him out. An hour lying there waiting for the VC to come and get him.

It was during that hour that JC learned what a fine friend his sense of smell was; and his sense of smell right now was sending out a red alert, because he didn't smell anything.

He heard the faintest tapping from the rear of the house. He followed it until he reached the back door. It was Szczepanski.

"What the hell are you doing?" JC hissed.

"The door was locked."

"Where are your fucking pick tools?"

"I forgot them."

JC figured it was fifty-fifty whether a jury convicted him of murder.

"You search the rooms to the left. I think the house is empty."

"What about that light?"

"A timer."

They made a quick sweep of all the rooms, finally bumping into each other in the kitchen.

"Maybe he went for a walk?" Szczepanski said.

"Just shut your fucking mouth, Tadeusz. Go through each room again, and check absolutely everywhere. He's small, so look in small places."

They spent another forty minutes checking the house.

JC shook his head. "You're sure he didn't sneak past you?"

"It was only five minutes, JC."

JC began to look for something, anything, that might tell him where Tran was.

There were a few empty hangers in the bedroom closet, but then, most closets had a few empty hangers. The bathroom seemed undisturbed: toothbrush, toothpaste, hairbrush, razor. The dresser drawers were all full of clothes.

There were no airline folders in the garbage. No numbers scrawled next to the phone. No magazines, or books, or travel folders left open. A neat, fucking house, with everything where it was supposed to be.

He went outside and looked through the trash but didn't find anything. There was nothing in the car, either.

First Weston, then Tran. He felt as if he were part of a magic act.

"Tadeusz, take the car and go call Taylor. Tell him we

missed, and he should get hold of Honeywell. Then get your ass back here."

"You gonna want some coffee?"

JC just stared at him.

Szczepanski saluted and hopped in the car.

JC leaned against the BMW and ran through the evening in his mind. First, Tran took off. Then, a minute later, he talked to Hawks. Then the goose chase. Then Tran returned home. Then Hawks was gone. Then Tran disappeared, but without his car.

And sometime during all that, the killer showed up to collect his money. Where had he come from? He didn't drive; there had been two men watching the road the whole time.

He walked over to the front door and turned on his flashlight. There, in the flower bed to the side of the door, was a footprint. He followed the track across the yard and down into the ditch, where he found footprints coming and going. Had Hawks gone after the killer?

He slid down into the ditch. The ground was a tracker's dream: soft and wet, with each footprint clear and deep. The killer was smaller than he was, and a good bit lighter. He took his time following the trail, stopping every now and then to listen.

A couple of hundred yards above Tran's house the tracks turned and went up into the park. He could see where the man had slid beneath the fence—the dirt was smoothed.

Twenty minutes later he found Kenneth Hawks. The kid was twisting and cursing, and straining against the ties.

"Get tangled practicing your Boy Scout knots, Kenny baby?"

"Fuck you, JC."

JC kicked him, hard. And when Kenneth protested, JC kicked him again, even harder. Then he slapped him twice. "How come you're not in your hole?"

"He was here, JC. A huge guy. The size of an ox."

"The size of an ox, huh?" JC smacked him again. "This ox drag you all the way over here from your hole?"

GARY FRIEDMAN

"I came here to get him, but all I had was a knife because you took my fucking gun. I could've shot him easy." He told JC about the dead radio.

JC smacked him again.

"Hey! Cut it out."

"You even think to try the On/Off switch?"

Kenneth stopped squirming. He couldn't remember whether he had tried the switch or not.

"This guy go into Tran's house?"

"Yeah. I saw him coming out the front door."

"But not going in?"

"Yeah, going in, too."

"He carrying anything?"

"I didn't notice. You gonna cut me loose?"

"Maybe I'll just leave you for the buzzards." He lit a cigarette. "What'd this guy look like?"

Kenneth thought a minute. "He was tall. Real tall. And big. A black guy. At least, I'm pretty sure he's black. It was hard to tell in the dark."

27

Eliot Brod didn't fly home with the money that Friday morning; he flew to L.A.

The first flight to L.A, United flight 1435, was booked; but he did manage to get a seat on the next flight, USAir flight 2702. It departed Oakland 7:00 A.M and arrived at the Los Angeles International Airport at 8:18. He had a small canvas carry-on bag with him, and a medium-sized box. He didn't have the half-million dollars.

The half-million dollars was sitting in a locker in the Oakland Airport. He planned to pick it up that afternoon and fly home.

USAir flight 2702 was six minutes late arriving in L.A. As soon as the plane had come to a stop, Eliot took the box and the bag and, along with everyone else, began the shuffle toward the terminal. Five minutes later he was standing in front of a locker. He removed a brown jacket from the canvas bag and put the bag in the locker, then he walked outside and caught a cab.

The cab ride took twenty-six minutes. He was dropped in front of a yellow house in a neat, middle-class neighborhood.

Eliot didn't know who lived in the house, but he did know that just a few blocks away there was a shopping center, and that in that shopping center was a store that sold bicycles. He had to wait ten minutes for the store to open.

At nine-thirty he walked in and bought a cheap bike, a lock, and a Swiss Army knife. He checked the main blade on the knife; it was reasonably sharp. He loaded the box and jacket on the handlebars of the bike, placed the knife in his pocket, and peddled over to Darrel Honeywell's house.

He knew Honeywell was in L.A. At least, he knew Honeywell had been in L.A. the day before, when he had met with L.A. police chief Daryl F. Gates. A report of the meeting had been on the late-night news. Honeywell had been trying to patch up differences between NAGO and the anti–assault rifle police chief.

At ten o'clock Eliot was around the corner from Honeywell's house. He locked the bike to a road sign, pulled on the drab brown jacket with the ACME DELIVERY SERVICE logo on the back, pulled on a pair of thin leather gloves the color of his skin, and walked around the corner. The Swiss Army knife was open in his hand, hidden by the box.

Honeywell's house was in a seedy part of the neighborhood. The houses were small, and a little run-down, the lawns and shrubbery beat up; most of the cars were several years old, at least. Eliot didn't see any teenagers around, but there were mothers and younger children on the street.

His plan, when Darrel Honeywell opened the door, was to step forward and cut his throat. From the street it would look as if he had just stepped inside to deliver the package.

He was outside Honeywell's house at 10:07. He walked up to the door and rang the bell, then opened the screen door and knocked. He hoped Honeywell was in, and he hoped he was alone.

28

Darrel Honeywell was sound asleep when the phone rang.

At first the ringing was part of a dream: a bell at an arcade, a prize bell. He had just hit his twentieth bull's-eye and was going for a record.

But on the third ring his record, and all his prizes, and the beautiful babe hanging on his arm cheering him on, began to dissolve.

By the fourth ring he was back in his own bed.

He jumped up. The clock glowed 1:26—1:26! What asshole was calling at that hour?

It was Patrick Taylor, and he was in a mood. JC had missed. The pickup had been made. And now the killer would be coming. He was to get back to Washington on the first flight.

"Are you alone?" Taylor wanted to know.

He was alone.

"I want you to go to a hotel for the rest of the night. And make sure you have your gun with you. And pack your suitcase now; I don't want you going back to your house."

Yes. Yes. Yes.

It was someone else speaking the words.

"Are you up?"

He was up.

"Is your head off the pillow?"

His head was in his hands, swimming in all the beer he had swallowed the previous evening. Did Mr. Patrick Taylor know what time it was?

"Just get your ass moving."

Darrel hung up the phone and pulled the pillow over his head. Taylor had fucked up his dream. The big tough president of the big tough National Association of Gun Owners shaking in his own boots. What a flyweight.

He pulled his .357 off the night table and checked to make sure he had a shell chambered. He did. He always did, except when he had a girl over. Girls were just too curious and too careless.

A Desert Eagle .357 magnum. Nine fucking shots, plus the one in the chamber. Enough to stop a fucking elephant.

He called the airport and got a seat on the morning flight. Then he went back to sleep.

At six the phone rang again. Patrick Taylor wanted to know why he was still there.

"Because my flight doesn't leave until ten."

"Well, make sure you don't miss it."

Darrel set the alarm for eight and crawled back under his pillow. The boss was getting to be a pain in the ass.

At 7:57 his eyes popped open; miraculously, he didn't have a hangover. He lay there gloating until the alarm went off, then he picked up the phone and called the cab company and arranged to have a cab pick him up at nine.

He lit a cigarette. He would take a long, hot shower, then shave, then cook himself a giant plate of bacon and eggs. Then he would pack a bag.

He would put his gun in the bag when he got to the airport and check the bag through. He didn't think the killer would try to kill him on the plane.

THE
END GAME

29

J C spent all day Friday looking for Tran.

He started by going house to house along Tran's road, telling each neighbor he was a private detective and Tran's family had hired him. Tran's brother had fallen ill, and the family was desperate to locate Tran.

But nobody knew where Tran was, and no one had seen him.

Then he called the cab companies. He felt sick when he saw the list in the Yellow Pages: fifteen companies in all, seven in the immediate area. How could such a dip-shit little community have so many cab companies?

But there had been no pickup of an Oriental between 9:45 and 12:00 anywhere in the vicinity.

He checked the BART stations. But with automated ticket sales, he didn't think he had a chance in hell of finding someone who had seen Tran; and even if he did get lucky, he still wouldn't know where Tran was now, only what direction he had been headed in.

He checked with the airlines, both at Oakland and at San Francisco. There was no record of a Tran Van Duong having

211

flown anywhere on Thursday, and no one by that name had a ticket for Friday or Saturday.

JC would have liked to send Szczepanski over with a picture, but the chance of finding the person who had sold Tran a ticket—if in fact he had flown anywhere—was about the same as finding a BART agent who had seen the man.

Not one of Tran's friends knew where he was. JC checked out the guys Tran bowled with, everyone he had phoned or who had phoned him, and the people he had sold his property to.

When JC stopped by the restaurant, Lee Hong also wanted to know where Tran was.

After that, JC was out of ideas. He had already called his credit-agency contact and asked him to keep an eye on Tran's credit accounts. But JC figured the chance of Tran using a credit card was about the same as the Chicago Cubs winning the World Series. The man had decided to disappear, and JC didn't think he would be able to find him.

There were lots of ways to disappear, especially for a few days or weeks, and especially if the police weren't looking for you. In fact, it wasn't all that hard to disappear forever if you were willing to suffer certain inconveniences, like using a different name, and starting over from scratch, and taking shitty jobs for cash, and never getting in touch with any friends from the past. If you went someplace you had never been before, and did things you had never done before, and made some minor cosmetic changes, like cutting your hair or growing a beard, then you might never be found for one simple reason: It cost too much to send someone to every corner of the earth with your picture to look for you.

At eight o'clock on Friday evening JC finally gave up. His throat was sore from smoking too much and talking too much, and he smelled, both from cigarettes and from sweat. Even if he could find Tran, it probably wouldn't do Honeywell much good. He doubted Tran knew where Weston was; and he doubted Tran could tell him where to find the killer.

He left Szczepanski to keep an eye on Tran's place and to follow up on a few last leads, and flew back to Washington.

* * *

"He'll be coming for Honeywell now," JC said.

He was in Patrick Taylor's office, slouched in a chair with his hand in his pocket, fiddling with a cigarette. He wondered if Taylor would fire him if he lit up.

Taylor nodded. Then he leapt up from his chair and smashed his fist down on the desk. "God damn!"

JC took his hand out of his pocket.

"God damn! This is America! The good guys aren't supposed to be chased around by the bad guys. We don't even know who this son of a bitch is. You sure he's black?"

JC shrugged. "That's what Hawks said. He also said the guy was huge; but the prints I found were made by a small guy."

"Jesus Christ! A black Houdini. First Brenden, now this. And how the hell could Tran *and* Weston disappear without a trace?"

JC shrugged again.

Outside the window the trees were leafing in, thick green healthy leaves. Taylor had the window open and a warm breeze was drifting into the room. It made JC sleepy. It was the sort of weather that cried out for a nap in the park. Except, now the parks were full of crack addicts.

"So, what do we do now, JC?"

"We let the police help us find these guys, Patrick. We can hide Honeywell for a while."

Taylor swiveled around in his chair until he was facing the window. JC wondered if *he* ever felt like taking a nap.

"You think the cops can find this guy?"

"Which guy?"

"The killer, for Christ's sake."

"If they can find Weston."

Taylor nodded. He was drumming his fingers on the arm of his chair. "What if we also set a trap for him? What if we use Honeywell to draw him out?"

"Sort of risky for Darrel."

"We can let *him* decide that."

"What about the police?"

"I'll call Bigelow today." He hit the intercom button. "Get Darrel Honeywell in here."

213

Five minutes later Darrel Honeywell sauntered in. The smell of gunpowder followed him.

"We got a problem here, Darrel," Taylor said.

Darrel slid into a chair.

"Seems there's someone out there planning to kill you."

"The same guy killed Brenden?"

"Looks that way."

"A nigger, right?"

"Might very well be."

Darrel snorted. "And you let him run circles around you, huh, JC?"

JC wondered if the killer would give him a cut if *he* killed Honeywell.

Taylor leaned forward. "Way I see it, Darrel, we have two options here. We can hide you and wait for the killer to go away. Or, we can use you as bait to draw him out. If we hide you, the killer might find you anyhow, or he might just hang back till you get tired of hiding and *then* get you. On the other hand, if we put you out front, we can control that, and when he makes his move, we can get him. You gotta decide."

Darrel whipped out his Desert Eagle. "I want to get this fucker *now*, Patrick. I wanna put a hole in him bigger than a whore's cunt."

JC snorted.

"I ain't scared of him, JC."

Patrick Taylor smiled. "That's good." He folded his hands on top of his desk. "Now, the convention's coming up in a week. This guy will know that, and he'll know you'll be there. He'll probably be there, too."

JC nodded. "And he won't have to ask who you are, because there was that nice picture of you a couple of months back in *Guns and Hunters*. Your address, too."

Darrel hadn't thought about that. It showed on his face.

JC laughed. "How's that grab you, kid? He knows what you look like and where you live; and you know he's alive."

"Fuck you, JC."

Taylor waved the worry away. "But that's about all he knows; and once he's dead, it won't matter. We got a lot of people, Darrel. Whenever you're out, we'll have you covered.

And we can plan the times you're out. I'll get you one of those vests that can stop a cannon. You'll look open; the killer will try; and we'll get him."

When they had finished discussing everything, Taylor called Bigelow. The Boston cop was out of the office until Tuesday, and, no, there was no way to get in touch with him.

"What about someone else?"

"It's Bigelow's case." And Boston hung up.

30

Manny Bigelow was not a happy man. His daughter, who was fifteen, wasn't speaking to him, and he didn't know why, because she wasn't speaking to him. This impasse was in its third week. His son, the nineteen-year-old, had been arrested for drunken driving for the second time in a month, and Manny wasn't sure he'd be able to get him off with just a warning this time. And his other son, the sixteen-year-old, was starting to use drugs. Manny had tried to talk to the kid about it, but as soon as he mentioned drugs, the kid denied he used them and walked away.

And his wife blamed him for everything.

He dunked his doughnut into his coffee and let the soggy piece dissolve in his mouth.

Why did cops have so much trouble with their families? Why were their kids always in trouble? He didn't know the answer.

He had spent the weekend with his wife and the two younger kids in the country north of Concord, New Hampshire. It was something they used to do, he and the wife, before they had kids; and something they had done with the kids when the kids were young. They used to play tennis and go fishing. They drank root beer in the general store, and ate candy bars, and browsed through the comic books. The boys had liked Spider-man; his girl, Archie.

They had had fun. They had been happy.

Now, as soon as they got to the motel, the kids tossed their stuff in a corner and disappeared; he didn't know where, and they wouldn't tell him. He had given up screaming at them two years ago. Threats had no effect. He was just glad they were still in school. In fact, dropping out of school seemed to be a threat *they* held over *him*. It scared him. And it confused him, because he didn't know what to do about it.

He lit a cigarette and finished his doughnut and coffee. Even though the past had been neither simpler nor easier, he longed for it anyhow. Maybe because he had already made it through.

The phone rang. It was his good friend Patrick Taylor, commandant of NAGO. His stomach rolled.

"What can I do for you, Taylor?"

"I've got some information you might find interesting."

"Which racetrack are we talking about now?"

"I found the man who had Brenden killed."

Manny poured himself another cup of coffee. "Are you saying it was a contract killing?"

"That's right."

"Did this guy confess to that?"

"Listen to this."

Taylor played him the tape of the conversation between Tran and Weston. "I'd call that pretty damning evidence."

"I'd call that a guy who was having trouble with termites."

"Listen, Bigelow, this is our man."

"What did you say his name was?"

"Tran Van Duong."

"Chinese?"

"Vietnamese."

"And you think he hired someone to kill Brenden?"

Taylor told him how JC had tracked down Tran, and then Weston.

"Sounds like your man JC has been pretty busy: illegal

wiretaps; subverting government employees; maybe breaking and entering."

"He had a job to do."

"So who killed Brenden? I'm biting my nails."

"We didn't find that out."

"So why are you calling? You looking for a donation to fight gun control?"

There was a pause as Taylor fought to control his temper.

On his end Manny Bigelow smiled. He could always tell when he was getting to someone.

"Listen, Bigelow, this turkey is getting ready to kill another one of my boys, and I want you to do something about it."

"Why don't you just lean on this Weston guy? Or Tran?"

There was another pause on Taylor's end of the line. "We can't find Weston. And now Tran has disappeared."

Manny Bigelow's grin widened. At last the reason for the call. "So you want *me* to find them for you. Is that it?"

"Yes."

Manny poured some sugar into his coffee and swirled it around with a swizzle stick. "How come this Tran wanted Brenden killed?"

"His daughter was one of the kids gunned down by that nut Mattox."

"Yeah, that's what you said. But why *Brenden*?"

"I don't know *why*. You can ask him when you find him."

Manny Bigelow pushed back his chair and put his feet up on the desk. "You were going to cowboy it, weren't you, Taylor? You were going to be a hero and nail Brenden's killer all by yourself. Am I right?" Taylor didn't say anything. "Of course I'm right. And you fucked it up, and showed your hand, and your suspects disappeared, and now all you have left is crap."

"Listen, Bigelow, I'm losing my patience."

Manny found the confession deeply gratifying. "Why should I clean up your crap, Taylor?"

"Because you're a cop, and that's what you get paid to do."

"Well, fuck you, cowboy." And Manny Bigelow hung up.

An hour later his phone rang. It was the captain's secretary, and he was wanted over in the captain's office, pronto. "Don't even finish your coffee."

219

Manny Bigelow sat back and lit a cigarette. It was wasteful not to finish things. Waste not, want not. Yes siree. He added a little more sugar to his coffee and gave it a stir.

"I want you to get going on this case, Bigelow."

The captain, my captain, did not invite Manny to sit. Manny sat anyway. His feet hurt from walking around all weekend searching for his kids. He took a quick peek around the office.

The captain's office was a lot like his office, except it was in the corner of the building and was about twice as large. It also had a rug, new paint, and the garbage can was empty. And there weren't any sticky circles on the desk where the coffee cup had been.

He lit a cigarette and crossed his legs.

"I want you to show these NAGO jerks every courtesy. When I talk to Taylor next time, I only want to hear how you've behaved like a Boy Scout. Do I make myself clear?"

"Like a crystal ball."

"Good. Give whatever you're working on to Milano. You're flying down to Washington today, right now; your ticket is waiting at the airport." He handed Manny Brenden's file. "Now, get the fuck out of here."

Patrick Taylor's office was a lot like Manny's captain's office, only about twice as big. And the carpet was thicker. And the desk, instead of steel, was out of some exotic hardwood that was probably on the endangered-species list. And the paneling—well, his captain didn't really have paneling in his office.

Manny rubbed his fingers over the arm of the chair—some sort of embroidered velvet. He didn't even want to know what it had cost.

"Listen, Bigelow, I know we fucked this up a little, but there's a killer out there getting ready to knock off another one of my boys. We got to do something."

Manny lit a cigarette. "What's this kid's name, again?"

"Darrel Honeywell."

"And where is he now?"

"He's downstairs."

"So why don't you just keep him there until the killer gets bored and goes away?"

Taylor nodded. "The thing is, he might not get bored and go away. We'd never know." He told Bigelow his plan: the convention; using Honeywell to draw out the killer.

Manny shrugged. "He's your boy. If you want to set him up as a target."

"What about tracking down Weston and Tran?"

"What about it?"

"The convention starts Friday. We're running out of time."

"You're breaking my heart."

Manny Bigelow didn't fly straight back to Boston. It wasn't often he got an all-expenses-paid trip to the nation's capital, and he intended to paint the town red.

He found a phone booth and called the airport and changed his flight to ten; then, he caught a cab to the Smithsonian Museum.

While Manny Bigelow was looking at old airplanes, JC was on the phone trying to get hold of Szczepanski and Big Mike. He got Big Mike first.

"Guess what, Mikey boy?"

Mikey boy set a finger over Sally Ann's lips. "You found the killer and shot him?"

"Close. The killer made the pickup and made us eat shit."

"So, how come you're calling?"

"Taylor's handing it over to the police. *They're* going to look for Weston."

Big Mike hummed.

"I want you to get on back here. We gotta baby-sit Honeywell now."

"Why don't you just lock him in the basement with a caseful of shells?"

"I'm thinking about that."

Big Mike let the phone slide onto the cradle. Sally Ann took his hand.

"Well, toots, I gotta get back."

Sally Ann gave him a good-sport smile. "One for the road, hon?"

JC had less luck reaching Szczepanski. It took nearly all night.

"Where the hell you been, Taddy?"

"Watching out for Tran, just like I'm supposed to."

"Good boy. Well, guess what? We're going to let the cops watch out for Tran now. You get hold of Hawks and get on back here. We got other problems."

31

About the time Manny Bigelow was catching the shuttle to Washington, Eliot Brod was stepping off a plane in Dallas, Texas.

The flight had seemed to take forever, partly because of delays, partly because even without delays Dallas was over fifteen hundred miles from New England, but most of all because he was sure the airline would lose the suitcase in which he had his gun.

When the plane came to a stop, he marched straight over to the baggage claim. Twelve minutes later the luggage arrived. Miraculously, his bag was the third bag off the plane. Sometimes, God was merciful.

He walked outside and caught a cab.

The Dallas landscape was nothing to write home about. It was flat and rolling, like stretched-out ocean waves, so that even from the height of the land you could only see as far as the next rise. What you saw were more churches, shopping centers, shoe stores, office buildings, and construction. Despite the economic slump in Texas, there were houses and buildings going up everywhere.

Eventually, the skyscrapers of Dallas came into view. They formed their own height of the land.

The cabby dropped him in front of the Holiday Inn. He paid what he owed; and after the cab had pulled away, he walked a block, caught another cab, and gave the name of a different hotel. A few minutes later he was checking in.

Grant DeBois was all smiles as he greeted Eliot Brod. The man was going to stay three days, maybe longer; and he was going to pay cash. The assistant manager liked people who paid cash, because not all the cash made it into the books. A clever and careful assistant manager could make an extra couple of hundred dollars a week skimming, just about enough to indulge his passion for young girls and coke.

"Business?" he asked amiably.

"I might move to the area," Eliot replied. He tried to look thoughtful.

"Why not?" DeBois agreed. "Everyone else is." He offered his best smile and wished Eliot a pleasant stay.

After the bellboy had dropped his bag in the room, Eliot locked the door and began to put away his clothes. Halfway down in the suitcase, wrapped in plastic so it wouldn't make his clothes smell, was the gun, or, really, the parts of the gun.

The gun had come from a man in Minnesota named Michael Michaelson. Michaelson ran a gun-repair shop. He also did custom work, any sort of custom work as long as it was for cash. Eliot had been buying guns from him for fifteen years.

He placed the parts of the gun in a medium-sized backpack. He had a second pack, identical to the first; he placed his biking togs and shoes, and a few plastic bags, in it. Then he finished putting away his clothes, leaving out a pair of chinos, a polo shirt, and his sneakers. He placed the empty suitcase and the pack with the bike gear in the closet, changed his clothes, picked up the pack with the gun, and walked out of the hotel.

The Greyhound Bus Station wasn't very far away, though it seemed part of a different town. Instead of upscale, well-dressed men and women, the garbage of the city stood leaning against the building. They eyed him as he passed: sportily dressed, scrubbed, obviously well off. Out of place. He could

224

feel their interest, and dislike. After dark he knew he would be a target.

He pushed his pack into a locker, dropped in his quarters, and made a note of the time. Then he went out and grabbed himself a couple of hamburgers.

Eliot spent the rest of the afternoon and the early part of the evening walking around Dallas. He took a turn around the Convention Center, a complex of buildings roughly the size of Rhode Island, and strolled through the adjacent Pioneer Park Cemetery. He walked through the empty box of the Kennedy Memorial and wondered how long it would be before they tore it down and put up a new office building. He walked through the underground walkways and the elevated walkways and decided it would be the perfect setting for a chase movie. Finally, he stopped at a tourist-information center and picked up a handful of maps and brochures. The pamphlets listed area restaurants, hotels, shopping centers, parks, museums, and historical sites, as well as a number of recreational possibilities, including day trips and outings.

It was dusk when he returned to his hotel. He showered and shaved and dressed for dinner. He had a reservation at one of Dallas's most exclusive restaurants. He had made the reservation two weeks before.

When Eliot had first come to Dallas to scout out the city and the Convention Center, he had imagined several possibilities for killing Honeywell: a shot on the street, à la Kennedy; a shot somewhere inside, or near, the Convention Center; or something at Honeywell's hotel.

But except for the Convention Center, where he knew Honeywell would be, Eliot didn't have the slightest idea which streets the guy would be on, or even which hotel he would be staying at; he wouldn't be able to find that out until the last minute. And while he didn't usually mind last-minute setups, usually *he* wasn't being hunted, too.

So at ten o'clock one morning, Eliot, in navy-blue blazer, white ducks, pink shirt, blue tie with a pattern of wood ducks, and white tasseled shoes, walked into the Dallas Convention

Center and presented himself to the secretary in the main office. His hair was cut short and carefully brushed; and he was sporting the sort of tan only those people with a great deal of leisure ever acquire nowadays, a yachtsman's tan—so what if it had come from riding a bike all winter? Tinted glasses just barely hid his eyes.

He handed the secretary his card: Wilson B. Cornwall IV of Providence, Rhode Island, and explained how he was in town visiting his sister, and had some free time and was in the neighborhood, and thought he would swing on by to have a look. He was the secretary of the National Association of Real Estate Brokers, and they were looking for a convention site for 1994, and—he realized this was last minutish—but was there someone to show him around a bit?

The secretary listened politely, and indifferently, as he wound his way through his explanation, and when he finally got to the point, she hit the intercom button. Half a minute later Dave Parkins was there. Eliot went through his spiel again. Dave Parkins looked him up and down and decided Eliot was probably who he said he was—who else would wear a pink shirt in Dallas?

"I'd be happy to show you around, Mr. Cornwall."

Eliot didn't invite him to use his first name.

"About how many people are we talking, here?"

"About eight thousand," Eliot said.

Dave Parkins smiled.

There were meeting rooms, and meeting rooms, and meeting rooms. Banquet halls. An arena. A theater. Exhibit halls big enough to store a fleet of airplanes in. Three levels, two wings, and the center halls. Thirty-five-foot ceilings.

They walked through the basement parking area and past the loading docks. Eliot wanted to see it all, and Dave Parkins was happy to show it to him. He offered statistics and stories along the way and answered all Eliot's questions, which were extensive and tended to focus on security. The tour took three hours.

At the end Eliot admitted he was impressed. He asked Dave

for his card, thanked him for the tour, and said he'd be in touch.

But Eliot hadn't been at all certain he'd be in touch.

At first, the Convention Center had looked perfect: big and sprawling, with scores of people milling around, and dozens of nooks and crannies to hide in. But after an hour the building had begun to look less sprawling. Every corridor had its closed-circuit camera; and there weren't all that many exits, and most of those were watched by security guards. And everyone seemed to be wearing a name tag. Even if he managed to slip into one of the NAGO events, someone inside might sense he was wrong. A lot of NAGO guys were combat vets, and combat vets had all kinds of antennae. It would be a foolish risk, because what would he do once he was inside, stick a knife into Honeywell? The man was sure to be guarded; in fact, there wouldn't be the slightest chance to get close to him.

Which meant a long shot.

The idea hadn't thrilled him; long shots sometimes missed. Far better to wait until Honeywell was alone, and *he* wasn't expected.

He had just about scrapped the idea of doing the job in Dallas, when something on the convention schedule caught his eye: NAGO had reserved a nearby rifle range for the weekend—open shooting for members all day Saturday and Sunday, except for three hours Saturday when a shooting competition would take place.

Maybe Honeywell would visit the range? There was nothing scheduled for Sunday. Maybe the man would be looking for something to do?

Eliot had thought about it. On the range he would just be another guy with a gun.

When Eliot got to the range at eleven o'clock the next morning, there were only a handful of people shooting.

He stopped his bike in the middle of the parking lot and took a look around. To his right the range stretched for four hundred yards. It was bounded on the sides by mounds of sand

and thick woods, and in the rear by a high earthen backstop. Just in front of the shooters, and slightly above the line of fire, was a wooden barrier. The barrier served to protect the surrounding neighborhoods from any shots aimed high.

The firing line and the parking lot ran for several hundred feet. To the left of the parking lot was a large field, and past the field, thick woods. The woods stood about a hundred yards away.

The road he had biked in on was the only road in or out.

Eliot watched the shooters for about twenty minutes. He was sure on the weekend of the NAGO convention there would be more shooters, a lot more shooters; and if Honeywell was around, every one of those shooters would be watched. The parking lot would probably also be watched, and maybe the woods beyond the parking lot. Which didn't leave a whole lot of places for *him*.

He turned back toward the firing line. A burst of gunfire had caught his attention.

One of the shooters was blasting away with an assault rifle, popping clip after clip into the gun. Even from the parking lot Eliot could see the sand kicking up downrange.

Downrange.

They wouldn't expect a shot from downrange, because who would be downrange while people were shooting? Only a lunatic.

He would have to find a spot off to the side, *far* off to the side.

He had hopped on his bike and pedaled off.

The land around the rifle range was mostly marsh and thickets and scrub. Eliot circled the streets, looking for a place to sneak onto the range that was both dry and out of sight of neighboring homes. When he found a spot that looked good, and when the road was clear of cars, he ran his bike into the woods.

Almost immediately he was up to his knees in water. He slogged forward, looking for higher ground. But now that he was off the road, it didn't look as if there *was* any higher ground.

228

He was more than a little concerned about snakes.

After a hundred yards, he heard the echo of gunfire. The land began to dry out a little. He passed a row of warning signs, and then a fence. When the woods began to thin, he got down on his stomach and wriggled forward.

To the left was the firing line; to the right the backstop.

He surveyed the ground in front of him: low mounds of dirt, mostly covered with brush and bushes; and winding between the humps, a series of gullies that had been cut by the seasonal rains. The gullies were just deep enough to hide him.

He slid into a trench and crawled along until he was about 150 yards from the firing line, then he inched his way to the top of a mound shadowed by an enormous bush.

Except for a spot near the middle of the firing line hidden by a dead tree, his view uprange was unobstructed. He took out a pair of binoculars. It would be an easy shot, especially if Honeywell stepped forward to shoot. The man would almost certainly be standing still.

He glanced around. He had waited in worse spots. He would be nearly invisible under the bush, and the leaves would protect him from the sun. He slid back off the mound and into the gully.

It would be a miserable few days waiting for Honeywell, especially since he didn't know if Honeywell would even show up. But if the guy *did* show, the job would be a piece of cake. The police might even decide it was an accident.

He had called Michael Michaelson that night, and had flown home the next day.

32

Bright and early Wednesday morning Manny Bigelow started making phone calls.

First he called Peter Weston; then he called Tran Van Duong. Neither man was home. So, Taylor *had* scared off his suspects.

Manny smiled. He was glad. *He* was rooting for the killer.

At nine-thirty he placed his first call to the Iowa County Sheriff's Department in Wisconsin. It took him only one hour to get through to the person he wanted. He explained what was up: an ongoing homicide investigation; a possible lead, except the man he was looking for was gone; maybe he was involved.

He gave the Wisconsin detective Weston's home address and business address, and the phone numbers. The detective said he'd get in touch when he had something.

Manny Bigelow thanked him.

It was still too early to call California, so, reluctantly, he scooped up the pile of paperwork covering the corner of his desk and pulled it forward. Twenty minutes later he was still fiddling with the ribbon in his typewriter; and after an hour, he despaired of ever getting the machine to work. He gave up and went to lunch.

At one-thirty he started calling California. This time he got through to the man he wanted in just forty minutes. He was on a roll. He told his story again: a possible lead in a homicide investigation; trouble locating the man; appreciate some help.

When he hung up the phone at 2:20, he wondered if he could get away with just going home for the day.

At the same time Manny Bigelow was silently cursing his typewriter, Eliot Brod was pulling on a pair of khaki slacks and a white polo shirt. The polo shirt was crisp and new (he had bought it the day before), but the slacks were a little worn; and his sneakers were not all that clean.

He picked up the backpack with his biking togs and slung it over his shoulder. The tinted glasses hid his wrinkles; and with the backpack, he looked almost collegiate—a graduate student who couldn't bring himself to go out and get a job.

He stopped at the bus station and dropped a few more quarters into the locker, then caught a cab to the SMU campus.

The ride was much the same as the ride into town from the airport: more churches, shoe stores, office buildings, and mini–shopping malls.

Eliot had the driver drop him off in front of the administration building. It was sunny and hot, and even with sunglasses the glare was almost unbearable.

A pretty coed walked by and smiled at him with end-of-the-school-year joy. He smiled back and headed in the direction from which she had come.

Eliot spent an hour strolling around the campus. He was lucky: Graduation was Saturday, and the place was filled with visitors. If the NAGO convention had been a week later, the campus would have been empty. All the other colleges in the area were already on summer recess.

Eliot liked college campuses. They were open, relaxed places with little or no security. It was rare to find the door to any building locked, and, if you didn't look too strange, and if you looked as if you knew how to read, no one seemed to mind which one of those doors you walked through.

He opened the door to the library and walked in. Libraries opened early and closed late. They were used by students, faculty, and members of the community. And they had bathrooms, and bathrooms were a good place to change your clothes.

He wandered around the building until he knew the layout. Not many students were inside, probably because classes were over, but maybe because it was lunchtime. He realized he was hungry himself.

Just to the west of the SMU campus was a small shopping area, a strip of stores that turned a profit mostly because five thousand students lived a block away.

Eliot stopped at a luncheonette and grabbed himself a sandwich and a glass of milk. Near the luncheonette was a clothing store; and near the clothing store was a bike store. When he was finished eating, he walked over to the clothing store and bought several pairs of gray chinos and several dark green work shirts. Then he walked to the bike store and bought a cheap bike and a lock.

Twenty minutes later, after having changed his slacks for biking shorts and his polo shirt for a T-shirt, he was pedaling toward the rifle range.

The place looked much the same as on his last visit, maybe the trees were a little greener. After a quick look around, he headed over to the spot where he planned to sneak onto the range. Thankfully, no one had cleared the land for a subdivision in the last two weeks. All he needed now was some place to leave his bike.

It took him forty-five minutes to find a supermarket near the range; he figured the distance at about a mile. He would measure it in the morning, when he came back to scout a trail from the road to his mound; he wasn't ready to face the horrors of the marsh that afternoon.

He walked into the supermarket and bought a can of juice and a box of raisins. Then he spent the afternoon pedaling around the Dallas suburbs gawking at the homes.

At six-thirty he was back at SMU. He locked his bike to a bike rack outside a residence hall. Ten minutes later he was on a bus headed downtown.

Thursday dawned bright and sunny in Dallas. But in Boston, after three days of summerlike weather, a cold rain was falling.

Manny Bigelow was in a bad mood. His elbow ached. It ached whenever it rained, which in Boston was too often.

He spent a minute rubbing the sore spot. The rubbing didn't help, but he did it anyhow, out of habit.

His elbow had ached ever since he had broken it—the dumbest accident imaginable. At the time, he had taken it as a sure sign of the beginning of old age.

He had been down in the file room going over some old notes. He was working on a case that reminded him of a case he had had ten years ago, a case he had never solved. The file drawer was open beside him, the file was spread across his arms, and he was bent forward trying to decifer his own rotten handwriting, when someone behind him called his name. He turned, a little too quickly. His extended elbow collided with the extended file drawer; the file drawer didn't give an inch. Four weeks later, when it was obvious even to him that the elbow wasn't going to get better by itself, he went to see a doctor. By then the pieces were nearly healed, all in the wrong places.

Dumb.

He took a sip of coffee and burned his tongue—the third time that week. He decided for safety's sake to take lunch in the office.

At eleven he was interrupted in his paperwork by a call from Wisconsin. Weston wasn't there, and his secretary didn't know where he was, but she was concerned. The man had left a note saying he would be gone a week or two, and hadn't been in touch since. That was almost a month ago.

"Did *he* write the note?"

"She says it's his handwriting."

"She got any idea where he might be?"

"Nope, but she's agreed to file a missing-person report, so we can start looking."

Manny thanked the Wisconsin detective and hung up the phone.

An hour later San Francisco called. There was no sign of Tran, but his house had been ransacked.

"The weird thing is, nothing seems to have been taken."

They were going to dust for prints. And they were looking for a private eye who neighbors said was asking after Tran on Friday. A composite drawing of the P.I. was being made.

"Any ideas?"

Manny had a very good idea where the person who fit that picture could be found. He gave the detective Patrick Taylor's number. It would be sweet justice if those NAGO fuckers got nailed for breaking and entering.

He poured himself more coffee and took three Tylenol. Then he started to look for Tran. Credit cards. Car-rental agencies. Airlines. He called in one of his detectives.

He wanted a list of every airport connected by direct flight to Oakland and San Francisco. Then he wanted to know whether a Tran Van Duong had flown out of the country from one of those airports anytime last Friday, Saturday, or Sunday.

The sergeant groaned. "You know how many flights that'll be to check?"

Manny could imagine. "Just get on it."

Then Manny Bigelow went home and was sick for the weekend. That Darrel Honeywell might be under an assassin's sights did not bother him in the least. He hoped the killer would use a bomb and get them all.

In fact, at that moment Darrel Honeywell was on an airplane en route to Dallas. Szczepanski was sitting to his left, JC to his right, and six other guys were scattered around. They wouldn't even let him go to the bathroom alone.

235

33

Eliot Brod spent Thursday morning on his stomach, crawling around the rifle range. The ground had dried out a lot in two weeks, so much so that he barely got his sneakers wet.

The first thing he did was mark a trail from the road to his mound. The woods alongside the rifle range were clumpy and thick, easily thick enough to get lost in, at least for a while. And while he had time to get lost on the way in, he definitely didn't want to get lost on the way out.

When he was finished with the trail, he started working on the mound. He would be lying there all day, which in itself would be a trial; but if a rock was sticking into his hip, each minute would be agony. He cleared and smoothed the ground, and scooped out a hollow for his hips; then, he stretched himself out and took a peek over the edge.

Not many people were on the range—he counted eight.

He pulled out a range finder and aimed it at the shooter nearest the middle: 170 yards. He had his rifle sighted in for 150 yards, which meant he might have to aim a tad high. No big deal.

He reached forward and cleared out the few dead twigs

that were in his way, then he laid down a piece of wood to serve as a rest for the rifle.

Eliot stayed where he was for thirty minutes. He knew from experience that a spot that seemed comfortable at first could become vastly uncomfortable after an hour, and sheer misery after four hours. It was hard to shoot straight when you were miserable, and even harder not to fidget.

After half an hour he rolled to the side and made a few adjustments to the hole—digging out a small rock he hadn't noticed before, and scooping out a little more dirt under one hip. When the fit felt right, he scattered a few leaves around so the hole blended in with the rest of the ground. Then he slid down into the gully. He wanted to have a second trail scouted out to the road, just in case.

It would take him one minute to break down the gun, three and a half minutes to get back to the road, one minute to change his clothes, and six minutes to jog back to his bike. A little more than eleven minutes. But after six minutes he would be away from the range, and after nine minutes he would be far away. He didn't think his pursuers would get organized that quickly; there was simply too much ground to cover, and it would take some time to figure out exactly where the shot had come from.

He pedaled slowly back to the SMU campus, changed his clothes, and caught a bus back downtown. After dropping a few more quarters in the locker, he went to lunch, and after lunch went shopping for his wife and daughter. He bought them each a dress, and for his daughter a small pocketbook; he also bought her a video game so she would know he still loved her. It took him two hours to find a pair of earrings for his wife.

Dinner that night was at Dallas's *most* exclusive restaurant.

He began with a crabmeat soufflé topped with mustard hollandaise. Then a plate of asparagus. Then slivered quail on puff pastry. By the time the quail was gone, he was grinning, probably because he was most of the way through a bottle of wine.

The waiter topped off his glass. Flaming leg of lamb in a wild mushroom sauce was next.

GUN MEN

By dessert, Eliot was feeling just fine. He decided to splurge and ordered a piece of chocolate-pecan torte with raspberry sauce. What was life without a little extravagance?

The tab was the cost of a small car.

Late Friday morning (very late Friday morning), Eliot rolled out of bed. He was only mildly hung over (a minor miracle).

He showered. Then went for a run. Then showered again. After a little breakfast (a very little breakfast), he went down to the front desk and paid for three more days.

Grant DeBois was delighted. "You're thinking *seriously* about moving here."

"There's a lot to see."

He waved Grant an *adios* and went for a walk, first to put some coins in the locker, then to a drugstore.

He bought a tube of the highest-rated sunscreen he could find, a small bottle of Tylenol, a first-aid kit (his good-luck charm—never leave home without one), eyedrops, a canteen, and a box of chocolate bars with peanuts. He dropped his goodies back at the hotel and caught a cab up to SMU.

The campus was jumping; and the parents seemed more excited than the kids, probably because they wouldn't have to pay any more tuition.

He stopped in at a party and helped himself to a beer and a couple of handfuls of chips. Around three-thirty he took a short spin on his bike. An hour and a half later he was back downtown. He ate an early dinner. At 6:37 he walked into the Greyhound Bus Station and picked up the pack with the gun.

The gun, the clothes he would need, the canteen, and everything else fit neatly into the pack. He set the pack in the closet, spent an hour stretching, watched part of a movie, and went to bed.

34

At 9:00 A.M. on Friday morning JC was standing outside the main entrance of the Dallas Convention Center. Even though he was from Texas, and even though he'd been there before, he was still awed by the size of the place—he'd been in cities that were smaller. He opened the door and walked in.

For three hours he toured the halls, and he didn't like what he saw. The place had more ratholes to hide in than there were cracks in a dried-up riverbed. It would be nearly impossible to protect Honeywell. He headed on back to where his people were waiting.

"We got a lot to do before six," he told them. "And we got some extra work to do, too."

He told them how NAGO personnel had been receiving death threats—letters, phone calls. The police had been notified, but the police weren't too excited.

"Which means we're on our own. So we'll be taking a few extra precautions."

He wanted the name and address of *everyone* entering the Exhibit Hall; and he wanted to be able to *read* those names and addresses. Tables would be set up in front of the doors.

"And if these people aren't local, I want to know where

they're staying while they're in town. And if anyone complains, just tell them we need to know who our friends are."

He also wanted a photograph of every man who wasn't accompanied by a woman or child. He had two good-looking girls in skimpy Texas cheerleader-style outfits to take care of that; and he was going to stand Big Mike next to them in case anyone objected to having his picture taken.

Each name would be checked, members against a membership list, nonmembers against phone-company records. And he wanted anyone who had joined NAGO within the last two months checked against phone-company records, too. JC hoped to God the killer wasn't a longtime member.

He also wanted his people to verify that nonmembers from out of town were staying where they said they were staying. And he wanted to know if anyone was paying cash.

The same checks would be made at the opening session, the annual meeting, and the banquet, even though they were members-only events. He also wanted the tapes from the surveillance cameras collected every day; and he wanted a few more cameras installed. He told them where.

When his people had finished taking their notes, he sent them off to get set up. Then he walked outside and began to look for those spots a gunman might wait.

Except for the opening session, the killer had no idea where Honeywell would be. That would have been fine if they were trying to hide Honeywell, but they weren't trying to hide him. They *wanted* the killer to find Darrel; and they wanted him to think he could do the job without getting caught.

What JC had to do was choose a place the man would like and parade Honeywell past. Or he had to find the place the killer had chosen, and make sure Darrel showed up.

He circled the Convention Center. How long a shot would the man attempt? One hundred-fifty yards? Two hundred yards? Even a hundred yards made a big circle.

He walked back inside and through each room NAGO would be using. Would the guy use a bomb? There was only one way to avoid a bomb: vary your routine. And even then, a man with time and patience would eventually get you—there were only so many routes to take.

He took the escalator down to the parking garage.

Would the guy try the garage again? It had worked once.

JC always figured it was a bad move to walk a trail where an ambush had taken place. He figured the VC, or whoever, would be waiting around for the man who didn't believe lightning could strike twice.

He headed back upstairs. They would skip the garage. And they would use a different door every day. There were more doors than days to the convention. A man with a rifle watching one door wouldn't be able to count on success.

Twenty-seven feet above him the ceiling lay in shadow. The ceilings were high in much of the Convention Center. He wondered if there were catwalks up there, or trapdoors? He would have to find out. Each closet, each window, would have to be checked. He would do it a room at a time.

He took one more turn around the Convention Center; but if the killer had been there, he couldn't feel it.

35

"I said, put the fucking gun away, Darrel." Szczepanski slammed shut the door of the refrigerator. The vase of flowers on top rocked precariously.

They were in the parlor of a hotel suite, high above Dallas. Off the parlor, like wings, were two bedrooms. Each bedroom had twin beds, a bath with Jacuzzi, a TV, a pair of easy chairs, a dresser with a large mirror, and two side bureaus. There was another bureau in the parlor, as well as a bar, a refrigerator, another TV, and two couches that opened into beds.

"Don't tell me what to do, Tadeusz. You ain't my mother, and you ain't in charge."

He slipped the gun back into its holster, then drew it quickly, taking aim at the TV.

"Pow! Pow! Pow!" A news anchorman fell dead.

Daniel Brooks looked up from his magazine. He was sitting on the couch farthest from the TV, and if he could have been on the other side of the wall, he would have been there. JC had hired him to help keep an eye on Honeywell, and he had been regretting his decision to take the job from the first ten minutes.

Another private detective was in the bedroom to the east,

guarding the door. The two other doors into the suite had been sealed.

"I want you to put that gun away now, before someone gets hurt." Szczepanski stepped between Honeywell and the TV.

"The only one who's going to get hurt, Tadeusz, is you, if you don't get out of my way." He whipped out the gun and pretended to shoot Szczepanski in the head.

Daniel Brooks watched in fascination. They were going to kill each other, and he would be able to go home.

"Put it away, Darrel."

"In a minute I'm going to put you away, you dumb Polack." Szczepanski grabbed him.

Darrel cocked the gun and set the muzzle between Szczepanski's eyes. Just then JC stepped into the room. He walked past them with hardly a glance.

"You guys playing chicken?"

Darrel looked at him and laughed. "Yeah, that's right, we're playing chicken. And guess who's going to lose either way?" He cackled.

JC picked up the phone. "You want burgers or ribs for dinner, Darrel?"

Darrel wanted ribs.

After JC called in the order, he walked over to Honeywell and put his arm around his shoulder.

"Now listen here, Darrel. I know it's bad just sitting around waiting, but I don't want this kind of squabbling. We got a guy out there getting ready to blow your head off. You want to get him, don't you?"

"Sure, I want to get him."

"Then you gotta do what I say. This boy ain't going to just walk up and say, draw, partner. He's going to try to shoot you in the back, maybe while you're in the Exhibit Hall checking out the latest Ruger, maybe while you're walking down the street. There's only two things he cares about: killing you, and not getting caught.

"Now I'm going to have guys around you all the time, but they've got to be a little invisible, otherwise our boy will get nervous and go home. You wearing that vest Taylor got you?"

"It's in my bag."

"Well, Christ, son, put it on. I want you to sleep in it. If this guy was after me, I'd sleep in a tank. You got to be ready."

"I'm ready. Long as I can carry my piece." He held up the .357.

"No problem."

"Then I'm ready."

JC walked to the window and looked out: The office building across the way was easily within range. He drew the curtains.

"We're going to have to establish a pattern for him, Darrel, give him something to work with; then he'll know where to wait. That's how a hunter does it when he's hunting alone: He figures out where the game will be, and picks his spot.

"Now he knows you're going to be at the opening session tonight. And he probably figures you'll go to the annual meeting and the banquet; so we won't disappoint him. The rest of the time we'll spend in the Exhibit Hall."

"What about the range, JC? They're gonna have those new assault rifles at the range."

"I can't cover you at the range."

"JC, I *am* going to fire those new assault rifles."

JC knew the range. When he was a kid, he had spent days there, firing his .22 and listening to war stories and hunting stories. It was in the middle of a swamp, very isolated; the killer would have a million places to hide. But it would also be hard for him to get away after the shot.

He looked at Honeywell's ratlike eager face.

"Okay, Darrel. We'll go to the range. Both afternoons. But you do what I say when we get there."

"No sweat. Long as I get to shoot."

People started filing into the Exhibit Hall at ten to six, and for four hours Big Mike, the girls, and six registrars checked the spelling of names, noted addresses, and took pictures, all with a smile.

NAGO secretaries would spend all night going over those names: the tall, the short, and the ugly. There was a phone line open to NAGO HQ in Washington, and from there people were calling across the country verifying addresses.

GARY FRIEDMAN

* * *

At 8:07 Darrel Honeywell banged the opening session to order. He welcomed everyone to Dallas, wished them a good time at the convention, and gave a short talk on the importance of pestering one's elected representatives—there to serve *you*! Then he introduced the first speaker, a retired general, and seated himself to one side of the podium.

From the side of the stage, hidden by a curtain, JC watched the crowd.

Lincoln had bought it in a theater, why not Honeywell? Maybe the killer had a sense of humor?

He had two men in the projection booth, a man at each door, and two men backstage; there were no hidden exits under the stage.

A very dull two hours passed as the general, two congressmen, a senator, and half a dozen prominent conservatives gave "right to bear arms" speeches. More than a few in the audience, emboldened by the camaraderie of like-minded men (and a few drinks), roared their approval at the most popular positions: an end to *all* restrictions on the sale and possession of firearms, including machine guns; an end to the import ban on assault rifles; an end to Ted Kennedy.

JC had Darrel Honeywell in bed by eleven.

248

36

Saturday broke sunny and cool.

Eliot was up early. He showered and shaved and pulled on a pair of beige slacks, an off-white cotton shirt, a dark tie, and a dark blue blazer. He ate a bowl of granola for breakfast, then grabbed the pack containing the gun and went to find a cab.

"Graduation?" the driver asked.

"My son," Eliot said proudly.

The driver looked in the mirror again.

Eliot grinned. "I got started early."

The cabby caught the wink.

They spent the rest of the ride talking about virgins and kids.

By nine o'clock Eliot was at the rifle range. And by nine-fifteen he was sitting behind his mound of dirt, putting together the gun Michael Michaelson had made. The gun was a nice piece of work: a rifle accurate to two hundred yards that could be disassembled and that was almost silent. It was mat gray, with green and buff patches.

He took the pieces out of their wrapping one at a time, screwing the barrel into the breech, sliding the stock into place. A huge silencer tube screwed onto the barrel. And a high-powered scope slid into mounting brackets; a pair of set screws ensured the scope would be in an identical position each time.

Eliot had test-fired the gun as soon as he had gotten back from Minnesota. It was very accurate: two-inch groups at 150 yards. And taking the gun apart didn't affect the sighting in the least; he had disassembled and reassembled it three times. The gun was as accurate as he was steady.

His only concern had been that the gun would sight differently in the Texas heat; it was still practically winter under the hemlocks outside his house. So one morning, when wife and child were gone, he had opened a window, set up a target, and fired one shot. By luck or chance, the bullet hit the center of a one-inch circle. He took it as a good omen.

He pressed the clip into the gun and chambered a round. Then he crawled up the mound and under the bush.

Men were walking around on the firing line getting things organized. He slid the gun onto the rest and watched them through the scope: Their heads were huge. With the rifle anchored, it would be an easy shot.

A couple of teenagers began to set out targets: half a dozen deer, a flock of turkeys, miscellaneous bad guys; three standard bull's-eye targets stood at a hundred yards.

The range would be open for NAGO members from ten to five, but from two to five there would be a shooting competition. He didn't think Honeywell would show up then. If *he* were Honeywell, he wouldn't show up at all.

Darrel Honeywell woke with a start. He was covered with sweat and for a moment didn't know *where* the hell he was. He had been dreaming, and the dream hadn't been good.

The hotel room came into focus. He closed his eyes and let his head fall back on the pillow.

His gun had jammed. His goddamn gun had jammed. Except, it hadn't been his gun; it had been a pissant .22 revolver.

He had been hunting, but not in the woods. In a city. Deer hunting. Except, there weren't any deer around, only people.

Thousands and thousands of people. So many people he couldn't breathe.

He had pulled out his gun to clear a path. But nobody moved. So he started shooting.

At least, he had tried to start shooting. That's when the gun had jammed.

The crowd moved closer, a crowd of angry black faces. A giant Negro standing in front of him with a gun. Brenden's killer.

He woke as the man pulled the trigger.

He reached under his pillow and pulled out the Desert Eagle. He had stripped and cleaned the gun the night before.

He popped the clip and cleared the chamber, then worked the slide a few times. It worked smoothly and perfectly, just like always. That gun would never misfire. He knew. He had fired it a thousand times without a misfire.

He pressed the shell back into the chamber, popped the clip into the gun, and tucked the gun under his pillow. Then he went back to sleep. This time he was hunting mice with a slingshot, and those times the rubber band didn't break, it rapped him on the hand as he let go.

A few minutes later JC came in and kicked him out of bed. Breakfast was waiting.

JC had been up for hours checking the first day's lists. Two thousand forty-seven people had passed through the door to the Exhibit Hall the previous evening. One thousand six hundred fifty-six members, and 391 others. Of the members, five had joined in the last two months.

JC had decided to call each man's home. He told the man's wife, or family, he was calling to let them know their husband, or son, had arrived in Dallas safely.

The calls were greatly appreciated.

JC had known they would be; it was the sort of thing that inspired loyalty among a membership. He just wished Taylor had been there to see what a fine job he was doing; he would probably have gotten a raise.

No one had answered the phone at one man's home. But since the man was in Dallas with a friend, and since he was staying at the Hilton and paying with a credit card, and since he was sixty and fat, JC figured he was okay.

The 391 others had been more of a headache. His people had been checking phone books all night. All but forty-five were listed at the addresses they had given. Of those forty-five, thirty-two lived where they said they lived but had unlisted phone numbers. Eleven of the remaining thirteen were staying in area hotels and paying with credit cards. His people were still working on the last two men.

JC studied their photos. Both looked to be in their thirties, and both looked fit.

He tore open another pack of cigarettes. Four to five thousand people would be passing through the Exhibit Hall that day; and the same number on Sunday. Probably, a third of them wouldn't be members. The thought made his stomach sour.

37

"Let's go, Darrel, you're going to make us late." JC was standing in the doorway, waiting.

Darrel leaned forward and gobbled down the last of his sausage and eggs. He still had to knot his tie. Then he had to take a shit. JC sent Szczepanski ahead to check the corridors. And he wanted one guy to stay in the room to make sure the maid didn't drop off a bomb.

Darrel checked his gun again, the fourth time that morning.

"He was in my dreams last night, JC. A big black fucker."

"He was black, huh?"

"The same guy who killed Brenden."

"You get him?"

"He got me."

"Was it quick?"

"Fuck you, JC."

They used the back door to the hotel. A car was waiting, a different car; the other car was parked out front.

Honeywell climbed into the back. JC got behind the wheel. He headed away from the Convention Center, then made a long loop back. When he reached Griffin Street, he hit the gas,

253

took a quick left onto Ceremonial, and pulled right up to the main entrance.

Do the unexpected. Yes, sir, that was JC's motto. Walk right in the front door.

He didn't clap himself on the back until they were all safe inside.

Taylor opened the annual meeting with a twenty-minute pep talk and rundown of the year's events. The best news was that membership was up significantly. He attributed this to a general panic among gun owners that their guns were going to be taken away.

"And they are," he warned, "unless we do something about it."

Scores and scores of antigun bills were working their way through state legislatures. Others had been introduced in Congress. He aimed his finger at the members.

"It takes money to fight these bills. A lot of money. And votes."

Which was why an increased membership was so important. It was no longer going to be possible to just sit back and trust to the inviolability of the Second Amendment. The mood of the country was shifting. Soon, the issue would be as simple as those who owned guns versus those who didn't. He banged his fist down on the podium.

"First, they'll take away these so-called assault rifles. Then *all* semiautomatics. Then handguns, then rifles, then shotguns. Are we going to let them do that?"

The shout of NO! was like a cannon going off.

Patrick Taylor smiled grimly.

Thankfully, NAGO had been vigilant. Despite numerous bills, in the last year not a single antigun law had been passed.

General applause and cheers.

"But this year will be harder."

Youth and training programs had to be expanded. It hardly needed to be said again: The earlier a child was introduced to firearms, the more likely that child was to own a gun as an adult. And he wanted his position to be perfectly clear: Girls had been left out of the equation for far too long. With more than half the country wearing skirts, NAGO needed to make a special effort to bring more women into the gun-owning community.

"*That's* where we'll find the members we need."

At the end of his report Taylor asked for a moment of silence to honor the memory of George Herbert Brenden.

The reports of the officers were next: finances; membership; youth, training, and marksmanship programs. There was an update on pending antigun legislation, both in Congress and in the state legislatures. Information sheets were passed out listing the names and addresses of representatives, as well as the bills in question and NAGO's position on those bills. Members were urged to write or call. It was pointed out that only one in ten members were vocal.

The membership passed a resolution calling for a mandatory jail sentence for anyone committing a crime while carrying a gun.

They voted to condemn the import ban that had been placed on assault rifles.

They voted to condemn the Maryland handgun law.

A motion to condemn the registration of machine guns was tabled until the next meeting.

Finally, nominations were taken for the office of president.

Patrick Taylor was nominated and seconded. Then two other men. The three names would appear on a ballot in the next issue of *Guns and Hunters,* the tabulation to take place in ninety days.

Taylor was relieved. In a three-way race he might win; the radical vote might split.

He walked to the podium, thanked everyone for coming, wished them a great weekend, and adjourned the meeting. It was 12:27.

As soon as Taylor gaveled the meeting closed, JC took Honeywell's arm and walked him into the crowd. Szczepanski was a couple of steps behind; the others were spread out.

They stayed with the crowd and walked right out the front of the building, through the Pioneer Park Cemetery (an act of

255

hubris?), and back to the hotel. It wasn't all that far, and JC
wanted to keep the killer off balance if he was tagging along;
he didn't want to set *too* much of a pattern.

He didn't notice anyone following them.

When they got to the hotel, Szczepanski went ahead to
check the elevator and the corridors, and to make sure the room
was secure. It was. JC found the beds made and the curtains
drawn back. He pulled the curtains closed again.

"Anyone show up?"

"Just the maid."

"You watch her the whole time?"

"Followed her around like a puppy dog."

"Good. Go get some lunch; and be back here by two."

They ordered up pizza for themselves. While they were
waiting for the food, JC called to see how things were going at
the Exhibit Hall.

Eliot Brod had a sip of water for lunch, half a candy bar,
and three Tylenol. He had a headache from the glare; and he
was getting sunburned, right through the leaves of the bush,
and right through the sunscreen.

All morning had been the same: men driving up and drag-
ging armload after armload of guns out of their cars. Pistols
and rifles and shotguns. If it was a gun, it was there. Even an
elephant gun; the range had rocked with the report.

Eliot couldn't begin to guess the number of shots fired, but
as the morning wore on, and more and more shooters arrived,
the noise grew until it was like thunder.

He swept the scope back and forth along the firing line,
and across the parking lot, looking for Honeywell.

At one-thirty the firing started to die down. Then it
stopped. Men came out and took down what was left of the
morning's targets and replaced them with standard competition
targets. Tables were placed along the firing line, and a few more
spotting scopes were set up.

Eliot studied the competitors. They were fiddling with their
guns and talking to one another. A crowd had formed behind
them, partly blocking off his view of the parking lot. He panned

the scope back and forth, looking at each face, peering into the parking lot for new faces.

At 2:08 the first group of shooters took their place on the firing line. More cars pulled into the parking lot.

And then, at a little after two-thirty, there was Honeywell. Eliot smiled. All things came to he who waited, as long as he who waited waited in the right spot.

Honeywell was standing there next to Wimpy—the guy he had seen in California—and someone else, someone he hadn't seen before. Muscleman.

Eliot set the cross hairs on the crown of Honeywell's head. But before he could get off a shot, the head was gone; Honeywell had started toward the range. For a moment he disappeared behind the tree that blocked the middle of the firing line. Then he emerged again, just behind the shooters.

Honeywell's head was huge in the scope, a rat's face, mean and nervous. He kept touching his chest—Eliot could see the bulge of a gun there.

He steadied the rifle and set the cross hairs an inch above the eyebrows. His finger was already tightening on the trigger when Darrel Honeywell's face was obliterated by another face. Eliot looked over the scope. Muscleman had passed between him and Honeywell. It had happened instantly, and with no warning. He was going to have to wait until Honeywell was standing a little apart.

He studied Muscleman through the scope: The man was constantly moving, turning this way and that, watching everyone; every minute or so he took Honeywell by the arm and moved him a few feet. The man moved smoothly, and Eliot figured he was probably dangerous. The man in charge. The man who was looking for him. The man who had found Peter.

Eliot counted three other people on the range besides Wimpy who seemed to be working with Muscleman. It was hard to be sure, because *everyone* on the range looked like a thug.

When JC first pulled into the parking lot, he drove straight to the end and stopped beside the clubhouse. He had Honeywell in the backseat, wedged between Szczepanski and Daniel

Brooks; he had a second car right behind him in case he needed help; and he had a third car sitting at the entrance to the parking lot, ready to block off the only exit if that became necessary.

He got out of the car and looked around. Dozens of men were standing by their cars comparing guns and drinking beer. Even more were on the range watching the competition; he figured three hundred, at least.

He told his men where he wanted them; then he guided Honeywell into the thickest part of the crowd.

It was like coming home. The range hadn't changed at all in thirty years: the clubhouse was the same beat-up shack; the parking lot was still unpaved; only the overhead wooden barriers were new. He wondered when they had been added. Probably, when the population of Dallas had started to creep out into the sticks. Probably, when some suburbanite's window got shot out.

He studied the shooters on the firing line. He had once won a match here, one of only two matches he had ever won. That had been a long time ago.

"Look alive now, Darrel. Every one of these guys is carrying a gun."

Darrel touched his hand to the Desert Eagle under his jacket.

JC stepped in front of him and scanned the parking lot and the field beyond. The field was empty, but the woods on the other side were only a little more than a hundred yards away. Would the killer be up in a tree?

"Keep moving, Darrel. Don't stand still."

He crossed behind Darrel and studied the range. Mounds of dirt formed a wall along the sides and back. A great, flat, empty space.

He shifted again, moving Honeywell with him. Most of the men in the crowd were watching the shooters, but some were just talking among themselves. He didn't notice anyone who particularly stood out. If a shot came out of the crowd, it would be difficult for the man to run, or even get rid of his gun, without being seen.

He scanned the parking lot again. A number of guys were standing alone by their cars. He positioned Honeywell so Szczepanski was between him and the parking lot.

Honeywell was looking pretty sour. "These guys are going to be shooting all afternoon, JC. *I* won't get a chance to shoot."

"Just breathe in the smoke, Darrel baby. You'll get your chance tomorrow."

They watched the competitors squeeze off their shots: handguns at twenty-five yards and fifty yards; standing rifles at a hundred yards. After an hour even Darrel Honeywell was bored. They were back in the hotel room by four-thirty.

When Darrel Honeywell left, Eliot Brod slid back off the mound he had been lying on. He popped the clip and cleared the chamber, then disassembled the gun, being careful not to get any sand in it. When the gun was wrapped in its cloth and plastic, he tucked it into the pack. Then he crept away from the range.

An hour later he was on a bus headed back downtown. And an hour after that he was soaking in a tub. The water was scalding and was just what he needed; every single muscle and every single joint ached from lying still for seven hours. When the bath began to cool off, he drained some of the water and ran in more hot.

They would be back tomorrow. And tomorrow he would shoot Honeywell.

He ran through the layout of the range in his mind. He would have to be ready the moment Honeywell got there; he would probably only have a second to aim and fire. He visualized Honeywell getting out of the car and pausing. Honeywell standing near the firing line. Honeywell stepping forward to shoot.

He wouldn't follow the man with the scope; he would just watch him. Sooner or later he would drift away from the others for a second, and that would be all the time he would need.

He let the water out of the tub, showered, and ordered up some dinner. Then he watched a movie on TV and went to bed.

38

At 7:00 P.M. Darrel Honeywell started in on the cocktails, and by 7:45 JC had relieved him of his .357 in the public interest. Darrel was past caring. He ordered another highball and staggered away from the bar. JC was right behind him. Szczepanski a little ways away.

The room was crowded, too crowded to protect Honeywell. It was the sort of situation that gave members of the Secret Service ulcers.

But JC wasn't working for the Secret Service, and while he hoped to get Honeywell through the weekend in one piece, he mostly wanted to get the guy who had killed Brenden and who had made him eat shit.

He had two men stationed at each door and more men in the kitchen. And he had checked with a Convention Center supervisor to make sure no one with less than two months' experience was working the room that night. He had already interviewed everyone at the Convention Center who had been hired in the last two months; he didn't think any of them had a sideline as an assassin.

An announcement was made that dinner was about to be served.

JC stepped forward and took Honeywell's arm and guided him to a table in the corner. The table had been reserved for NAGO personnel, and JC personally knew everyone sitting there. He helped Honeywell into a chair. Szczepanski slid into the seat on the other side. The two waiters at the table were NAGO employees.

From where he was standing, JC could see the entire hall. What he saw was a roomful of half-tipsy men playing musical chairs. He waited until everyone had found a seat, then sat down himself.

Shrimp cocktail. Onion soup. Salad. Steak with baked potato and peas.

The shrimp were rubbery, the onion soup salty, and the salad starting to wilt; but, hey! at least he wasn't paying for it.

He checked the room again. Things had quieted down now that people had started to feed; only the waiters were walking around. He couldn't help but notice that most of them were black, which made him extra glad he had his own men working the table. He started in on his steak.

A tray fell just to his side.

JC was out of his chair and behind Honeywell even before the silverware had stopped ringing. Darrel looked up at him.

No one had fired a shot, and no one had made any threatening moves.

JC felt like a fool. He patted Darrel on the shoulder and settled back in his chair. Suddenly, his steak didn't seem so appealing, even though it was cooked perfectly.

"I need to use the john, JC."

JC looked at him. Honeywell was a fine shade of jade.

"Take his arm, Tadeusz."

Szczepanski grabbed Honeywell by the arm and hoisted him out of the chair.

JC had Szczepanski check each stall; he wanted the room empty before Honeywell went in. Darrel almost didn't make it.

JC winked at Szczepanski. "What'sa matter, Darrel? That onion soup sitting a little funny?"

Darrel started to puke again.

Szczepanski laughed. "He'll have lots of room for dessert."

"I wanna go back to the hotel, JC."

"There's still dessert."

"I don't want any dessert."

"Yeah, but we do."

They cleaned him up and dragged him back to the banquet hall. He was asleep as soon as they dropped him in the chair.

The pecan pie and vanilla ice cream were waiting.

JC picked up his spoon just as the keynote speaker began his address: an hour of hunting and fishing stories, and backwoods advice, mostly about keeping your powder dry and your knife sharp. Darrel snored through it all. They had to half-carry him back to the room.

After Honeywell was settled in bed, JC went to see who had visited the Exhibit Hall that day. There were over four thousand names on the list. Extra people had had to be recruited to help sort through them all.

JC sifted through the pile of photographs. At one o'clock in the morning, after yet another fruitless day, all this security seemed like a ridiculous waste of time. Not only would the killer be crazy to visit the Exhibit Hall, he would be crazy to be in Dallas at all. He could wait. A month. A year. In a year Honeywell would be walking around all by himself again.

Sunday morning was a repeat of Saturday morning: breakfast in the room; then over to the Convention Center.

JC dragged a very hung-over Darrel Honeywell to a lecture on pistol shooting. After that they toured the Exhibit Hall.

Handguns. Shotguns. Rifles.

JC wanted to take a look at the new 9mm semiautos.

Darrel Honeywell snorted. "Those are TV guns, JC. In real life they wouldn't stop an old lady."

It was the first sign that Darrel was going to make it. He pulled out his Desert Eagle.

"If you want a semiauto, try this."

He handed the gun to JC, who almost dropped it, it was so heavy.

They went to see the 9mms anyway.

Every major gun manufacturer had a booth. Ruger. Beretta. Colt. Browning. Smith & Wesson. Remington. The amount of weaponry, and ammunition, was staggering.

At one o'clock they headed back to the hotel room. JC ordered up some lunch, then went to see how his people were doing with the Exhibit Hall list. Now that it was daytime, and he had had some sleep, the list didn't seem like such a bad idea.

Four more men couldn't be accounted for, a total of six, with the two from the first day. He glanced at the photos. For some reason, he didn't think his man was among them. He memorized the faces anyway.

And he wanted Big Mike to personally find out who the hell these guys were if they happened to show up again.

At two-fifteen he collected Honeywell and headed out to the range.

39

Eliot Brod was a happy man; the sun had just disappeared behind a band of clouds, and the clouds only looked as if they were going to get thicker. He figured it would be raining by evening.

He took a sip of water, then wet his fingers and dabbed his neck; the skin was on fire. His eyes were on fire. It made it difficult to focus through the scope. Eyedrops had helped a little, as had some Tylenol, but things were still a little blurry. He had once missed the chance for a shot because his eyes were blurry; it had taken another three weeks to get the man.

He wiped the sweat off his forehead and ate a candy bar.

All day they had been blazing away on the range. Hundreds and hundreds of men with every weapon imaginable. But mostly with assault rifles. He was half-deaf with the noise. And once or twice he had nearly been shot when a round went particularly wide.

He swept the scope back and forth. Most of the men on the range were in their forties, or older. Vets, he guessed. Reliving the good old days.

He was glad he didn't live in the West, where men were men, and were ready to prove it.

He stopped the sweeping motion. There they were—right on schedule. He picked out Honeywell. The man was moving toward the firing line, weaving in and out among the crowd; he stopped directly behind the tree that blocked Eliot's view.

Eliot steadied the scope. He could just see Honeywell's head; it bobbed into view every couple of seconds. The man seemed jumpy. And he seemed to be arguing with Muscleman. Muscleman wasn't looking at him but was scanning the range, studying the other shooters.

Eliot was glad *he* was two hundred yards away. He didn't doubt Muscleman would sense something wrong with him.

He set the cross hairs back on Honeywell. If he could squeeze off a shot when the guy rocked out from behind the tree, he would have him.

"You are not going to go up there and shoot," JC said.

"You bet your ass I am."

"In two minutes your ass is going to be in the trunk of the car."

Darrel laughed. "You're not going to start a brawl, JC, not here in front of all these members."

He pushed past Szczepanski and walked right up to the firing line. A dumpy little guy with glasses and a beer belly was popping another clip into a rifle.

"Hey, pal, lemme give it a try, huh?"

The man squinted up at him. "I know you?" He wasn't smiling.

Darrel smiled. "Name's Darrel Honeywell."

The man leaned a little closer. "I seen you on TV? On Oprah Winfrey?"

"You think I could give it a try?"

"Just lemme finish the clip."

He emptied the gun shooting from the hip, one long sweep from left to right.

"Great gun. Really great gun." He handed it to Darrel.

The rifle was warm, almost hot. And it *was* a really great gun. Darrel knew all about it: the Colt AR-15A2 H-BAR. A beautiful weapon. There was an even better version, a real sniper's rifle—the Delta H-BAR. A gun well worth the extra five hundred bucks. A gun that had been range-tested for accuracy before it was sold. One-inch groups at a hundred yards.

He flagged down one of the ammo guys and grabbed a handful of clips.

Eliot Brod couldn't believe his eyes. His man had moved out from behind the tree and stepped right up to the firing line; now, no one could possibly pass in front of him.

He took a deep breath and found Honeywell in the scope. Conditions were almost perfect, just a bit of distortion from the heat coming off the ground, but not enough to worry about. He set the cross hairs between Honeywell's eyes, raised his aim slightly, breathed out, and started to squeeze the trigger.

JC was having a fit. Suddenly, Honeywell was no longer part of the crowd.

He glanced quickly left and right to see if anyone had noticed, or was showing particular interest. A hundred men were readying their guns. He looked back at Honeywell, already popping in a clip.

Behind Honeywell the range stretched for four hundred yards, and all of a sudden it didn't seem so empty. There were dips in the land, and, along one side, mounds covered with bushes. Bushes and brush and trees and heavy shadow. He figured the distances. Some of the trees weren't even a hundred yards away. An easy shot. And a clear shot to the shooters with no risk of detection, because *who* would be downrange? No one. The killer would be alone.

"Son of a bitch!"

He stepped forward and grabbed Honeywell and jerked him back into the crowd.

Eliot Brod cursed.

"I need fifteen minutes, Darrel. Just fifteen minutes. Then you can shoot until your shoulder falls off."

"Let go of my arm, JC." He shrugged JC's hand off his arm.

JC grabbed him again. "You little fuck. I'll rip your arm

right out of your shoulder. You give me fifteen minutes."

It finally dawned on Darrel that JC *might* rip his arm out of his shoulder. He was looking kind of mad. "Okay, JC. Fifteen minutes. Whatever you want." He took a look around. "You see something?"

JC turned to Szczepanski. "You stay between him and the range. Right here." He placed Szczepanski where he wanted him. "And when he steps up to shoot, stand right behind him. And face this way, so you can watch the crowd. You got that?"

"Sure, I got it."

"Make sure nobody swings a gun in his direction."

"Where you going?"

"Just do what I said, goddamnit."

Eliot wiped the sweat off his forehead and peered over the scope. Honeywell was back in the crowd, behind the tree again. Why had he stepped back? He had been ready to shoot. Muscleman had said something to him.

He looked through the scope. He could see Wimpy, and part of Honeywell. But not Muscleman.

He swept the scope carefully along the firing line and the parking lot. Muscleman was gone. Gone where? The guy had been positively frantic when Honeywell stepped forward to shoot. Hadn't he known the man was going to do that? Wasn't he prepared to cover Honeywell on the firing line?

He imagined himself standing where Muscleman had been, looking at Honeywell and the range beyond. Obviously, Muscleman had seen some spot he *didn't* have covered. A spot downrange. Was that where he was headed now?

Eliot slid back down the mound and into the gully below him. He wasn't going to wait around to find out. Honeywell could wait for another day. He ripped apart the gun and stuck the pieces into the pack. Then he started crawling downrange along the gully. It was time to use his emergency escape route.

As soon as he started down the gully, Eliot realized his mistake: Though the gully was deep enough to hide him from the sight of those on the firing line, the bullets they were firing didn't travel along the line of sight; they curved *down*! And the farther he went downrange, the more those bullets would drop.

He pressed himself into the dirt and wriggled forward as quickly as he could. It was eighty long yards before there was a turn that would take him out of the line of fire, and the way the bullets were kicking up the sand in front of him, he wasn't sure he was going to make it. He cursed himself for being stupid.

It took Eliot almost a minute to crawl those eighty yards. Just as he turned away from the range, he felt something hit his left leg, low down in the calf. He ignored the pain and kept crawling until he was hidden by a mound of dirt.

His ankle felt wet. He grabbed the pant leg and pulled it up. There, on the inside of his calf, was a small, ugly hole oozing blood. He turned his leg over. The exit hole gaped up at him, a steady stream of blood pouring out.

He pulled out a handkerchief and tied it around his calf as tightly as he could, tucking the knot into the wound. A proper bandage would have to wait. Then he picked up the pack and took out the parts of the rifle and put them back together. He would have to kill Muscleman, because if he didn't, Muscleman would certainly kill him. There was no way he could outrun the man now.

When the rifle was assembled, he crept to the top of the nearest mound and peeked over the edge. He had a view of the firing line, but not of the mound with the bush. He crawled up a higher mound: The mound with the bush came into view. He studied it through the scope. He could see the depression he had been lying in, as well as about ten feet of the gully he had followed in. He didn't doubt Muscleman would find the trail that led to that gully.

He smoothed out the dirt on the top of the mound and set down a broken branch to serve as a rest.

The brush was thicker than JC had expected. Brush and thickets and bog and trees. He had swung wide so he wouldn't be seen, and now, with the clouds blocking the sun, he was having trouble keeping parallel to the range. He glanced at his watch. He was running out of time. He pushed through a bush and cut straight across a wet spot. He kept his eye to the ground, only glancing up occasionally; he didn't want to miss any tracks.

But after eight minutes there hadn't *been* any tracks, and he was beginning to wonder if this walk in the woods was just another goose chase.

And then he saw it: a broken branch, and beneath the branch a footprint in the soft earth—the same size print he had seen in the ditch by Tran's house. The guy was there! He had finally caught up with the bastard.

He began to follow the tracks, moving quickly. In a minute he had reached the edge of the trees.

The noise from the range was incredible. He pulled out his gun and crouched down.

The trail led behind a mound of dirt and into a gully. He searched the mounds in front of him. The man would certainly be camouflaged and difficult to see.

But all he saw was dirt, and bushes, and brush.

He slid into the gully, moving forward half a step at a time, always scanning the ground ahead. The dumbest thing a person could do was follow a trail with his nose to the ground. That was a good way to bump into a tree.

In another minute he was at the edge of the range. Where the hell was the guy? There was no place left to go. He cocked his gun and eased past a mound, and saw something that made his stomach heave.

He had seen the same thing once before, in Vietnam, the day he had been ambushed by that sniper: the tracks, and then the backtrack in a different direction.

He had considered the possibility of a backtrack; but from where he was standing, it had seemed impossible. Now, he noticed the deepish gully that cut the ground at the very edge of the range. The killer had done his homework.

The other time the sniper's gun had jammed. This time JC didn't do as well.

The M855 bullet ripped into the side of his head just as he was turning. It tore off part of his ear and shattered his skull, then broke into two pieces as it was designed to do. One piece went clear through his head, taking a good portion of his brains with it. The second, lighter, piece rattled around inside, finally coming to rest by his nose. JC never felt a thing. He didn't even know he was dead.

Approximately two thousand M855 rounds would be fired that day on the range.

Even before JC had stopped twitching, Eliot had the gun apart and in the pack. He pulled out the small first-aid kit (so much for talismans) and took out a wad of gauze, the Merthiolate, a compress, and the roll of adhesive tape. He cut away the blood-soaked handkerchief with his knife, soaked the gauze in the Merthiolate, and stuffed it into the wound. Then he placed the compress on top and taped it in place, carefully overlapping the compress with the tape so the blood wouldn't run down his leg.

When he reached the road, he changed into his jogging shorts. A little mud over the top of the tape dulled the whiteness and made the bandage look a couple of days old. His leg hurt, but not unbearably. He was sure it would get worse.

It was a long walk back to his bike, and even though he took it slowly, by the time he reached the supermarket, his leg was throbbing badly. He bought a bottle of aspirin and took four of them, then he climbed onto his bike and headed back to the SMU campus. He was glad the Texas landscape was flat, because he didn't think he could pedal uphill with one leg.

The campus was nearly empty, just a last few students packing up their cars. He cleaned himself up and changed.

He had planned to get rid of the gun that evening, burying it somewhere; but it was three or four hours until dark, and he didn't dare wait that long. In four hours his leg would be useless.

He stepped outside and down to the road. Just across the street was a storm sewer. He looked around. Nobody was anywhere nearby.

He walked over to the sewer and bent down as if to tie his shoe; then, using the pack as a shield, he let the parts of the rifle slide through the grate. They would be found eventually, but eventually didn't matter, because like all of Michael Michaelson's guns, this one was untraceable.

He didn't throw away the plastic stock, because it would have floated. And he didn't throw away the scope, because he wasn't sure if it would float. Instead, he wrapped them in a bag and dropped the bag, and the pack with the bloody clothes, in a dumpster. Then he walked to the bus stop. He needed to find a pharmacy that was open.

It took twenty minutes, and five shots of vodka, to clean the hole in his leg.

First, he washed away the dried blood and dirt. Then he soaked some gauze in alcohol and, using the eraser end of a pencil, forced it into the wound, first from one side, then from the other.

Even after five shots of vodka his body began to shake uncontrollably. When the shaking finally stopped, he washed out the wound with alcohol again. Then he repeated the process with Betadine.

After that, it was all he could do to bandage his leg. He swallowed half a dozen aspirin and crawled into bed.

40

"I don't give a fuck where JC is, Tadeusz. *I'm* hungry, and *I'm* going back now."

It was 6:10, and the last car had left the range fifteen minutes before. There hadn't been any shooting for an hour.

Szczepanski walked the length of the firing line again.

"JC?"

It was more a call than a shout.

"JC?"

The sound echoed strangely on the empty range.

Finally, he shouted out JC's name, but if JC could hear, he wasn't answering.

Szczepanski walked back to where Honeywell and the others were waiting.

"Okay. But we'll leave one car; he has the keys, anyhow."

They piled into the other two cars and drove back to the hotel. Szczepanski called Taylor and told him JC was missing; then he ordered up burgers and ribs. They sat around eating and watching the tube, and waiting for JC to get back from wherever he had disappeared to.

At eight o'clock Big Mike walked in the door. "Taylor wants us to check the range again, Tadeusz. Let's go."

They left Honeywell in the room with Daniel Brooks and a couple of other guys and drove back to the range. The car was still there.

Szczepanski walked over to the firing line and started calling after JC.

"Where were you standing when he took off, Tadeusz?"

Tadeusz looked around. "We were standing right here."

"And he headed toward the road?"

"He started off that way. I was watching after Darrel."

Big Mike started toward the road, keeping an eye on the ground at the edge of the woods.

But there had been so many men tromping back and forth that day that it was hard to see anything, especially in the gloom. It began to drizzle.

"You should have started looking for him earlier, Tadeusz, while it was still light. Why the hell did you go back to the hotel?"

"I had to keep an eye on Darrel."

"He could've helped you look."

"He was going to leave!"

"You should have let him. Go get the car."

Szczepanski ran and got the car. They called Taylor from a pay phone, and Taylor called the police.

"You say he's been missing how long?"

"Six hours."

"That ain't very long. This here Jamison Conners a grown man?"

"He's forty years old."

"You check the bars over there?"

"He's a private investigator. He was on a job. He wouldn't have just taken off."

"Maybe he found something interesting to investigate? Know what I mean?"

"Look, I want to file a missing-person report."

"You'll have to come down to the station. Eight o'clock tomorrow morning would be fine."

"How about right now?"

But the desk sergeant had already hung up.

274

Patrick Taylor started making phone calls.

An hour later the Dallas Police Department was busy putting together a search party complete with dogs; by midnight they were out at the range and organized. Taylor had sent Szczepanski and Big Mike over to help, as well as six other NAGO men. It was raining hard now.

They swept the firing line in both directions, then they swept the field behind the parking lot, then the edge of the woods along the road. Finally, they started searching the woods.

When they found JC four hours later, the rain was coming down in sheets.

"This the guy?" The sergeant aimed his flashlight at the body.

Szczepanski took one look at JC's head and puked up the ribs he had had for dinner.

"What's his name?"

"JC."

"That a joke?"

"Jamison Conners."

The sergeant looked at his watch and made a note of the time in his book.

"Okay, I want this area cleared. We already made a mess for the Homicide boys. Brown, you and Dawson stay here and guard the body."

Officer Brown groaned. "Come on, Sarge. It's raining like a bitch."

Sergeant Bill Burke grinned. "It sure is, ain't it? Lucky thing you're wearing your galoshes." He took Szczepanski by the arm. "I got a few questions, son."

At first light, the Homicide detectives were checking over the area. But with the rain, and all the tramping around that had gone on the night before, there wasn't much to see: only JC, his brains, and his gun—still cocked.

When the photographer was finished taking his pictures, they carted the body away. The preliminary examination was done by noon. By then, Eliot Brod had been in the air two hours.

41

"**W**hat the hell do you mean it was probably a stray from the range?" Patrick Taylor felt his control beginning to slip. What was it about police lieutenants that disagreed with him?

"That's what it looks like, Mr. Taylor. A .223. Probably fired from an assault rifle."

"I tell you, we got an assassin out there."

"The man on the knoll, huh?"

"Say, what?"

"Assassin theories don't play real big down here in Dallas, Mr. Taylor. Know what I mean?"

"This guy's already killed one of my men. This makes two."

"You got this assassin's name? A description?"

Taylor was silent.

"You got anything?"

"Maybe he's a big black guy."

The lieutenant chuckled. "A big black guy, huh? Is that light black or dark black?"

Taylor didn't say anything.

"Now if I knew who was on that range yesterday afternoon,

I could maybe get a match on a particular weapon. But I *don't* know who was on that range."

"It was open shooting to members." Taylor tried not to sound defensive.

"A bunch of grown men playing Rambo." The lieutenant clicked his tongue. "The way I figure it, Mr. Taylor, is your man was downrange on a rifle range at a time when everyone and his brother was cutting loose with enough firepower to fight a small war. Seems quite possible a stray could of hit him, especially since half those boys were a little stewed at the time and probably not shooting too straight. Know what I mean?"

"You're not even going to check this out, are you?"

"I tell you, Mr. Taylor, ain't nobody called in reporting a big black guy walking around the streets of Dallas with an assault rifle. Not even a little black guy."

"And the fact that his body was found *downrange* from where his brains were lying? Doesn't that bother you?"

"Now, that surely does, and that could be a real thorn. But if your man had been standing or crouching when he was hit, the force of the slug could have spun him around; he might have landed anywhere. I've seen that before."

"I tell you, he was hunted down. You must have found some tracks out there?"

"It rained awful heavy last night, Mr. Taylor. And that ground's a bog anyway; a good bit of it was under water this morning, and the rest had been pretty badly trampled by the search party, which is why we like to send out our search parties when it's light."

The lieutenant paused so Taylor wouldn't miss his point.

"What I'm trying to say, Mr. Taylor, is that unless you can give me something more than what I have, which is nothing, I got nothing left to check out."

"I'll get you more."

"You do that now. Have a nice day."

Patrick Taylor slammed down the phone. Except for the accent, and the "Mr.," this guy could have been Manny Bigelow's twin brother.

He stormed over to where Darrel Honeywell was being kept.

"I want him out of here now." He pointed at Szczepanski and Big Mike. "Get him on a plane and get back to Washington. I'll see you tomorrow night."

He was already late for the afternoon session of the board.

42

Patrick Taylor got back to Washington late Tuesday night. First thing Wednesday he got a call from Manny Bigelow.

"Hear y'all had a bit of trouble down there in Dallas over the weekend."

Taylor decided not to rise to the bait. "What have you got for me, Bigelow?"

Manny lit a cigarette. "Nothing but more bad news, brother. Just bad news. Your little Oriental friend, the mastermind behind all this business..."

"What about him?"

"He went home."

"What do you mean, he went home?"

"He flew from Honolulu to Hong Kong, and thence to Ho Chi Minh City, what used to be Saigon in the old days."

"He's in Vietnam?"

"Yup. Been there over a week. Probably being rehabilitated, or whatever, right now, even as we speak. Sold the works before he left. But, then, you already know that." He poured himself a cup of coffee. "By the way, the Sheriff's Department out there tells me his house was ransacked. Know anything about that?"

"No, I don't."

"Breaking and entering is a crime, you know."

"Is that a fact?"

"It surely is, even in California."

"He leave behind a note or anything, saying why he went back to Vietnam?"

"A farewell video? They didn't find anything. But they talked to a couple of his friends. Seems he's been depressed since his daughter died. Second time he's lost a child. Just an unlucky sort of guy."

"He could've been a lot more unlucky. How'd he get to Hawaii?"

"Must have flown."

"Don't you know?"

"He wasn't listed on any flight coming in. We're checking with the crews. Maybe he used another name."

"Now why would he do that?"

"Now how should I know without asking him?"

In fact, that was exactly what Tran had done.

After he dumped the case of bricks, he drove home and picked up a suitcase he had packed earlier. Then he walked out the door and started down the road. Just above where Szczepanski was waiting, the road forked. He took the turn and in a few minutes was scrambling up a hill to the top of the ridge. On the other side of the ridge was another road. In less than an hour he was at the Lafayette BART station. An hour after that he was at the San Francisco Airport. He arrived in Honolulu as the sun was coming up.

"You manage to track down Weston?" Taylor asked.

Manny Bigelow emptied a packet of sugar into his coffee. "Now Weston, that's a sad story. A man can't hardly take a vacation."

"Come on, Bigelow, just get on with it."

"He died in a skiing accident."

"You're amassing quite a pile of corpses, Lieutenant."

"Only one of them is mine."

"Where the hell was he skiing in May? New Zealand?"

"Up in Calgary. Spring skiing. Very popular. You can get a nice tan, though it seems you have to be careful in the morning; it can be a bit icy before it warms up."

"Jesus Christ, Bigelow. We have three dead people and a guy hiding in Vietnam. Don't you believe me yet?"

"Lots of people die every day. That doesn't make it a conspiracy, more like a coincidence. A guy goes skiing. He's a beginner. Takes a few lessons, gets on a slope that's a little too tough and a little too icy, and runs into a tree."

"A fucking tree?"

"The body wasn't found for a week, not until someone else ran off the slope in the same spot. Must be a bad spot. He was alone, so there wasn't anyone to report him missing. And he worked for himself, so no one cared when he didn't show up, except maybe his secretary. And since she could sign the checks, she didn't care all that much. Seems this isn't the first time he's taken off, though she allowed this was the longest he'd ever been away. But maybe he was having a good time. The Mounties found a few girls up there he had gotten kinda friendly with. Know what I mean?"

"And that's it?"

"They went through his files and diaries and stuff. Nothing under assassin. He put in burglar alarms for a living. Custom jobs. Must've paid pretty well; he was carrying a fair amount of cash when they found him."

"How much?"

Manny Bigelow put his feet up on his desk. "Eight grand."

"Eight grand!"

"Some guys like a heavy wallet. Makes them feel big. He also had about twenty G's in his safe-deposit box. Must have done some jobs off the books."

"The killer probably gave him a cut. I want you to keep going on this. Have you started to check the names in those files?"

"That would take years."

"Get some help."

"Listen, Taylor, with the shit I have for evidence, I don't *want* to check those names. Even if I found Brenden's killer, I couldn't prove anything."

"You're a real fighter, Bigelow."

"The fight's over."

"I want a look at those files."

"They're not mine to show you."

"You son of a bitch. You've been a real help on this, right from the start."

Manny Bigelow smiled. "Always glad to be a help. Y'all have a nice day now." And he hung up the phone.

That day, Governor Deukmejian of California signed into law a bill outlawing over fifty kinds of assault rifles.

43

The next six months weren't great for Darrel Honeywell.

All summer he walked around with an itchy finger, pulling out his gun at every sound. That made the people around him nervous; and when he almost shot a congressman, Patrick Taylor decided it was time to send him home. By then Darrel was ready to go.

But on the flight back, his .357 stowed in a suitcase in the luggage compartment, he began to feel exposed. The killer was still out there. The killer knew what he looked like and where he lived. Those had been JC's words, and now JC was dead.

He glanced at the people in the neighboring seats. Had they been stealing looks at him?

By the time Darrel was standing outside his front door, his imagination had run positively riot.

He pulled out his gun and swung the door wide.

He checked each room, each closet. He checked under the bed. But there hadn't been anyone inside his house since he'd left, months ago. He opened a window to air the place out. Then he closed the window. The killer might sneak in that way.

Each time he returned home, he checked the house; and

if he heard a board creak, or some other unfamiliar sound, he checked the house again, imagining that somehow the man had found a way in.

It got so bad, he spent the whole day with his gun drawn. He wouldn't watch TV, or listen to the radio, because they made too much noise. At night he left the lights on; and even then, he couldn't fall asleep unless he'd had a few drinks.

But nothing happened in September. And nothing happened in October.

And by the time November rolled around, Darrel Honeywell realized nothing was ever going to happen: Tran was gone, and so was the killer. Strangely, he felt let down.

He began to have his few drinks at dinner. Then he moved them up to lunch.

The drinking began to interfere with his representation of NAGO. He missed appearances, and sometimes showed up drunk. Finally, he was fired.

On December 14, Darrel Honeywell stumbled home after a night of preholiday carousing. He unlocked the door, turned on the hall light, and staggered up the stairs to his bedroom. As he reached the second-floor landing, the heel of a palm shot out and whacked him in the side of the head. Darrel buckled.

Eliot Brod slid one hand under Honeywell's chin, placed the other hand on the back of his head, and twisted hard. The pop was like a .22 going off.

Darrel tumbled back down the stairs.

Eliot waited five minutes before checking for a pulse. Then he stepped out the door, closed it, and walked the six blocks to the all-night grocery where he had left his bike.